# NEVER YOUR GIRL

USA Today Bestselling Author

## JENNIFER SUCEVIC

Never Your Girl

Copyright© 2025 by Jennifer Sucevic

Published by Tangled Hearts LLC



This is a work of fiction. Names, characters, businesses, palaces, events, locales, and incidents are either the products of the author's imagination or used in a fictitious manner. Any resemblance to actual persons, living or dead, or actual events is purely coincidental.

Original Cover Design by Mary Ruth Baloy at MR Creations

Special Edition & Illustrated Cover by Claudia Lymari at Tease Designs

Editing by Shauna Stevenson at Ink Machine Editing

Proofreading by Sisters Get Literary Author Services

Interior Formatting by Silla Webb at Masque Publishing

Join my Newsletter here!

# WESTERN UNIVERSITY CHAT APP

FragileLikeABomb

So, do you message every random profile you come across, or am I just special?

ColdAsIce17

You caught me. I couldn't resist. The username? Chef's kiss.

FragileLikeABomb

Fragile and LikeABomb felt on-brand. I'm complicated.

ColdAsIce17

Complicated or dramatic?

FragileLikeABomb

Aren't they the same thing? What's your excuse for ColdAsIce?

ColdAsIce17

Thought it sounded cool. Pun intended.

FragileLikeABomb

Did you consider literally any other options?

ColdAsIce17

EmotionallyUnavailable17 was taken.

FragileLikeABomb

That one hits a little too close to home.

ColdAsIce17
Guess that makes us a perfect match.
FragileLikeABomb
Oh no. Absolutely not.

HOLLAND

A digital chorus of beeps and dings sweeps through Slap Shotz like a wave as the buzzing of my phone coincides with dozens of others. In the split second before I read the message, I catch the shift in the room. The way conversations die mid-sentence, the collective intake of breath, the sudden tension that crackles through the air like static before a storm.

ANONYMOUS MESSAGE

> Make sure someone sends the hockey ho penicillin in the morning. We all know she's gonna need at least one dose. Maybe two.

Damn.

Shots fired.

I shouldn't smile.

I really shouldn't.

But there's something darkly satisfying about watching the mighty fall, especially when that fall involves Bridger Sanderson. The same type of texts have been terrorizing him for months now, and no one has been able to trace their source.

Not the tech department.

Not campus security

Not even the chancellor himself.

As far as I'm concerned, Bridger deserves it.

If I didn't believe in karma before, I certainly do now.

"Oh boy," my bestie, Willow, mutters from where she's sitting across from me. "That's not good."

"Says who?" I arch a brow, not bothering to hide my amusement.

Willow tips her head in Bridger's direction. "Probably him."

Near the bar, I can feel Bridger's presence like a physical weight. He's been brooding in the same spot all night, radiating the kind of darkness that makes people give him a wide berth.

Not that I've been watching.

Much.

Our eyes meet across the dim space, and that familiar jolt of awareness hits me like a sucker punch. His gray eyes narrow, and I respond with my middle finger, a gesture that feels childish even as I do it.

"Real mature," Willow says dryly.

"What can I say? I have my moments."

She flicks a glance at him before refocusing her attention on me. Questions and curiosity swim in her blue depths. "Are you ever going to tell me what happened between you two?"

I take a long sip of my root beer to buy time.

Not deterred in the least by my silence, she lifts a brow, prodding me for an answer. Only then do I grudgingly say, "Nope."

"Ahhh. Now we're finally getting somewhere." She holds her hand up. "Stop. We're bordering on information overload. Why must you be so dang chatty? It's *such* a personality defect."

I roll my eyes as a smile trembles around the corners of my lips.

I love Willow to pieces, but she doesn't need to know the gory details of what happened between Bridger and me. Most of the time, I wish I could scrub them from my memory.

I'm saved from further interrogation when my phone chimes with a work reminder. Thirty minutes until my shift starts at a job my best friend doesn't even know I have.

"I need to head out," I say, already gathering my things.

"Already?" Willow frowns. "We've only been here for an hour."

"Yeah." I tuck an errant strand of hair behind my ear. "You know I can only handle being around these guys in small doses. Unfortunately for you, I've reached my quota of hockey players and drama for one night."

"Want company?" she offers. "We could watch a horror movie like we used to. I'll let you pick the goriest one, even though we both know I'll have nightmares for weeks."

The offer makes my chest ache with nostalgia.

I miss those days.

Now that Willow has a boyfriend, everything has changed.

"Nah, you stay here and celebrate with your man." I force lightness into my tone that I don't feel. "This week has been exhausting. I probably wouldn't make it through the first murder. And that's my favorite part."

"I'm sorry, did you just say murder?" Maverick McKinnon's eyebrows shoot up. "Should someone warn Bridger?"

"Please." I grab my bag, glad for the excuse to shield my expression. "If I were going to murder Bridger Sanderson, I wouldn't be foolish enough to incriminate myself by talking about it. And you'd never find the body. No body, no murder. Isn't that how it works?"

"That's..." Maverick glances at Willow. "Concerning."

"Don't worry," my bestie says, tipping her face toward him with a softness that brings a small, wistful smile to my lips. "We were talking about movies."

He brushes his lips across hers, whispering something that makes her giggle, and just like that, they're in their own little world. I watch them for a moment, torn between genuine happiness for my best friend and a loneliness that cuts bone-deep. Willow deserves this—deserves *him*—after everything she's been through. But sometimes I miss when it was just us against the world.

My phone buzzes again.

Twenty-five minutes until my shift starts. Randi's face flashes through my mind. My boss could make a drill sergeant cry with one perfectly arched eyebrow.

"I'll see you tomorrow," I say, already backing away.

Willow surfaces from her Maverick-induced haze. "Let me know if you change your mind about that movie."

"I won't." The words come out softer than intended as I turn away to weave through the crowd, dodging familiar faces and wondering, not for the first time, what Willow would say if she knew where I was really going.

Everyone has secrets, but mine feel heavier lately.

"Taking off already?" Garret Akeman materializes in front of me, all cocky grin and practiced charm. "The night's just getting started."

"Yeah." I shift my weight, uncomfortably aware of Bridger's gaze burning into my back from the bar. "I think we both know Slap Shotz isn't my scene."

He glances around with disinterest. "Maybe I'll come with you. We can chill for a while."

I shake my head. "Sorry, not tonight."

"Why not?" His jaw tightens as his eyes sharpen. "You have better plans?"

"As a matter of fact, I do. With my pillow," I tack on to soften the blow. My gaze strays to the bar, only to find the tall defenseman watching us. "I'll catch you later."

"Yeah, sure," Garret mumbles as I slip past him into the night air, sucking in a deep breath that tastes like freedom. Being around Bridger does this to me. It sets everything inside me spinning until I can barely breathe. Two years later and I still can't shake him, no matter how hard I try.

My ancient Toyota grumbles to life on the third attempt, and I pat the dashboard like a faithful pet. "Just a little longer, baby. Keep it together."

The drive to the Envy Room feels like crossing a border between worlds. Here, I'm not Holland Tate, college student just trying to scrape by. I become someone else entirely.

The club's exterior is understated elegance. It's nothing like the neon-soaked dives people imagine. Inside, Rocco mans the door in his usual suit and ever-present aviators, gold chains glinting around his neck.

"You're cutting it close, Tate," he says with a flash of a smile.

"Yet still technically on time." I glance toward the bar where

Randi sits with her laptop, looking like a CEO who took a wrong turn and ended up running a strip club. Her raised eyebrow speaks volumes.

After she took a chance and gave me this opportunity, she's the last person I want to disappoint.

Once inside the club, the dim lighting and thumping music are familiar, almost comforting. A few of the girls wave as I head to the dressing room.

Two years ago, I could never have imagined this place and the people in it would feel like family, but that's exactly what they've become. These girls are more like older sisters. They've given me the necessary skills to not only survive but thrive in this world.

Along with the one that lies outside these walls.

The dressing room is where I shed one identity before slipping into another. Each piece of Lavender Smoke's costume feels like armor, from the black, lacy bustier, the barely-there bottoms, and the silky purple wig that turns me into someone else.

Someone who's untouchable.

Heavy, smoky makeup follows. Since I've never been a girl to wear eyeshadow, blush, or lipstick, it took months of practice to perfect. Thankfully, Jade and Megan were patient teachers. The most fascinating part is watching Holland Tate fade with every stroke of the brush, replaced by the persona I've grown to love over the past year.

It's what allows me to step out of my comfort zone and onto the stage three nights a week. Holland Tate wouldn't be caught dead strutting around and taking off her clothes for a bunch of horny men.

Lavender Smoke, on the other hand, has zero issues with that.

For a price.

One that pays my tuition, rent, and groceries in full every single month.

"Looking good," Megan says, adjusting her own wig beside me.

My phone buzzes with a message from *ColdAsIce17*, and something in my chest loosens. It's ironic that the person who knows me best is someone I've never met.

COLDASICE17

Just wanted to check in and see how you're doing.

A smile tugs at my lips as I type back.

ME

I'm good. Just hustling for a living. How about you?

COLDASICE17

The usual. Ready to run away from it all yet?

My fingers hover over the keys. With him, I don't have to pretend.

ME

Every day. But someone's gotta make sure the bills get paid, right?

The banter is easy, our messages laced with sarcasm, but there's a warmth that lies beneath the surface that keeps me coming back for more.

"Holland!" Jade's voice cuts through my thoughts. "You're up in five."

I shove my phone in my bag, taking one last look in the mirror. Holland Tate stares back at me for a moment before disappearing completely, replaced by someone stronger, someone who doesn't flinch when the music starts.

Time to give them a show.

# BRIDGER

My gaze tracks Holland as she weaves through the crowd at Slap Shotz, all long legs and that flame-red hair that haunts my dreams. She moves like she's ready for war with her chin held high and shoulders back, all the while radiating a touch-me-and-die energy that makes most guys steer clear.

Then again, Garret Akeman isn't most guys.

I watch him intercept her, stepping into her path with practiced ease. She doesn't immediately eviscerate him, which is… interesting.

Or maybe the word I'm searching for is "concerning."

Something hot and ugly twists in my gut when she actually smiles at him. The exchange looks too comfortable.

Almost familiar.

I get along with most of my teammates. And up until recently, I didn't have a problem with him either. But Garret's decided to ride my ass and gun for my position on the team.

The guy can take a flying leap if he thinks I'm just going to roll over and give it to him without a fight.

Her gaze flicks to me for a split second before she dismisses me entirely. That single glance hits like a body check, leaving me winded. Then she turns back to Garret, saying something that makes him lean in closer.

My brows pinch.

*Are they friends?*

*Or worse, more than that?*

Their conversation flows a little too easily, and something about that irritates me. With a tilt of my head, I study the pair more carefully. It's tempting to stalk over there and put the kibosh on whatever game Garret is trying to run.

Over the past couple months, Holland has become my number one suspect in the messages that have been wreaking havoc in my life.

As I stare at them, another thought slams into me.

*What if she isn't the only one behind them?*

*What if she has an accomplice?*

Months of anonymous texts, and now Holland Tate is getting cozy with my biggest rival on the team.

Coincidence?

I don't fucking think so.

A heavy hand lands on my shoulder. "You're doing that thing again," Steele says, sliding onto the barstool next to me.

"What thing?"

"That thing where you look at Holland like you're trying to solve a murder and commit one at the same time."

I tear my gaze away from where she's slipping past Garret toward the exit. "I don't look at her like anything."

"Right." Steele flags down the bartender. "And I'm not about to order another beer just so I can stick around and make sure Lilah gets home safe."

"At least admit you're into your best friend," I say, trying to deflect attention from my own drama.

"Sure. I'll do that as soon as you admit you're not over Holland."

My phone buzzes before I can tell him where to shove that thought. My father's name flashes on the screen. It's his third call tonight.

Steele's expression softens. "Your old man?"

"Yeah." I rub the back of my neck as the tension coils tighter. "I should go deal with this."

"Want backup?"

"Nah." I nod toward where Lilah is laughing at something by the pool tables. "Go save your 'friend' from whatever frat boy she's hustling."

His eyes narrow. "She's not hustling anyone."

"Keep telling yourself that." I stand, tugging my cap lower. "Try not to murder any of her admirers while I'm gone."

A few people reach out and pat my shoulder, congratulating me on winning our first playoff game. It takes more effort than usual to smile and thank them before escaping out the door.

The drive to my father's house is a blur of streetlights and nerves. It's the last place I want to be, but there isn't much choice in the matter. When Richard Sanderson, or *Dick* as I like to call him, demands your presence, you show up, whether you want to or not.

By the time I park outside the sprawling brick Tudor on campus, there's so much dread pooling in my gut that I'm practically drowning in it. I grip the leather steering wheel, willing myself to pull it together before releasing a steady breath.

The sooner I get this over with, the quicker I can get the hell out of here.

That's the only thought I can focus on right now.

The front door creaks open like a warning. Inside, the house is silent. Oppressive. It's always felt more like a museum than a home. I learned at a young age that warm, fuzzy family moments don't happen within these walls. These days, I only come when summoned, like now.

I find him in his study, exactly where I knew he'd be. Richard Sanderson is nothing if not predictable. He stands at the window, bourbon in hand, power stance perfectly calculated.

Everything about the man is calculated.

"You're late," he says, voice cold.

I straighten to my full height, refusing to shrink in his presence like I did when I was a kid. "We were celebrating our win."

He finally turns, his sharp eyes taking me apart piece by piece. "Yes, I watched part of the game. You played like shit." His lip curls. "And then, on top of that, yet another embarrassing message. I'm tired of making excuses for you to the Board of Regents. You're just hell-bent on humiliating me at every turn, aren't you?"

My fingers curl into fists. "You do realize that I'm not the one sending them," I say through gritted teeth. "I'm just as tired of this as you are."

He sets his glass down with a sharp clink that echoes through the room. Three long strides and he's in my face, bourbon breath hot against my cheek. "That's not the point. You're a direct reflection of me, and right now, you're making me look like a fool. You can't even manage your own life."

Even though I know better, I can't stop myself. "Maybe if you just backed—"

The slap cracks across my face before I can finish. My head jerks to the side, copper flooding my mouth where my teeth cut into my cheek. I force myself to remain still, refusing to give him the satisfaction of a reaction.

"You really think I should back off?" His voice drips venom. "How can I do that when you're so incompetent?" A pause, then the killing blow. "Just like your mother."

I bite my tongue, swallowing down both blood and rage. He always brings her up when he wants to gut me. And it works like a charm every time.

"Clean up your act," he says, voice eerily calm. "Or I'll make sure you regret it. Now, get the hell out of my sight."

It takes everything in me not to snap, to throw a punch, to finally fight back. But that's exactly what he wants. Proof that I'm the failure he says I am. Instead, I turn and walk out, each step measured and controlled until I'm back in my car.

Only then do I release the breath I've been holding as my hands shake on the steering wheel. My phone buzzes, and for a second, panic spikes, thinking it's him.

But it's not.

It's her.

FRAGILELIKEABOMB

Sorry to leave you hanging. You still alive over there?

The simple message feels like a life preserver thrown into raging waters. She has no idea how perfect her timing is or how much I need this connection right now.

My cheek throbs as I type back.

For the first time tonight, I finally feel like I can breathe.

ME

Barely. Family drama.

FRAGILELIKEABOMB

On a scale from 1 to vodka, how bad?

A chuckle escapes me. It's genuine and unexpected. The swirling in my stomach eases just a fraction.

ME

Bourbon. The expensive kind. Neat.

FRAGILELIKEABOMB

Ouch. Want to talk about it?

I hesitate. Talking to her feels dangerous, but I can't stop. I'm drawn to this girl, even though I don't know who she is. Or maybe it's *because* I don't know. It's so much easier to be honest with someone who doesn't know me.

Bridger Sanderson.

The chancellor's son.

ME

Not much to say. Just tired of being a punching bag.

FRAGILELIKEABOMB

There's only so much you can take before
you snap and hit back.

Her words crash over me. It's like she's reached into my mind and pulled out the exact feeling I couldn't put into words. No one understands me the way she does. How ironic is it that we've never met? I guess that's part of the attraction. The safety of anonymity that lets me lay my soul bare.

This girl knows all my deepest, darkest secrets.

Even the ones Steele isn't privy to.

ME

Sometimes it feels like I'm tap dancing on the
edge. You're the only one who keeps me
sane.

There's a pause long enough that I wonder if I've scared her off with my honesty. Then her reply lights up my screen.

FRAGILELIKEABOMB

Same. You ever want to walk away, let me
know and I'll walk with you.

My chest tightens, her words breaking through my walls in a way that nothing else could.

ME

Thanks.

FRAGILELIKEABOMB

Anytime.

Enough of the heavy stuff. It's time to lighten the mood a bit.

ME

Pretty sure thinking's overrated, you know?

FRAGILELIKEABOMB

Probably.

Before I can fire off a response, hers pops up.

FRAGILELIKEABOMB

So stop overthinking. You don't have to carry everything alone.

And just like that, the weight pressing down on my shoulders lifts a fraction. She has a way of making me feel like maybe I'm not as alone as I thought.

ME

You're incredible, you know that?

FRAGILELIKEABOMB

Nah. Just telling it like it is.

I stare at her message for a long moment as a rare sense of peace settles over me. It's amazing how one person—someone I've never met—can keep me grounded when everything else feels like it's spiraling out of control.

ME

Thanks.

I drop my head against the seat as her words echo in my mind, and then Holland's face flashes behind my eyes. That's all it takes to destroy the delicate peace blanketing me.

I have the sneaking suspicion that I know exactly who's behind the messages.

My fingers rise to touch my cheek.

Now I just need to prove it.

HOLLAND

"Are we still grabbing lunch at the Union?" Willow asks as we cut across campus for our ten o'clock classes. The sun is out in full force, and the warmth feels good on my face.

"Yeah, pretty sure," I say.

"Pretty sure?" Her eyebrow lifts.

I huff out a breath. "Yeah, I've been trying to get ahold of Vivienne. If she doesn't text back within the next hour, I'll need to pop home and make sure she's still alive."

I wish I were kidding.

"Oh. Everything good on that front?" The concern in Willow's voice makes my chest tight. She's seen enough of my mom's greatest hits to know what "checking on her" usually means.

"I sure as hell hope so."

"Well, let me know. You don't mind if Ava joins us, do you?"

"Not at all. She's cool. I like her."

Willow's eyes widen with mock astonishment. "Wow. Look at you branching out and broadening your social horizons. I'm so proud of you."

A smile teases my lips. "If I'm not careful, I might just get sucked into your little girl gang."

"The horror." She gasps, slapping a hand over her mouth. "What would your high school emo self say?"

I bump her shoulder. "She'd probably write a very angsty poem about it."

My stomach does an odd little flip as Varner Hall comes into view. After two years of avoidance, it feels like everything with Bridger Sanderson is coming to a head.

"All right, I'll see you in a couple of hours." With a wave, Willow takes off toward the tutoring lab for a shift. She gets a dozen or so yards away when Maverick throws his arm around her shoulders before tugging her close.

For just a second, I pause and watch them.

A smile blooms across Willow's face as her boyfriend brushes his lips over hers.

As reluctant as I was to like him, I can't help but admit that he's been good for her. He's aware of her childhood leukemia diagnosis and doesn't treat her like she's made of glass that will crack under the slightest bit of pressure. Even her family has backed off.

Well, sort of.

Becks, her mother, would never willingly take a step in retreat.

"Coveting your bestie's boyfriend, huh?" The dark voice hits me like a physical touch. "That's low. Even for you."

I jump, spinning to find Bridger close enough that I can count the silver flecks in his gray eyes. His cologne wraps around me, woodsy and familiar enough to make my heart stutter. I force myself not to take a giant step in retreat, refusing to give him the satisfaction.

"Hardly." I meet his gaze, ignoring how my skin prickles with awareness.

His lips curve into an infuriating smirk. "You sure about that?"

Instead of responding, I roll my eyes and stride away, hoping to put a little bit of distance between us.

No such luck. He falls into step beside me, his long legs easily matching my pace. "FYI, I'm onto you, Tate."

"Oh?" I keep my eyes forward, focusing on Varner Hall. "What exactly are you onto? Wait, let me guess. You dug out your old Scooby-Doo Mystery Kit and you're hot on the trail of Mr. Carswell, the bank president?"

"Haha. You're hilarious."

I flash him my sweetest smile. "Thanks. I try."

He leans closer, his breath warm against my ear. "I know what you've been up to, and when I get the proof, I'm going to make your life a living hell."

"Promises, promises." I suppress a shiver that has nothing to do with fear. "Good luck with that."

"Just know I'm watching you," he says as we climb the steps to Varner.

"Careful, Sanderson. Someone might think you care."

A group of hockey fans descends on him, giving me the chance to escape. I slip into class, claiming my usual spot by the window. Bridger strolls in a few minutes later. He ignores the girl trying to wave him down as his gaze locks on me like a heat-seeking missile.

"Did you seriously think you were going to get away from me that easily?" He looms over my desk.

"That was the hope."

He turns to the guy next to me. "Mind if I sit here?"

The traitor practically trips over himself to give up his seat. Bridger slides in, his thigh brushing mine as he settles. "I'm going to be all up in your business until I can prove you're behind the messages."

"Wow." I shake my head. "You really are delusional. How sad. You might want to seek treatment before you descend into total madness." I blink and force my eyes wide. "Or is it too late for that?"

"Unfortunately not." He shifts closer, his scent making my head spin. "I think you've been holding a grudge for two long years."

With a snort, I swivel to face him. "For what? One lousy lay?" I arch a brow as color floods his cheeks. "Do you really think sex with you ruined me for all others? I'm all like—*boo hoo*, I don't get to have Sanderson's dick on the regular." I roll my eyes. "Give me a freaking break."

A muscle tics in his jaw. "Funny, I didn't hear any complaints from you in the moment."

"Well, a tutorial of the female anatomy just seemed rude at the time."

"Then you gave one hell of a performance." His voice drops lower until it's rough around the edges.

"Consider it an act of mercy." My tone is casual, but my pulse is pounding in my ears. "I just wanted to speed things up. It was late, and I was tired."

He leans in, close enough that I can feel the heat radiating off him. "I think we both know I could prove you wrong."

"Too bad you won't be given the opportunity to try." My gaze flicks to the bruise on his cheek. "Let me guess, bar brawl over an eager bunny?"

Dark emotion flashes in his eyes before it's quickly masked. "Nailed it."

Something in his tone makes my stomach curdle, but before I can analyze it, Dr. Abbott launches into his lecture about our final project. Once this semester ends, I'll never have to deal with Bridger Sanderson again.

Thank fuck.

"You'll be paired with a classmate," Abbott announces, his gaze sweeping the room.

My muscles lock. He's going alphabetically. I frantically search my memory for anyone between Sanderson and Tate but come up empty.

"Bridger Sanderson and—"

*Please don't say me.*

*Please don't—*

"Holland Tate."

My pen clatters to the desk. Bridger turns, his gaze burning into my profile.

"I couldn't have planned this more perfectly myself," he whispers, satisfaction dripping from his tone.

I force my features into something resembling calm, choking down the urge to scream. We can't be within three feet of each other without verbal warfare breaking out. How the hell are we supposed to work together?

The second Abbott dismisses class, I'm out of my seat and

heading for his desk. I feel the weight of Bridger's stare burning a hole through my back as he takes his sweet time packing up.

"Miss Tate?" Abbott looks up. "Questions about the project?"

I clear my throat, aiming for reasonable rather than desperate. "Just one. Is there any way I can work alone? I'm willing to do everything my—"

"I'm afraid not." His smile is tight. "In the real world, you won't get to choose your colleagues. Consider it a lesson in learning how to play nice with others."

The condescension in his tone makes me grit my teeth. "Got it. Thanks for the insight."

I turn to leave, only to find Bridger leaning against the wall outside the room, waiting like a predator.

He falls into step beside me. "Looks like you and I are stuck together for the next couple weeks, Tate."

"Apparently." I don't bother hiding my irritation.

His lips twitch. "Told you I was going to stick to you like glue."

I stop short, spinning to face him. "Let me be crystal clear, Sanderson. I don't like you. And I sure as hell don't want to be anywhere near you."

He tilts his head, eyes darkening. "That wasn't always the case, now was it?"

My spine stiffens. Even at five-ten, I have to crane my neck to meet his gaze. "That was a long time ago."

"And yet…" His voice drops lower, turning silky, when he finishes with, "Sometimes it feels just like yesterday."

"No, what it feels like is ancient history." I step closer, jabbing my finger into his chest. "Not to mention completely forgettable."

"So you keep saying." His hand catches mine before I can pull back, his thumb brushing over my knuckles. The touch sends electricity shooting up my arm. "I think we both know that's a lie."

I yank my hand free, ignoring how my skin tingles where he touched me. "You have absolutely nothing I want." I turn away, desperate to escape before he realizes just how much he's able to affect me. "Now, if you'll excuse me, I have better places to be."

His low chuckle follows me out into the sunshine. I pull out my phone, trying to focus on my mother's radio silence rather than the lingering warmth of his touch.

I give her number two more tries before accepting that I'll have to make the trip home. The forty-five-minute drive gives me way too much time to think.

About what Bridger's hand felt like on mine.

About my mother's latest crisis waiting to happen.

About how my life seems to be one endless cycle of damage control.

Our tiny bungalow comes into view, looking exactly like it has since I was a kid—

slightly neglected but still standing. A black plastic ashtray sits on the railing, cigarette butts spilling over the edges despite my constant lectures about lung cancer.

While I've never doubted her love for me, the woman will never win mother of the year. She's more of a dreamer. An eternal optimist who floats through life in a bubble of her own making. Her superpower is her ability to find lowlifes and try to turn them into her next great love interest.

What Vivienne has yet to realize is that she won't find Prince Charming at the bottom of her beer glass at a local corner dive bar.

And it wouldn't be the first time she's taken off for a couple days without so much as a word.

So, Vivienne being MIA isn't necessarily something to be overly concerned about. But I still feel compelled to stop home at least once a week to make sure she's alive and paying the bills on time. Even when I was a kid, it felt more like I was the parent and she was the child.

I'm sure it doesn't help that she was only sixteen when she got knocked up. When she couldn't tell her parents who the father was, they kicked her pregnant ass out of the house.

And it's been the two of us ever since.

Every so often, someone tries to be a third wheel, but it never lasts long before they end up ditching her. Mom is a lot to handle. She's fun for a week or so, but then it becomes a little much.

I peer through the windows but see no signs of life. My heart clenches with that familiar fear. The one that whispers maybe this time she's really gone too far.

When I test the front door handle, I find it unlocked.

How did I end up with all the self-preservation skills and my mother got zero?

The living room tells its own story. Beer cans are scattered across end tables, there's a half-empty bottle of Boone's Farm—Mom's signature drink when she's entertaining—along with a glass smeared with bright-red lipstick.

"Mom?" I call out, my voice echoing through the quiet house. After a beat, I try again, louder.

A shuffling sound comes from her bedroom. The door creaks open to reveal my mother, hair disheveled, wearing an oversized white T-shirt.

"Holland?" She blinks at me. "What are you doing here so early?"

She steps into the hallway, carefully pulling the door closed behind her until it clicks.

"Mom, it's almost noon."

She glances toward the window like the sun might be playing tricks on her. "Really?"

"Yeah." My gaze darts to the closed bedroom door. "Is someone else here?"

Her face lights up like a kid on Christmas morning. "Oh, honey, I met the most fabulous man." She hugs herself, practically vibrating with excitement. "I think he might be the one."

That's when I notice the gap in her smile where a tooth should be.

"What the hell happened to you?"

Her hand flies to her mouth, expression turning sheepish. "I had a little accident when we came home from the bar the other night."

"Jesus. Are you all right?"

She waves off my concern. "I'm fine. It was so stupid. I tripped on the walkway and hit the cement face-first."

"You'll have to call the dentist—"

"Oh, I don't know if I'm going to bother. Dale says it adds character."

I stare at her, wondering how this is my life. "Mom, you can't walk around like that."

"You're making a big deal out of nothing. You didn't even notice at first."

My gaze catches on a worn leather vest thrown over a dining room chair. Before I can reach for it, Mom's voice turns sharp.

"Don't touch that! Dale was really weird about it."

The stone in my gut turns to lead. "Please tell me he isn't part of a biker gang."

Her eyes widen with childlike excitement. "How did you know?"

"Mom..."

She drops her voice to a conspiratorial whisper. "They call him Jigsaw, but he won't tell me why."

When I continue staring, she bounces on her toes, making the oversized shirt ride higher. "Hey! Are you seeing anyone? He's got some friends who seemed nice. Maybe we could double date!"

"Absolutely not."

She rolls her eyes. "You're so judgy, Holland. You really need to chill out and live a little."

I press my lips together, swallowing back all the things I want to scream.

About responsibility.

And consequences.

Or how I've spent my entire life watching her "live a little" before cleaning up the aftermath.

"Look, I need to take off." I force my voice to remain steady. "I just wanted to stop by and make sure everything was good. If you'd answer your phone once in a while, I wouldn't have to go out of my way to check up on you."

She closes the distance between us, cupping my cheek in her warm palm. "Aww, but I'm glad you did. I enjoy seeing your pretty face. I love you, baby girl."

And just like that, my anger melts into resignation. Nothing is ever going to change with Vivienne. She is who she is.

"I love you too."

She smiles, the gap in her teeth making her look vulnerable in a way that breaks my heart.

"I'll let you know what the dentist says. I'm sure between the two of us, we can figure out a way to pay for it." I can already see my savings account draining, my carefully built safety net dissolving.

"Okay. And think about the double date. Dale said his friends have a real thing for curvy redheads."

"I'm way too busy with school to date." Or get tangled up with a biker.

"Sounds awfully boring."

"Yup, that's me. Boring."

I press a kiss to her cheek before heading for the door, my chest already tight with the need to escape.

To breathe.

"I'll let you know what the dentist says."

"No worries."

I almost snort. That's Mom's mantra. *No worries.* And somehow it always works out for her.

For me? Not so much.

Back in my car, I'm about to turn the key when my phone lights up with a notification from the college chat app.

COLDASICE17

Thanks for your message the other night. It was exactly what I needed to hear. I don't know how you knew, but... thanks.

Warmth blooms within me, pushing back against the cold weight of responsibility. Our connection might only exist through words on a screen, but it's the one thing in my life that feels real.

Important.

This guy understands me like no one else.

And I get him too.

ME

I'm always here for you.

His reply comes instantly.

COLDASICE17

Same. Just know that this thing between us matters to me.

A lump rises in my throat. My guard slips as I type back.

ME

I feel the same. Our relationship is one of the only things that keeps me sane.

There's a pause before he responds.

COLDASICE17

Good to know. We might not have much, but we have each other.

His understanding wraps around me like a blanket, making me feel safe and warm. He might be a stranger, but he sees me in ways no one else does. Between my mother's chaos, Bridger's threats, and the weight of everything I'm juggling, these conversations are sometimes the only thing that feels real.

The only place I can truly be myself.

ME

Life, family, relationships—they've never come easy. Remember when you asked if I wanted to walk away from it all? Today is definitely one of those days.

I start the car, grateful that at least one thing in my life makes sense, even if they're just simple messages. As I pull away from the house, I try not to think about the dentist bill waiting in my future, or the project I'll have to suffer through with Bridger.

One crisis at a time.

That's all anyone can handle, right?

BRIDGER
SANDERSON
17
17
7
WILDCATS

The puck whizzes past my stick while my mind replays the last mass text and my father's reaction. We haven't spoken since that night.

The silence is blissful.

Out of all the possible suspects on this campus, one name keeps circling my thoughts like a shark in bloody water.

Holland Tate.

Her parting shot after class still burns.

Nothing about our sexual encounter was forgettable.

Not that I'd ever admit it, but I obsessed about that night for months. The way her body—

"Sanderson!" Coach's whistle pierces the air. "What the hell was that? My grandmother has better hands, and she's been dead ten years." He jerks his head toward the bench. "Akeman, show him how it's done."

Perfect.

Garret fucking Akeman.

At the beginning of the season, he'd been gunning for Ryder McAdams's spot before getting it through his thick head that he didn't have a shot. Now he's turned his attention to mine.

He glides onto the ice, all cocky attitude and unearned confidence. "Don't worry, Coach. I got this."

I clench my stick so hard, my fingers cramp. One punch. That's all it would take to wipe that smirk off his face.

In the end, the few seconds of pleasure it'll give me won't be worth it.

Especially if my father catches wind of it.

I drop onto the bench and guzzle down some water before silently stewing. It's a relief when Coach ends practice and everyone files off the ice.

My mind tumbles back to the beginning of the season and how epic I thought it would be to play the sport I've always enjoyed, with guys who've become more like brothers to me.

Fast forward six months, and my life feels more like a living hell I can't see my way out of.

I push into the locker room and throw my stick in the holder near the door. The place is already thick with the scent of sweat along with humidity from the showers.

With a huff, I settle on the bench to unlace my skates before shoving them in my locker. Next comes the jersey and chest pad. Just as I'm peeling off my elbow pads, Garret saunters over with a white towel slung around his hips and a shit-eating grin quirking his lips.

"Rough practice, huh?" he says, leaning against the locker beside mine. "Better watch it, or I'll be taking your place on the second line."

I stiffen. There's no way in hell I'll allow that to happen.

"Fuck off, Akeman."

His eyes light up as his smile broadens. "Nah, don't think I will. It's about time Coach realized the only reason you have a place on this team is because of your old man."

I almost snort but rein it in at the last second.

This guy doesn't know what he's talking about. My father didn't lift a finger or make any phone calls to get me on this team. I earned the position on my own. If Dick had his way, I wouldn't be wasting my time playing college hockey.

But I'm not about to share that with this douchebag.

It's none of his business.

Ignoring him, I strip off the padded pants and stuff them in my locker.

When he continues to stare, I snap, "Is there something else you'd like to add?"

He shrugs, the picture of nonchalance, but there's an edge in his gaze, as if something is bristling beneath the surface, scratching to get out.

"Nope."

"Great." I strip off my jock and head to the showers.

I've always been even-tempered, but I've found myself snapping more than usual lately. Everything that's been happening has been slowly building within me like a geyser.

By the time I return to my locker, most of my anger has drained away.

Half of the guys have already taken off.

"Any interest in grabbing something to eat?" Hayes glances my way as he shoves his feet into slides.

I pull on my hoodie. "Can't. I'm meeting someone at the library to work on a project."

"Bummer."

"Yeah." It's probably for the best. I wouldn't be good company right now. "I'll catch you back at the house later tonight."

He takes a step before faltering, his gaze meeting mine. "You doing okay?"

I jerk my head in a nod and force a brittle smile. It feels like I've been doing that more often lately. "Yeah, it's all good."

"You sure about that? Because I'm here if you need to talk." He glances down the row of lockers until his gaze lands on Garret. Mine does the same. "We might be teammates, but I have no problem kicking his ass." Hayes gives me a lopsided smile before raising his voice so that it carries. "In fact, it would be a real pleasure."

"Suck my dick, Van Doren," Garret yells back.

"Nah. Too small. I like a meatier cock."

All right, that does it. My lips lift into a genuine smile when Garret glares and gives him the finger.

Only Hayes would say something like that.

It makes me realize just how much I'm going to miss him next year.

I grab my backpack and head out of the locker room with Hayes at my side. "How's everything going with Ava?"

My mind is still blown that they're officially an item. And that Coach didn't bury him somewhere deep in the woods where his body will never be found.

"Couldn't be better."

I shake my head. "Can't say I ever thought the day would come when you settled down." There's a pause before I add, "But you seem happy. I'm glad for you."

Some of the humor that's always present in his eyes fades, only to be replaced by solemnness.

It's a scary look on him.

"I love her," he says simply. "And one day, I'm going to marry the girl."

My eyes widen. "Wow."

"Yup." The seriousness melts away as he flashes another grin. "All right, man. I'm going to take off."

And then Hayes is gone, jogging to his Ford Bronco. The truck is a throwback from the nineties, but he loves it. Even when he can afford a brand-new vehicle, it's doubtful he'll ever get rid of it.

With a huffed-out breath, I head to the library to meet up with Holland. Even thinking about the green-eyed, auburn-haired girl pisses me off.

All right, so maybe it does a little more than that.

For two years, she's been an itch I haven't been able to scratch. An unexpected closeness sprung up between us. One I found myself gravitating to as much as I wanted to run away from it.

By the time I reach the library, the need to see her thrums through me like that of a steady drumbeat.

As much as I want her to confess that she's the one behind the messages, I want her to admit that I'm not the only one haunted by what happened between us.

HOLLAND

5

# HOLLAND



I read over the message again, letting the words sink into my bones. It's almost eerie how Ice knows exactly what to say, how he sees straight through my carefully constructed walls to the mess underneath. I've never experienced this kind of understanding with anyone else.

Not even Willow.

Most days I feel adrift, like I don't quite fit anywhere. The weight of responsibility has been crushing me for so long, I've almost forgotten what it feels like to breathe freely.

My fingers hover over the screen to reply when a shadow falls across my table. I look up to find Bridger Sanderson looming over me, and just like that, the peace from Ice's message evaporates.

He drops into the chair across from me without a word.

When my stomach dips, I tell myself it's irritation and not the lingering attraction I can't seem to kill. I slip my phone into my bag, trying to ignore how his eyes track the movement.

"Who were you texting?" The question comes out sharp, almost possessive.

"That would be none of your business." I shove the phone deeper into my bag. "Can we just get started? The sooner we hash this out, the quicker I can move on with my life."

His lips twitch as his gaze lingers on my bag for a beat longer before he nods. "Fine by me, Tate. Not like I'm any more thrilled to be partnered up with you." He leans back in his chair and folds his arms over his broad chest. "Just to be clear, if you think I'm going to get stuck doing all the work, you're delusional."

Barely do I resist the urge to bare my teeth and leap across the table at him. "Let me get this straight. You actually think I'd rely on *you* for my grade? I'd rather chew broken glass than take that risk."

His eyes darken before the corners of his mouth lift into something that almost resembles a smile, and for a second, I forget why I can't stand him. Until he looks at me with that infuriatingly smug expression and I'm reminded of the reason.

With a huff, I flip open my laptop and bring up the assignment details.

"Abbott wants a mock business pitch," I say. "We've got two weeks to come up with an original concept, research the market, and put together a full financial plan."

I reluctantly glance up only to find him watching me. When our eyes collide, a shiver dances down my spine.

"As usual, I'm way ahead of you, Tate. I read over the rubric and already have a list of potential ideas."

I pop a brow. "Oh?"

Well, color me surprised.

"The first one is a digital platform that pairs college athletes with local businesses for sponsorships and endorsements."

Even though I secretly think it's an interesting idea, I roll my eyes. "Of course your brain would go there first. What else do you have?"

"How about a sustainable clothing line that only uses recycled and eco-friendly materials? The pitch could focus on filling a growing demand for green fashion that targets Gen Z and Millennials who care about the environment."

Damn. That's actually good.

I'd rather rip out my own vocal cords than admit it, though.

"Hmmm. I suppose that could work." When his brows rise, I add, "Let's just say I don't totally hate the idea."

His eyes narrow.

The fact that I can annoy him so easily calms me in a way nothing else can.

"I jotted down a few others," he grinds out. "Should I continue?"

I wave a hand. "Nah. We'll just go with that one. I'm sure you mentally taxed yourself coming up with the first two."

"Not even close. I've got six other ideas ready to go. Want to hear them?"

A small smile spreads across my lips. "Nope. That'll work."

He taps his fingers on the table in a slow and deliberate rhythm as he contemplates me. "Are you certain?"

"Positive."

He grunts before moving on. "I'll take product development and financials. You can handle branding and social media." There's a pause before he adds, "You know, the fluffy stuff."

"Fluffy stuff?" Is he kidding? "I didn't realize financial projections could be done by someone who skated through his math classes because his daddy's chancellor of the university."

A muscle pops in his jaw before ticking a mad rhythm, but he doesn't miss a beat. "Daddy's never done a damn thing for me. And I didn't realize you'd want to tackle market research. Do you even know the difference between organic cotton and recycled polyester?"

"I know exactly what they are," I fire back, my blood starting to boil. As much as I hate to admit it, arousal blooms in my core. It's so sick and twisted.

Am I seriously getting off on our verbal sparring?

The answer to that question is yes.

Yes, I am.

I quash it before continuing. "And I understand that we need them both if we want to stand out in a market that's oversaturated with people trying to be 'eco' without any actual commitment. How about you handle social media and branding, and I'll work on something with a little more substance."

Bridger leans forward, his gaze sharp. "Sounds like you've got a lot to say about people who *pretend* to care about sustainability. Let me guess... personal crusade of yours?"

"It's called integrity, Sanderson. Try looking it up sometime."

He laughs, the sound low and annoyingly attractive. "Fine, Tate. Have it your way. You take product development and the financials. I'll figure out what our branding and social media presence will look like. Just know that you better bring A-level work. There's no way I'm taking a hit to my grade just so you can attempt to prove something."

"Excuse me? I'm a four-point-oh student and can run academic circles around you." When he opens his mouth to argue, I raise my hand. "You know what? Let's stop bickering and just get to work. We're wasting time." I can't resist tacking on, "Not to mention brain cells. And you have so few to spare."

Satisfaction floods through me when his lips tighten into a thin line and he growls out his response in one snappy syllable. "Fine."

Even though it's tempting to glance at him, I force myself to open a new document on the computer and start typing notes. With his gaze pinned to mine, ignoring him feels impossible.

After a handful of silent minutes, he finally opens his own laptop and gets to work. Just as I lose myself in an industry report, he says, "We should probably look for eco-friendly influencers."

"That was my thought as well. Do you follow any?"

"Nope."

"I guess it would have been more helpful if our project focused on something fluffy and meaningless like what the next viral challenge was," I say innocently, scrolling through lists of eco-conscious brands for inspiration.

"Whatever you say, Tate," he mutters. "Just make sure your influencer buddies know what they're actually selling."

"Oh, don't worry," I reply, voice saccharine-sweet, "I'll even teach you how to do a sustainable brand launch without blowing the budget on a massive ego trip. If you're not careful, you just might learn a thing or two."

His smirk never falters. "Huh. It kind of sounds like you should take the fluffy stuff after all."

Before I can come up with a scathing comeback, our phones buzz simultaneously. Bridger glances at his cell, and his expression hardens. I reluctantly fish mine out of my bag to see a new anonymous message lighting up the screen.

ANONYMOUS MESSAGE

Looks like Sanderson is getting downsized from the hockey team. Apparently Daddy's money and power can't buy everything. Hey, Sanderson… Don't let the locker room door hit you in the ass on the way out.

I glance back at him as fury leaps to life in his eyes.

For just a second, I almost feel sorry for him.

It's one thing to deal with someone like Bridger head-on but quite another to continually get shit on by some faceless troll on a public forum. The entire university is reading that message.

And what did it even mean?

Did Bridger get benched?

Or worse, cut from the team?

Before I can come up with something to say, he scowls and holds up his phone. "Just fucking admit it, Tate. You're the one behind this, aren't you?"

My mouth drops open as my eyes pop wide. "Excuse me?"

He leans in, pressing against the table that separates us, as his expression turns thunderous. "Save the innocent act for someone who'll buy it. I know you've had it out for me since—" His words fall off and his jaw tightens. I blink as a mixture of sorrow and regret flash in his eyes before being quickly masked. "Whatever game you're intent on playing ends right now."

A burst of anger flares to life inside me that's fueled by two years of buried resentment and hurt. "Do you seriously think I'd waste my time or energy messing with you? Please. Like I told you before, what happened between us didn't mean anything, and it certainly wasn't something I thought twice about. Hate to burst your bubble, but it was just as boring and unforgettable as every other interaction we've had."

His jaw clenches as his expression hardens into an unreadable mask. "Kind of coincidental that you mentioned my daddy and seconds later, this message with the same reference pops up."

I stare at the cell in his hand.

Yeah... it is an odd coincidence. I can see how it could paint me in a suspicious light.

I straighten on the chair and notch my chin higher. "It wasn't me. I know you don't think much of my word, but I swear it wasn't."

"Well, you're right about one thing." He tosses the cell onto the table, where it clatters. "I don't think much of your word."

The silence between us stretches until it turns taut and electric. When I can't stand another second of it, I shove my chair back and pop to my feet. There's zero point in us going around in circles.

"You know what? Screw this and screw you. I'm out of here."

My hands tremble as I snap my laptop shut and shove it into my bag. Before I can haul it onto my shoulder, Bridger leaps to his feet.

"You're not going anywhere until I get some answers."

His fingers close around my upper arm, holding me in place.

Shock floods my system as my gaze drops to his hand. "What the hell do you think you're doing?"

"We're not done talking," he grits out.

My pulse quickens as I stare up at him. He's so close that it would be impossible not to feel the heat radiating off his body. A yelp escapes from me as he steers me toward the shelves, guiding me into the stacks, away from prying eyes. Even though my legs are long, I have to hasten my steps to keep pace with him.

"Bridger!" I hiss, trying to yank my arm free, but his grip remains tight.

Punishing.

We turn another corner before he grinds to a halt and locks his other hand around my upper arm before taking a step forward, forcing me to retreat until my spine meets the cold metal of the bookcase. My breath catches as he swallows up the space between us until his hard body is pressed against my softer one.

It's so tempting to shift against him.

Instead, I force myself to remain perfectly still.

"What the hell do you think you're doing?" My voice comes out far breathier than intended as I hold his gaze, refusing to back down.

His gaze searches mine before dipping to my mouth.

"I don't know," he admits, sounding strangely confused. "I'm tired of feeling this way where you're concerned."

I swallow hard, almost afraid to push out the words but needing to know the answer just the same. "Feeling what way?"

I couldn't be more aware of how close we're standing or the hard length of his erection that juts against my abdomen. When I have to stifle the urge to wriggle against it, I realize that it's been a couple months since I had sex.

Clearly, that's the only reason I'm so turned on.

It has absolutely nothing to do with Bridger Sanderson.

I can't stand this guy.

*At all.*

My pulse quickens as his gaze lingers on my lips. When my tongue darts out to moisten them, his eyes darken, and a groan rumbles up from his chest. The sound of it strums something deep within my core.

Without another word, his mouth captures mine in a kiss that's all heat and fury. As tempting as it is to give in, I keep my lips clamped together. The frustrated growl that breaks loose from him is sweet music to my ears.

It's only when he nips my lower lip that I open my mouth on a gasp. It's just enough for him to force his way inside until his tongue can tangle with mine. The kiss is nothing like the ones we shared in the past. There's not an ounce of softness to be found. It's hard and demanding, bursting with everything neither of us are willing to voice out loud.

I don't realize that he's released my arms until his hands rise to cup my cheeks so I'm held firmly in place.

He pulls away just enough to mutter, "This. *This* is exactly what I can't forget about."

Before my brain can process the words, his mouth reclaims mine, devouring it. When he deepens the caress, my defenses crumble, giving way to the heat and chaos we always seem to generate. I've never felt anything like it before, and I'm scared to death I won't feel anything like it again.

He can't be the only one capable of stoking this fire to life inside me.

That's exactly when reality crashes down on me. It takes every bit of strength I possess to shove him away. My breathing turns harsh as I stare at him in shock. Every beat of my heart pumps a mixture of anger and something far more dangerous through my bloodstream.

"I'm not the one behind the messages," I whisper, my voice thick. "But I wish I were."

With that, I shove past Bridger, leaving him in the shadows of the stacks as I stalk away, my head a mess of confusion and anger.

Exactly what I don't need where this guy is concerned.

# WESTERN UNIVERSITY CHAT APP

# BRIDGER

By the time I reach the house, my mind is still tangled up in Holland Tate. No matter how hard I try, I can't shake the memory of that kiss. The heat of it, the way she looked at me with fire in her eyes one second and ice the next. No one else on the planet crawls under my skin the way that girl does.

As much as I hate it, a sick part of me enjoyed every second of it.

The usual chaos greets me when I step inside our house. Maverick and Hayes are tossing a football across the living room while Ryder and Riggs are battling it out on *Madden*.

Steele emerges from the kitchen with a beer in hand. Concern flashes in his eyes as soon as he spots me. "I take it you saw the latest message?"

I drag a hand through my hair. "Unfortunately."

He winces. "Sorry. That was harsh. How are you holding up?"

"Couldn't be better." I pull out my phone and scroll through the familiar thread of messages, looking for clues as to who's behind them. "It doesn't mean a damn thing, right?"

He levels me with a hard look. "Bro. Stop blowing smoke up my ass."

Yeah, I didn't think he'd buy it.

His expression darkens as he steps closer. "To insinuate that you're getting benched or cut from the team is bullshit."

The reminder ignites my anger all over again. I'd been so consumed by Holland.

By the taste of her.

The feel of her.

So much so, that I'd almost forgotten about Coach pulling me.

"Is it?" The words come out sounding bitter.

"You know it is. It was one shitty practice." He taps my temple with his finger. "Don't let it fuck with your head. We both know that's when problems start."

He's right. Once doubt creeps in, it's all downhill from there. Hockey is just as much of a mental game as a physical one.

Maybe even more so.

I scan the living room. Teammates are sprawled across couches and girls are floating around, looking for attention. "Whoever's behind this knows what happened at practice. It has to be someone on the team." My jaw tightens. "Or they're being fed information."

What I've learned these past few months is that paranoia is a real bitch. Especially when you're looking at guys you've known for years, wondering if they were ever your friends to begin with.

Steele straightens, his usual easygoing demeanor vanishing. "Come on, man. You really think it could be someone on the team?" His gaze sweeps the room. "No way would any of them do that to you."

"How'd they know Coach pulled me from the scrimmage?"

"It could've been anyone in the stands. Practice isn't private."

True enough. Which means we're back to square one.

"Whoever it is has a real hard-on for you," Steele continues. "And the messages keep getting more personal. It only makes sense that it's someone you know."

My mind circles back to green eyes and auburn hair, to the way Holland felt pressed against me in the library stacks. The taste of her still lingers on my tongue.

"What if it *is* her?" The words come out rough. "She's the only one who has a reason to hate me this much."

Steele's eyebrow lifts. "Are we back to Holland Tate again?"

"She refuses to admit it, but I think she's bitter about what happened between us."

"I don't know." He looks torn between support and skepticism. "You've confronted her and she's denied it. There's not a shred of proof. Does she even have those kinds of computer skills? Or know someone who does?"

"It's more of a gut feeling." But doubt simmers beneath my certainty. "I need to keep a closer eye on her. That way, when she slips up, I'll be there."

"And how exactly are you going to do that? Last I checked, she couldn't stand to be in the same zip code as you."

I shrug, but my mind's already spinning. "I'll figure something out."

He shakes his head, taking a long pull from his beer. "I hate that this is happening to you. You don't deserve it."

I clap his shoulder, managing a half-smile. "I appreciate it."

Instead of joining the guys, I retreat to my room and pull out my phone. Deep down, there's a part of me that wonders if I'm too blinded by my emotions to see Holland clearly.

*What if I'm wrong?*

All I know is there's an irresistible force between us that I can't fight. I can still remember the way she dropped her guard enough for me to catch a glimpse of the real Holland Tate. At the time, it scared the hell out of me. I told myself it was best to bury the uncomfortable feelings she roused and walk away.

Now, here I am, right back where I started. A tangled mess of regret and attraction with a few added layers of anger and suspicion. She's camped out in my head, and no matter what I do, I can't evict her.

When I scroll through my messages with *FragileLikeABomb*, I feel that same pull, that same twisted sense of connection. The way she gets under my skin. It's different from Holland but somehow just as intense.

It doesn't make sense.

I reread our latest exchange, wondering why her words always strike such a familiar chord. She knows things I've never told anyone else.

Things I can barely admit to myself.

My fingers hover over the screen before I type.

ME

> What do you think it takes to really trust someone? How do you know when they're being real with you?

Maybe I'm asking because Holland's denial has me questioning my instincts. Deep down, I want to believe her. I want to believe she wouldn't strike out and hurt me so publicly.

Her response is cautious, like she can sense my mood.

FRAGILELIKEABOMB

> Trust is messy. People lie, even when they don't mean to. Sometimes it's about protecting yourself… or someone else. Why do you ask?

Her words hit a little too close to home.

She's right.

Sometimes it's all about self-preservation.

ME

> What if lying is all you've ever known? What if you're just trying to keep things together?

There's a pause. When her next message comes through, it's softer. Like she understands exactly what I mean.

FRAGILELIKEABOMB

> Then maybe you haven't met the right people yet. The ones who don't need the lies. Sometimes trust is just… surviving, you know? Getting through each day in order to conquer the next.

My chest tightens. There's something about her words that feels meant for me, not just my screen. Before I can respond, she sends another message.

FRAGILELIKEABOMB

> Guess it's hard to tell who to trust when it feels like everyone's hiding something. Sometimes I think we even hide the truth from ourselves. Anything to make life easier.

I stare at the screen, letting her words settle into the parts of me I usually keep locked away. It's like she knows what it's like to carry secrets that weigh you down, to wear a mask just to get through the day.

FRAGILELIKEABOMB

> Are you good?

I draw a deep breath into my lungs and hold it until they burn.

ME

> Yeah, I am. Thanks.

FRAGILELIKEABOMB

> No problem. That's what I'm here for.

ME

> I'm glad you are.

I second-guess myself as soon as I hit send. This is the most real I've been with anyone, and it makes me feel like my skin is too tight for my body.

Just when I consider ending the conversation, another message pops up.

FRAGILELIKEABOMB

> Enough heaviness for tonight. Let's keep it light. Favorite movie. Go.

A smirk tugs at my lips as the tension drains away.

ME

> Not telling. You'll laugh.

FRAGILELIKEABOMB

Now you have to tell me. Come on, spill.

I hesitate, then type it out, feeling ridiculous but strangely relieved when I hit send.

ME

Fine. Die Hard. Maybe it's not a Christmas movie, but it's my guilty pleasure.

Her response is instant.

FRAGILELIKEABOMB

Die Hard?! All right, I'll give you points for taste. But I'll bet you've never watched The Breakfast Club.

ME

What? Please. The Breakfast Club is a classic.

FRAGILELIKEABOMB

We might have more in common than I thought. Scary.

I let out a breath I didn't realize I was holding, feeling lighter. The emotions about Holland still simmer beneath the surface as I tell myself that this thing with FragileLikeABomb isn't dangerous.

How could it be when it's anonymous?

Detached.

Safe.

Maybe like she said, it's one of the lies we tell ourselves to make it through to the next day.

HOLLAND

# HOLLAND

"I'm sorry, he did *what*?" Ava's coffee cup freezes halfway to her mouth, her eyes wide. "Bridger actually accused you of posting those anonymous messages online?"

"Yup," I say, shrugging with an indifference I don't feel. "Apparently, I'm living rent-free in his head. Evil plan accomplished."

Willow bites her lip, giving me one of her careful looks, the kind that makes me want to squirm. "So, what really happened with you two anyway? Because the daggers you shoot at him aren't exactly subtle, and now he's accusing you of, what, cyberstalking?"

I roll my eyes as a slight twist of unease settles in my stomach.

"Nothing happened. At least—" The words stick in my throat. "Nothing that matters."

They continue to stare.

"Fine." The admission feels like glass in my mouth. "Freshman year we hooked up. Once. And before either of you say anything, just know that it was an accident and totally meaningless."

"An accident?" Ava's eyebrow arches. "Did you trip and fall on his—"

"Don't." My lips twitch despite myself.

"Are you sure it was meaningless?" Willow's voice softens. "Because from where I'm sitting—"

"Trust me, it was nothing." The words come out too sharp, too fast. "He's an egotistical asshat who thinks I'm obsessed with him. Like I have time for that."

"Or maybe," Willow ventures carefully, "you're both still a little hung up on each other?"

I turn my glare on her. "The only thing I'm hung up on is how he ghosted me like I was some random puck bunny."

Shit. I didn't mean to say that.

"Hold up." Ava straightens. "He ghosted you?"

"It doesn't matter." I glance at the clock, and relief floods me. "I need to go. Mom stuff."

"Holland—"

"Say hi to Vivienne," Willow calls as I grab my bag.

Guilt twists in my stomach as I meet her eyes. For a second, I consider spilling everything. About the club, about Ice, about how that night with Bridger meant more than I've ever admitted to anyone.

Instead, I run.

The Envy Room is already packed when I arrive, the parking lot full of expensive cars belonging to men trying to buy what they can't have. Rocco gives me his usual chin lift as I pass, which I return. We're both people of few words.

The dressing room thrums with conversation and the muffled

bass from the club, but I barely notice. My mind keeps circling back to Bridger. To the hurt in his eyes before he masked it with anger. To the way he'd pressed me against those library shelves like he couldn't decide if he wanted to kiss me or kill me.

"You look ready to commit murder." Jade drops into the chair beside me. "Bad day?"

I let out a sharp laugh. "Something like that."

"Let me guess... Boy trouble?"

"You're two for two." I open the tube of lipstick, hoping the physical action will shut down the mess raging in my head.

"Holland." Randi's voice cuts through the chatter. She stands by the door, all sleek power in stilettos, her gaze locked on me.

When she crooks a finger, I follow.

"Is everything all right?" she asks once we're in the hallway, her tone softer than her expression.

I blink. "Yeah, why?"

She leans against the wall, arms crossed. "Because you've got that look I see right before girls start making mistakes. The one that says their head's somewhere else entirely." Her eyes narrow. "I'm not in the business of letting my girls look lost on stage. Ruins the fantasy and kills the tips."

I open my mouth to deflect, but something in her expression stops me. "There's just... a lot going on. But it's nothing I can't handle."

"Listen." She steps closer, voice dropping. "The day you walked in here, you had purpose. Pay your bills, take care of yourself, get where you need to be. Don't let anyone, especially some boy, mess with that."

My throat tightens.

She sees way more than I want her to.

"You've got something special, Holland. You're smart and driven." A small smile plays on her lips. "In a lot of ways, you remind me of myself at your age. Don't lose sight of your goals because some guy's got you twisted up inside."

I swallow hard. Randi built this place from nothing and turned judgment into power. She's everything I want to be. Strong, untouchable, and in control.

"Thanks," I manage. "I won't."

She gives me a long look before nodding. "Finish getting ready and then get out there and kill it."

As she walks away, her words linger, rooting themselves deep in my brain.

She's right. I can't allow myself to get distracted. Not by life's curveballs, and definitely not by a certain gray-eyed hockey player who keeps finding his way into my thoughts.

Even though I don't want it to, Bridger's face flashes through my mind. The way he looked at me right before his lips crashed into mine. The feel of his muscular body pressed against me, pinning me to the bookshelf. Instead of allowing my brain to trip down that path, I shove the memories away and paste a smile on my face.

Back in front of the mirror, I apply my makeup, each brushstroke a layer of armor against the turmoil in my head. By the time I'm done, the person looking back at me is one I barely recognize. She's bold and untouchable. Every inch the woman who can handle anything, even Bridger Sanderson and his accusations.

Just as I'm about to get up, my phone buzzes, and I glance down at the screen.

*ColdAsIce17.*

I've come to look forward to these messages more than I ever imagined, and tonight, they help ground me. Bridger might think I'm out to ruin him, but Ice sees past all that. He gets me on a level that most people never will.

COLDASICE17

Sorry for not responding right away. You know I'd never leave you hanging.
Rough day?

A small smile tugs at my lips, and for a moment, I let myself relax. I type back before I can overthink it.

ME

> Unfortunately. Let's just say it's been one of those 'who needs enemies when you've got assholes in your life' kind of days.

His response is quick.

COLDASICE17

> Sounds like someone's giving you trouble.
> Need me to break some kneecaps?

A snort escapes from me.

*ColdAsIce17* has that way about him. He's sarcastic, sometimes blunt, but there's always an undercurrent of sincerity and protectiveness that's impossible to ignore.

ME

> Not sure anyone's worth that much effort.
> Just some arrogant prick who thinks he's got me pegged.

COLDASICE17

> Ahhh. One of those. Annoying.

ME

Exactly.

There's a pause before his next message rolls in. It's a question that makes my pulse skip.

COLDASICE17

> So, what's his issue?

I stare at the screen, my stomach tightening as memories flood back.

The night Bridger and I spent together, along with the way he ghosted me afterward. All the hurt, confusion, and bitterness come rushing in, and for a second, I want to confess everything.

Instead, I chicken out.

ME

> No clue. Guess some people just need a villain. Always happy to oblige.

There's a pause that feels heavier than usual.

COLDASICE17

> Funny. I know exactly what you mean. But, hey, sometimes people only see what they want to.

His words hit deeper than they should, like he knows exactly what it feels like to be misunderstood, to be judged before you've had a chance to explain. I have the sudden need to know more. Who he is and why he gets what no one else seems to.

ME

> Exactly. Doesn't matter what you do or say, they've already decided who you are. Makes life exhausting.

"Holland, you're up." Randi's voice cuts through my thoughts.

I set my phone down and let my eyes fall shut, pulling in a deep breath to steady myself. Whatever I think I want, whatever emotions threaten to surface, none of it changes the truth.

Not with Bridger.

Not with Ice.

Nothing will alter the reality of where things stand.

As I step out of the dressing room, a faint flicker of hope sneaks in. And I wonder, just for a moment, if there will ever be a time when I let myself believe in something more.

Something real.

# BRIDGER

When another mass message lights up my screen, I swear under my breath. I don't need to open it to know it's going to be another shot aimed straight at me. Whoever's behind these messages knows exactly where to hit the hardest, twisting things just enough to make me question everything.



I slam my phone down, pacing my room as anger knots in my chest.

"Fuck, dude." Steele watches from my bed, worry etched on his face. "It never ends. Why can't the tech department just shut the server down?"

"I'm done waiting for the university to handle this." I grab my keys, already moving. "I'm going to take care of it myself."

Before he can argue, I'm out the door and in my car, heading toward Holland's place near campus. I have no idea what I'll say when I see her, but I can't sit around watching my life get picked apart one message at a time.

As I pull up, I spot Holland leaving the townhouse. The red glint of her hair catches the porch light as she strides toward her car. With her attention focused on the phone in her hand, she doesn't notice me. It's so damn tempting to confront her now and force her to admit what she's been up to, but my curiosity stops me from acting on impulse.

I follow at a distance as she heads toward the north end of town. When she pulls into the parking lot of a well-known strip club, I almost miss the turn.

There is no damn way Holland Tate is headed to a place like this.

Unless she figured out I was following her and is fucking with me.

Now that, I believe.

My brow furrows as I take in the sign and rows of expensive cars lined up in the lot. My black BMW fits right in. Anticipation clogs my lungs as I wait for her to slam out of the car and confront me.

There's a part of me that relishes the idea of finally having it out with her.

Except, Holland never glances my way. She gets out of her car and strolls through the door like she owns the place. I sit stunned, watching as she disappears inside the building without so much as a backward glance.

What the hell is she doing in a place like this?

Meeting someone?

Working part-time as a waitress?

A hundred questions flood my brain, and not a damn one of them makes sense.

I wait a few seconds, debating if I should go in or wait out here in the parking lot.

In the end, my gnawing curiosity overrides my irritation. I glance around the inside of my car before finding a ballcap and tugging it low over my forehead as I step out of the vehicle and make my way to the entrance.

A guy in a slick suit and sunglasses at the door gives me the once-over. "ID?"

I slide my license from my wallet and hand it over. He glances at it for a second or two before studying my face and returning it.

"Enjoy yourself."

"Thanks," I mutter, knowing there's no possibility of that happening.

My gaze slides over the interior. Dark wood lines the walls, giving the place a warmth I hadn't anticipated, almost like it was designed to be inviting and intimate. The lights are dim and strategically placed, casting a soft, warm glow that makes everything feel private. Deep crimson velvet booths curve along the edges of the room, each one secluded, with plush cushions and polished black marble tables that catch the light from flickering candles.

Instead of the stale, smoky scent I'd imagined, the air is faintly spiced. Amber maybe or something else that feels unexpectedly sophisticated. The bass-heavy music thrums through the space, vibrating up through the floor in time with the rhythm of colored LED lights outlining the room. I can feel the steady pulse in my chest. It all adds to the surreal, almost hypnotic atmosphere.

The stage draws my attention. It's raised and round, with an LED-lit walkway stretching out toward the crowd. It feels like something out of a luxury Vegas club. A polished brass pole stands in the center, catching the light from above, while rich indigo curtains frame the stage, giving it a dramatic, theatrical look.

This place is designed to make you forget the outside world. Every detail is precise, intentional, crafted to make you feel like you've stepped into another reality. One that's a hell of a lot more exclusive and glamorous than I imagined.

I make my way toward the bar, all the while trying to blend in. A bartender with soft-pink lipstick and a bright smile pours a drink without me asking.

"I haven't seen you around before. What's your name, handsome?" she purrs, sliding the drink my way.

I pull the cap lower, giving her a brief smile before scanning the room again. "First time. Just looking for someone."

"Oh, aren't we all," she says with a laugh, her gaze lingering before she drifts away.

I take a sip as my gaze sweeps over the tables, half expecting to see Holland tucked away in a corner with some old dude. But there's no sign of her anywhere.

Five minutes pass and I glance at my phone, growing antsy.

After ten, my impatience is stretched thin.

Maybe this was a mistake.

Maybe she was onto me the entire time and slipped out the back door.

I wouldn't put it past her.

She's definitely wily that way.

Just when I consider leaving, the music shifts. It's more of a low, sultry beat that fills the room as the stage lights dim. The female announcer's voice rolls through the speakers, smooth and slick.

"Please welcome... Lavender Smoke."

My gaze snaps to the stage as a figure emerges from the shadows, her hair a sleek lavender bob that frames her face, casting her features in a surreal, dreamlike glow. It takes a second for my mind to play mental catch up and the realization to sink in.

I'm barely able to breathe.

Heavy makeup transforms her into someone almost unrecognizable.

Someone confident and unattainable.

She's wearing an outfit that's practically painted on, strappy and shimmering with each calculated step. The sight is like a punch to the gut.

*Holy shit.*

Holland moves with assurance as her hips sway in a rhythm that matches the pulse of the bass. Every step is controlled and measured, as if she not only owns the stage but every eye in the room.

And it's true because I can't fucking look away.

More than that, I don't *want* to look away.

My focus is locked on her.

On the way she moves.

On the calm, unbothered expression that's so different from the guarded, sharp-tongued girl I've come to know.

Holland's gaze skims over the crowd, cool and detached, but she doesn't make eye contact with anyone. She's untouchable, commanding every inch of the stage with an ease I've never seen before. Almost as if this version of her was always there, hiding beneath the surface, waiting for the perfect moment to step into the light.

I'm struck by the sheer contradiction of it.

The girl who once told me with a laugh that she couldn't dance to save her life is here, moving like she's born for the spotlight.

It's not just the shock that hits me.

Possessiveness rushes through me as I realize every guy in this place is watching her the same way I am.

My jaw clenches as she reaches up and slowly slips her top off with a practiced movement. Her gaze remains distant, almost detached, like she's somewhere else. Jealousy coils tight in my gut as the audience starts whistling, tossing out crumpled bills, their eyes glued to every sway of her hips.

The simmering anger inside me blazes, but I can't ignore the other part that's darker and feels a lot like fascination. As much as I hate to admit it, she's fucking incredible. The way she moves, the way she owns that stage.

I've never seen Holland look more powerful.

More in her element.

I down the rest of my drink. My grip on the glass is so tight, it's a surprise when it doesn't shatter.

The lights shift again as her set ends and she saunters off the stage, slipping into the shadows as the music fades. I release a shaky breath, the fury and twisted thrill of finding out one of her secrets burns through my veins.

When my phone buzzes in my pocket, I ignore it.

I have to find her.

I need to know what the hell she's doing here.

At the very least, this is leverage.

Holland Tate isn't as bulletproof as she thinks she is.

HOLLAND

pplause rings through the club as I finish my last spin. Every time I step off that stage, there's this high. A total rush. When I'm out there, I feel like someone else.

Someone powerful.

A version of myself that can command every eye in the room.

I see the way men look at me. The lingering stares. The propositions disguised as compliments. There's no way I'd ever take them up on it, but there's something about the power in it, in knowing I can make them look but they can never touch.

It's heady in a way nothing else has ever been.

And then, of course, there's the money.

A prickle of unease skates down my spine as I head backstage. It's like I can feel someone's heated gaze following me. The intensity of it is unsettling. I scan the room before I push through the curtain, but no one stands out.

My shift passes quickly with two more performances. After wiping off the heavy makeup, Lavender Smoke disappears, and Holland Tate is once again back in charge.

"See you this weekend," Rocco says as I slip past him. "Don't get into too much trouble."

"I'll try not to," I say with a chuckle.

"Need an escort to your car?"

I shake my head. "Nah. It's all good."

As I push through the exit into the cool night air, another wave of unease washes over me, and I sweep my gaze over the dimly lit parking lot. Maybe I should have taken Rocco up on his offer. Another step and I sense his presence before I spot his familiar broad-shouldered frame half-hidden against the wall, lurking in the shadows.

I falter as my eyes widen.

He's the last person I expected to find loitering outside the Envy Room.

"Bridger?" His name comes out on a gasp as he saunters closer. His gaze is sharp and intense. The smirk that tugs at his mouth is more dangerous than any offer I've received tonight. "What the hell are you doing here?"

"Funny. I was just about to ask you the same question," he says, glancing at the building. "Interesting choice of side job."

I force my pulse to settle, and roll my eyes. "Don't you dare judge me. Not when you're lurking around here like some kind of creeper."

"Oh, I'm not judging," he says, stepping closer and lowering his voice. "Just wondering what else you might be hiding."

"For fuck's sake, are we back to that again? Do you really think I have the time or interest to waste on you?" I sneer. "Seriously. Get over yourself."

"If you're not the one behind it, why are you so defensive?" He closes the distance between us, and his scent surrounds me. Sandalwood and cedar, a combination so familiar it sends a pang straight through my chest.

"You're unbelievable," I shoot back.

"And you're hiding something," he snaps.

The heavy silence that stretches between us is thick with unspoken words. I can't help but watch him warily as my heart pounds with an intensity I refuse to acknowledge.

He's not just under my skin.

He's tangled in every thought and feeling.

Impossible to shake loose or pretend he doesn't exist.

Only now am I able to admit it to myself.

My breath hitches when he reaches out to tuck a strand of hair behind my ear. I freeze as his gaze drops to my mouth. That's all it takes for memories of what happened at the library to surface.

Just when I think he might lean in and kiss me, I take a quick step in retreat. "Go to hell. I'm out of here."

"Not so fast, Tate. We have more to discuss."

"Wanna bet?"

He smiles, and his teeth flash in the darkness. "Actually, I do."

I straighten to my full height and glare at him. I'm almost afraid to ask, but I just want to get it over with. "Okay then, spill."

He swallows up the small bit of distance I managed to put between us. "You and I are going to be spending a lot more time together."

I blink, thrown off by the response. "Excuse me?"

"I want you with me 24/7."

A gurgle of panicked laughter spills from my lips as I cross my arms over my chest. "You're actually crazy. Why would I agree to something so insane?"

"Because," he says, voice dropping, "if you don't, your little secret won't be so secret anymore. My personal details won't be the only ones flying across campus."

My mouth falls open as I stare at him. Rage bubbles beneath my skin as his words sink in. I can't resist calling his bluff. "You wouldn't."

He raises a brow. "Eager to test that theory?"

*Fuck.*

"You're a real asshole, know that?" I growl.

"Actually, I do."

It's so damn tempting to flip him off and walk away, but he's seen too much, and if he tells anyone...

I don't even want to think about it.

How I choose to support myself is no one else's business but my own.

I swallow hard and square my shoulders. "What, exactly, does '24/7' mean?"

A slow grin curves his lips. "It means you're with me, at my side and in my bed, so I can keep tabs on you. If you're not the one behind the messages, it shouldn't be a problem, right?"

"I already told you that I don't have anything to do with them."

He studies me, doubt flickering in his eyes before his expression hardens. "Then prove it."

With a scowl, I toss my hands up. "How am I supposed to do that?"

"By helping me find the one who's been making my life hell," he says, his gaze steady and unyielding. "Work *with* me instead of *against* me. Think you can do that for a change?"

I release an unsteady breath and contemplate my options. What I really want to do is tell him to go fuck himself, but he's got me cornered. And by the look in his eyes, the bastard knows it.

It's almost a shock when I hear myself bite out, "Fine. When does this start?"

"Tonight." Satisfaction glints in his silvery eyes.

What I hate even more than that is the way my pulse quickens with the knowledge that I'll be at Bridger Sanderson's mercy.

Not in my wildest dreams did I ever imagine that happening.

It's like a nightmare come true.

I shift my weight as defiance curls my lips. "And when you finally realize I'm not the one you're after? What then?"

He doesn't flinch, just shrugs. "We part ways. Until then, you're stuck with me."

# BRIDGER

I follow Holland through the parking lot, each step charged with restless energy that coils tighter by the second. She shoots a glance over her shoulder as she reaches her car.

Her icy glare is sharp enough to cut glass. "Is it really necessary for you to follow me home, Sanderson?" She spits my name like poison.

With a shrug, I lean against the side of her car. "That's what 24/7 means. You're a smart girl. I thought you'd understand that."

Her expression darkens, and I can tell she's close to snapping. I have no idea why I enjoy provoking her so much. It's twisted. A therapist would probably have a field day with the thoughts that run rampant through my head where this girl is concerned.

It's a surprise, and maybe even a disappointment, when she doesn't rise to the bait. With a roll of her eyes, she slides behind the wheel. It takes a minute or two for her engine to turn over.

My brows rise as the vehicle coughs and sputters. "Are you sure this thing will make it back to your place?"

Her response is to give me the finger.

I can't help the chuckle that slips free.

As soon as she backs out of the space, I beeline to my own car and tail her through the winding streets. The drive is just long enough for guilt to rear its ugly head and have me second-guessing myself.

It's not too late to put the kibosh on this half-baked idea. Holland would be more than thrilled to forget about this arrangement I'm forcing her into. I won't say a word about her working at the club, and I'll go back to pretending I don't think about her more than I should.

But...

I don't want to.

And I really fucking hate how much I don't want to let go of the opportunity that's fallen into my lap.

Holland Tate has managed to burrow deep beneath my skin, and I'm going to get her out one way or another.

Fifteen minutes later, we pull into the parking lot of her town-house. With another chilly glare aimed in my direction, Holland slams the car door with more force than necessary before marching up the steps. She doesn't bother waiting for me. I follow her inside the small entryway before shutting the door behind me as she stalks through the dark interior.

"Make yourself at home," she says, her tone dripping with sarcasm as she gestures around the living area. "Oh, wait. I don't actually want you here."

Instead of settling in the living room, I follow her to her bedroom, leaning against the doorframe and scoping out her private space. "Nice to see you're warming up to this arrangement."

She mutters something unintelligible under her breath before yanking open a drawer and tossing articles of clothing into a bag. Her movements are stilted and her jaw remains tight. Not once does she glance my way.

"How many days should I pack for?" she asks in a clipped tone.

I shrug, pretending like I haven't already imagined her at my place and in my bed or haven't considered the havoc that's going to come with having her all up in my business. "Guess that depends on how long it takes for us to catch the culprit." I wink. "That is, if it's not you."

A growl vibrates in her chest as her lips twist into a scowl. "Right. Because I'm the architect of all your problems. Totally forgot about that. Thanks for the reminder."

"Guess that's what we're going to find out," I say, stuffing my hands into the pockets of my jeans as I watch her throw a few more items into her bag.

I can't help but glance around her room with more interest. It's nothing like I expected. There's a worn leather armchair in one corner, stacks of books and notebooks piled high on the floor. A sketchpad tossed carelessly onto the chair catches my eye, the pages slightly bent and smudged.

Without thinking, I gravitate in that direction before reaching down and picking it up. Intricate sketches of landscapes, portraits, and half-finished scenes fill the pages, each line careful and precise.

They're good.

Actually, they're better than that.

There's a rawness to them, an intensity that pulls me in and captures my attention.

"You draw?" I glance up.

"No," she snaps, grabbing the sketchpad from my hands and shoving it into her bag as color floods her cheeks.

I pop a brow. "Clearly, you do. I didn't realize you had a hidden artistic side."

She looks away, shoving another shirt in her bag. "Shocker that you're not exactly perceptive."

There's a bite to her words.

I hate to admit that she might be right.

Holland's always been a mystery to me, a combination of sharp edges and soft curves that never quite added up. She's too much, too real in a way that makes me uncomfortable.

I settle in the chair and watch her. "Is it some big secret?"

Her hands still for a second but she doesn't look up. "Not a secret at all. The people who matter in my life know about it."

Ouch.

"Did you ever consider me one of them?" The question is out before I can stop it.

Her gaze is hard when it slices to mine. "After all this time, why does it even matter?" Before I can tell her that it doesn't, she adds, "Let's get something clear. We're not friends. You're blackmailing me because you think I'm out to ruin your life. At some point, you'll realize it's not me. And then won't you feel like an asshole?"

Her words hit harder than I expect, and something that feels very much like regret unfurls inside me. I'm caught between wanting to pull her closer and wanting to protect myself from what she's capable of.

"This could be over with before it even starts if you'd just come clean." My voice is quieter than I intend. "Just admit you've been fucking with me, and I'll let it all go. I won't even press charges. I just need it to end."

She lets out a humorless laugh before zipping up her bag and throwing it over her shoulder. Sadness flashes in her eyes before it's quickly masked. "I'm not going to admit to something I haven't done."

With that, she pushes past me into the hallway without another word. I follow, still trying to piece together what's real and what's just a façade.

When it comes to Holland, I'm not sure I'll ever know.

As soon as the townhouse is locked up, she beelines to her vehicle, stubbornness and tension etched across her expression. "I'll follow you back to your place."

"Actually," I say, holding her gaze, "you'll ride with me."

With a roll of her eyes, a puff of air bursts from her. "So now I can't even drive my own car? What if I need it? How am I going to get to work?"

I glance at her death trap of a vehicle. It wouldn't surprise me if it was held together with paperclips and bubblegum. "I'll drive you."

"Awesome. Now I have my own personal chauffeur. Things just keep getting better and better."

A grin twitches around the corners of my lips. "Aren't you lucky?"

Her glare hardens. "Luckiest girl in the world."

I pop open the passenger door of my BMW and extend my arm. "Your chariot awaits, madam."

With a snort, she slips past me before settling on the leather seat. "Chariot, my ass."

Once she's situated, I close the door and hustle around to the driver's side.

Who would have ever thought Holland Tate would be sitting in my car and sleeping in my bed at night?

It all feels a little surreal.

And yet, I still can't bring myself to regret the impulsive decision to bind her to me.

The drive to my place is made in silence as thick tension permeates the small space. Each unspoken word stretches uncomfortably between us as she stares out the window. Her expression might be unreadable, but I can feel the anger and frustration radiating off her in suffocating waves.

It's strangely intoxicating.

The moment we pull up in front of my place, Holland bolts from the car before I have a chance to kill the engine. My attention stays riveted to her as I follow her up the stairs to the front porch.

She pauses outside the door, glancing at me with a dubious expression. "Can't say I ever thought I'd be shacking up at the hockey house."

*And I'd fucking kill the guy she shacked up with.*

The thought is so unexpected, it catches me off guard.

I bite back the sharp retort and reach around her, opening the door before muttering, "That makes two of us."

She's close enough for the rosemary and mint scent of her shampoo to slyly wrap around me. It's so damn tempting to lean in and inhale a big breath of her.

But I don't.

*Are you fucking kidding?*

*Of course I don't.*

She'd probably junk punch me if I did. And then she'd kick me while I was curled up in the fetal position on the ground.

Her eyes narrow. "Did you just sniff me?"

*Fuck.*

I feign ignorance. "What? Of course not."

I wasn't kidding about the junk punching.

With a frown, she stalks inside the entryway before taking in her surroundings. Her body stiffens when she notices a couple of my younger teammates making themselves at home on our couch. There's a girl or two cuddled up next to each of them. Their gazes stray to us, and I'm treated to a round of chin lifts.

Holland's upper lip curls with disgust as she hitches her bag higher on her shoulder. "Just to be clear, I don't plan on hanging out with your friends."

"I wouldn't expect it."

"So, what happens next?" she asks, her tone turning to more of a challenge. When I continue to stare, she tacks on, "Care to share what nefarious plans you have in store for me now that you've dragged me back to your evil lair?"

I force a slow grin at the description. "What's wrong, Tate? Frightened?"

The thought of Holland at my mercy and fingertips any time I want sends a rush of pleasure through me.

Her eyes blaze with a heady mix of anger and defiance. This is one girl who will never turn tail and run. With her, it'll be a fight to the death.

"Just remember that I'm here because you blackmailed me, not because I want to be anywhere near you."

Unable to help myself, I crowd her personal space.

And just like I expected, she doesn't back down. Her furious gaze remains steady and her jaw stays tightly clenched.

"Keep telling yourself that, Tate. At the very least, be honest with yourself. There's a reason you didn't walk away."

Her cheeks flush a pretty pink color as she continues to hold her ground. "Don't delude yourself, Sanderson. I'm here because I don't want people all up in my personal business. There's no other reason than that."

On some level, I believe her. Holland has always been private. Her circle of trust is almost nonexistent. But she's also not the kind of person who does anything unless she ultimately wants to.

I study her expression. "Do you realize that you have a tell?"

Her face scrunches at my change in topic. "Excuse me?"

"Your left eye twitches when you lie. I noticed it a few years ago. I always thought it was interesting to see when you were being honest and when you were lying."

"Fuck off, Sanderson. You don't know what you're talking about."

"Holland?"

We swing toward the soft voice. Willow stands there, Maverick at her back, both wearing identical expressions of confusion.

When neither of us respond, Willow's brows pinch together. "What are you doing here?" Her gaze darts between us. "With Bridger."

Holland stays motionless.

I don't think I've ever seen her at a loss for words.

"We've been seeing one another," I blurt.

Willow blinks. "I'm sorry, could you please repeat that? For a moment, I almost thought you said that you two were together. As in... *together*."

"Yeah, that's right."

Willow bursts into laughter. "Shut up. No, you're not." Her gaze remains focused on her roommate. "What are you really doing here?"

The moment I wrap my fingers around Holland's forearm, electricity sizzles between us. Her body jerks, wide eyes slicing to mine, filled with confusion and something darker.

I tug her closer before slipping my arm around her waist. "Go ahead and tell them, babe."

Her mouth opens and closes a few times, like a fish gasping for its last dying breath. Any other time, it would be hilarious.

Just when I think I'll have to step in and do all the talking, she whispers, "It's, um, true. We're together."

Willow's eyes widen. "No way."

Holland's teeth scrape across her lower lip. I'm pretty sure she's dying a slow death inside. "Yeah. We're..." She gulps. "Together."

"I... don't understand."

Maverick's lips tremble with smothered laughter.

Dickhead.

Holland's cheeks are fire-engine red as her tongue darts out to lick her lips. "I..."

I've never seen Holland flounder so much in her life. Taking pity on her, I cut in. "We've been secretly seeing each other for a couple weeks."

Willow levels me with a hard-edged stare. "Why?"

"Why?" I repeat, not understanding the question.

"Yeah." She plants her hands on her hips. "You two can't stand each other." Her attention slides back to her friend as she points at me. "You've made your feelings for him *very* clear."

Holland nods, acknowledging her past comments. "I, um... It's like you said earlier. There was more to it buried beneath the surface."

Hurt flashes in Willow's eyes. "Why didn't you just tell me that when we were talking about it?"

Holland's shoulders collapse. "I just needed to get it figured out before we made anything public." Her expression hardens as she side-eyes me. "I'm really sorry."

I give in to impulse and press a kiss to her cheek before burying my face against the side of her neck. "Oh, sweet cheeks. There's no more keeping our love to ourselves. We can yell it from the rooftops if we want."

Her voice dips, becoming more of a grumble. "We don't want to do that."

"Are you sure, love muffin?"

She glares as her tone turns menacing. "One hundred percent positive."

"Well, I think it's time for us to go upstairs and"—I waggle my brows—"*you know*."

Holland narrows her eyes before smashing her lips together. I can almost see the smoke billowing from the top of her head. "Talk?"

"Sure. Maybe afterward."

"I'm going to kill you with my bare hands." She snaps her teeth at me.

I glance at Willow and Maverick. "Threatening bodily harm is her love language."

"I don't make threats. I make promises."

When that bone-chilling comment is met with silence, I steer Holland toward the staircase. "On that note, we're going to skedaddle." I lift a hand in a wave. "Have a good night."

We're halfway up to the second floor when Willow says, "We'll talk more in the morning, Holland."

"Now *that* sounded like a threat," I say beneath my breath.

"Because it is."

As soon as we cross the threshold and step inside my room, I close the door. Not even a second later, Holland whirls around and punches me in the gut. It happens so fast I don't see it coming until it's much too late. I do the only thing I can and double over as the air leaves my lungs in a rush.

# WESTERN UNIVERSITY CHAT APP

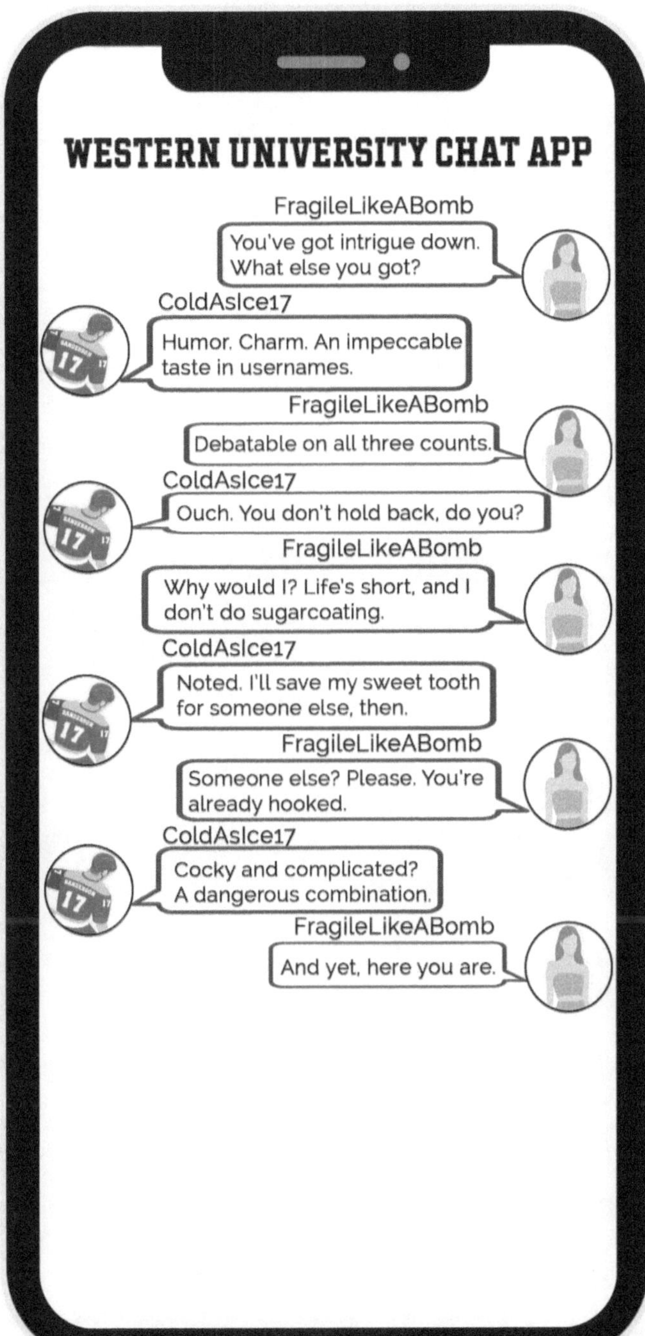

HOLLAND

"What the hell was that for?" Bridger wheezes, clutching his abdomen. He might be all hard, chiseled muscle, but I aimed well. One of Mom's exes was an amateur boxer, and he taught me how to throw a proper punch. It's come in handy more times than I care to admit.

"For telling our friends that we're together," I snap, crossing my arms over my chest and glaring.

"Did you have a better explanation as to why you were stepping foot inside this house with me?" His voice is still breathless, but there's that damn smirk again. The one that makes me want to simultaneously punch him and—

*No.*

Just punch him.

"If you'd given me a moment, I'm sure I could have pulled something out of my ass!" I huff. "And what the hell was with all the nuzzling and *sweet cheeks* shit down there?"

"I thought it added authenticity to the story. You know, really sold it."

With narrowed eyes, I jab a finger toward him. "We don't have a story. Now everyone's going to think we're having sex."

"Hate to break it to you, muffin, but most people who are dating do that sort of thing."

"Except we're not actually dating. And we're certainly never going to do *that* again."

He straightens as challenge sparks in his eyes. Not only is it sharp, it's dangerous enough to make my stomach flip. "You sure about that?"

I tighten my arms around myself, as if they're some kind of shield against the way his words crawl under my skin. "Positive."

His gaze drills into me as the corners of his lips curl in a way that makes my pulse stutter. The tension is only broken when he shrugs, moving toward his dresser. "Suit yourself, *sweet cheeks.*"

"Stop calling me that!"

Ignoring me, he pulls off his shirt.

My gaze drops before I can stop it, taking in the hard planes of his chest and the subtle dusting of hair that leads down—

Nope.

I'm definitely not looking there.

My cheeks heat as I whip around and rummage through my duffel bag, racking my brain for a way out of this mess.

Nothing comes to mind.

"What exactly do you think you're doing?" I demand without turning around.

He chuckles. The sound is low and infuriating. "Getting ready for bed. What's wrong? It's not like you haven't seen it all before."

I mutter under my breath, yanking out a tank top and shorts. With my back turned to him, I strip off my shirt and bra, trying not to think about the fact that he's just a few feet away. The thin black tank slides over my head, hugging my curves as I pull down my leggings. The heat of his gaze feels more like a physical caress.

Hoping that it's just my imagination, I glance over my shoulder and then scowl when I catch him watching me. "Do you mind?"

He flashes a grin. One that's full of mischief and meant to irritate. He knows all my buttons to push. "Not at all. Please, continue. It was just getting interesting."

"Turn around, Sanderson," I snap.

He raises a brow, clearly enjoying himself. "For someone who strips in front of an audience, you're surprisingly shy."

"That's a *job* that pays the bills," I bite out with an icy glare that hopefully shrivels his balls.

He smothers the laughter brimming on his lips. "Relax, Tate. You can have a little bit of privacy while I use the bathroom." He grabs something off the dresser before strolling out.

It's not until the door clicks shut behind him that I realize I've been holding my breath. A shaky exhale leaves my body as I lean against the bed for a moment and try to calm my racing heart. Being around Bridger feels like standing too close to a fire. Warm, dangerous, and impossible to ignore.

I shake off that disturbing thought and quickly strip off my leggings and underwear. I've never been able to sleep in panties. They're way too constricting. Guess that's coming back to bite me in the ass.

I toss them into my bag and zip it up before running my fingers through my hair.

It's almost crazy to believe how much my life has been turned upside down in one short hour.

When the door creaks open, I spin around. My breath catches when I see him wearing nothing but boxers. Somehow, he's even more chiseled than two years ago. Every line of muscle, every sharp angle, looks like it was carved from stone. My mouth goes dry, and I force my gaze to the ceiling, pretending I didn't just eye-fuck him.

"Ready for bed?" he asks, his voice rougher than usual. The gravelly tone of it sends an unwelcome shiver cascading down my spine before pooling like warmed honey in my core.

I nod stiffly, not trusting myself to speak, and climb into bed, tugging the blanket up to my chin. He follows, sliding in on the other side. The mattress dips beneath his weight. The space between us feels nonexistent, every movement amplified. I'm painfully aware of the heat radiating from his body and the soft rustle of fabric as he adjusts the pillow.

The silence that stretches is suffocating. I squeeze my eyes closed, trying to block out the fact that he's lying right beside me and I can feel every shift of his body, every subtle intake of breath.

"You okay over there, Tate?" There's a tightness to his voice that makes me wonder if he's having second thoughts about forcing me into his bed.

"Couldn't be better," I bite out, not bothering to open my eyes. "This is exactly how I wanted to spend my night."

"Could've fooled me."

With gritted teeth, I turn my back to him and stare at the wall. Already, I know it's going to be a long-ass night. I can't focus on anything but the sound of his steady breathing while mine feels erratic, like I've run a marathon.

As much as I want to hate him, as much as I tell myself that there's nothing between us, I can't shake the way my body reacts to him. The way he seems to draw me in no matter how hard I fight it.

The worst part is, I'm pretty sure he knows it.

BRIDGER
SANDERSON
17
17
WILDCATS

The first thing that registers when I wake up is the warm weight pressed against my side. My brows pinch together as I blink against the weak sunlight streaming in through the window.

What the hell happened last night?

I haven't had a one-night stand since someone decided to stalk my every movement and post it online for the world to comment upon.

I carefully turn my head and glance at the girl sacked out beside me. That's the moment everything from last night slams into me with the force of...

Well, the force of a Holland Tate sucker punch to the gut.

I still can't believe she did that.

On second thought... yes, I can.

Holland is a ticking time bomb, waiting for the right moment to detonate.

It's all part of her charm.

My gaze lingers on the sleeping woman, studying her in the quiet of the morning as her thick auburn hair spills across the cream-colored pillowcase like a fiery halo. She's all sharp edges and defiance when she's awake, but here, in this moment, she looks peaceful.

Softer.

Vulnerable in a way she'd probably throat-punch me for noticing.

Her long lashes fan across her cheeks, and her lips—Jesus, those lips.

Full, plush, and just slightly parted, like she's in the middle of a dream.

Unable to help myself, I reach out and run my fingers through a loose tendril of her hair, marveling at the silkiness of the strands. My mind drifts to what those lips would feel like on me. I can still remember what they felt like two years ago, but it wasn't nearly enough to satiate the deep craving inside.

What if I hadn't gotten scared and run?

What if I'd stayed?

And we started something real?

My jaw tightens as I shove the thought away.

There's no sense dwelling on things that can't be changed.

Still, the sight of her in my bed both unsettles and satisfies me at the same time.

Someone needs to explain how that's possible.

Better yet, how do I make it stop?

I drop the lock of hair before sliding carefully from the bed, not wanting to wake her. I need space to breathe, to think, to wrap my head around what I've done.

Just as I'm about to leave the room, I glance back.

It's impossible to ignore the pull, the way she's somehow rooted herself in the parts of me I thought were untouchable. The steady rise and fall of her breathing is the only sound in the room. For a moment, I stand frozen, watching her.

She looks peaceful, her features soft and relaxed in sleep, a stark contrast to the fire and sharp edges she carries when awake.

The sight of her tangled in my sheets feels right in a way it shouldn't.

The most fucked-up part of all this is that I don't regret blackmailing her.

Not even a little.

I like having Holland Tate at my mercy.

Five minutes later, I'm dressed and heading downstairs. The last thing I need is to be late after Coach was up my ass at practice. As I hit the bottom step, I freeze.

Ryder, Hayes, Riggs, Steele, and Maverick occupy the couches, looking strangely serious. Ford, Colby, Wolf, and Madden, my teammates who don't live here, are perched on chair arms.

The low hum of conversation dies as they notice me, and a heavy silence follows.

My eyes narrow. "Why aren't you guys at practice?"

Ryder clears his throat, shifting uncomfortably. "We thought it best to have this conversation here. First of all, you should know that we all care about you." He glances at the others for backup. "And we only want the best for you."

I blink. "Umm... okay."

"And you've been going through a lot lately," Ford adds. "We get it."

A chorus of murmurs fills the room.

"Get what?" I step closer as tension coils in my gut. "What the hell are you talking about?"

Hayes clears his throat. "With the messages and your father..."

"What is this? An intervention?" I glance around, waiting for someone to crack a smile. Instead, that comment is met with crickets. My eyes widen. "Oh my God, this *is* an intervention."

"I don't think it's necessary to slap a label on it," Wolf says, his expression solemn.

"For what?" I bark, crossing my arms over my chest. "I'm not drinking any more than you fuckers. I don't have a gambling problem. And last time I checked, I wasn't hoarding stray cats in my room."

"Not yet anyway," Ford mutters.

Wolf rises to his feet, drawing my attention back to him. "Is it true?"

"Is what true?"

"Are you actually dating Holland Tate?"

For fuck's sake. Is that what this is about?

I press my lips together. "So what if I am? Is it really that big of a deal?"

"Yeah, it kind of is." Wolf drags a hand over his shaved head.

Steele smothers a laugh with a cough. I glare at him, knowing he won't be any help. After the text I shot him last night, he's the only one who knows the truth. And the bastard is enjoying this way too much.

"Look," Ryder steps in, face earnest, "you've been under a lot of pressure lately. We get it."

"Do you?" I growl. "Because it sounds like you're all one bad joke away from staging an exorcism."

"We're just worried," Maverick adds. "Everyone knows you hate Holland Tate. A few weeks ago, you threatened to wring her neck."

"I don't hate her," I snap, but their dubious glances tell me I've already lost this battle. "You guys don't know what you're talking about."

"Don't we?" Colby pipes up. "It's not exactly normal to go from despising someone to dating them overnight."

"We've been seeing each other on the down-low," I blurt before scowling at him. "Kind of like someone I know who secretly married a reality star in Vegas?"

He shrugs. "In my defense, I had no idea who she was."

"I think we can all agree this relationship came out of nowhere," Ryder interjects, trying to keep the intervention on track. "We just want to make sure you're good."

"I still think it's a cry for help." Ford leans forward. "Blink twice if she's got something on you and you're being watched."

"Shut up, Hamilton."

Wolf steps closer, arms crossed. "With everything you're dealing with, no one would blame you for going off the deep end."

From the corner of my eye, I catch Steele's shoulders shaking with silent laughter. Any second he's going to lose it and roll around on the floor.

"I appreciate the concern," I grind out, "but everything's under control."

Except nothing could be further from the truth.

I look around at my teammates. These guys are the ones who've always had my back. The truth sits heavy on my tongue, but I can't risk one of them letting it slip. This thing with Holland is too precarious.

Instead, I give them a small piece of the story. "Something happened with Holland a couple years ago," I admit, voice low. "And she's always been there, in the back of my mind. Whatever this is between us needs to run its course. All right?"

They stare at me, and for a second I think they'll keep pushing, but then Ryder nods. "Okay."

"Okay?" I blink. "That's it? No more with the third degree?"

"We're still concerned," Maverick says, rising to his feet. "But if this is your way of getting closure, we'll support it. Even if you're not thinking clearly."

"Or at all," Ford adds with a smirk.

"I, for one, think their relationship is a match made in heaven," Steele finally chokes out between laughs.

"Can we get to practice now?" I glare at them all. "Or are there more feelings you'd like to share in the circle of trust? I'm sure Coach would love to hear why his entire first line can't be bothered to show up on time."

They all groan and shuffle toward the door.

Ford pats my shoulder as he passes. "Don't worry, man. If it all goes south with Holland, cat adoption is still a viable option."

I flip him off but can't help smiling.

The truth is, I have no idea what the hell I'm doing with Holland. But for now, I don't have any other choice but to fake it until I figure it out.

Or until it blows up in my face.

Whichever comes first.

HOLLAND

# 13

My eyelids flutter open to find Willow's face looming way too close for comfort.

"It's about time you woke up," she says, perched on the edge of the bed. "I've been waiting here for at least fifteen minutes. I was about to start poking you."

"That wouldn't have ended well for you," I slur, trying to find my bearings. It feels like I've been hit by a bus. "You're never going to believe the crazy dream I had."

She lifts a brow. "Is it any crazier than reality? The one where you're dating Bridger Sanderson?"

I'm sorry, did she just say *dating Bridger Sanderson?*

I bolt upright and—

*What the fuck?*

The navy walls of an unfamiliar room swim into focus. "Oh shit. Looks like it wasn't a dream after all." I flop back, dragging the pillow over my face as I contemplate the merits of suffocation.

"Oh no, girl. We need to talk about this."

Oh God.

"Can we *please* do that after I've downed a gallon of coffee?" My voice comes out muffled.

"Absolutely not. I've had almost ten hours to let your news sink in, and I'm still in shock. You and Bridger? This isn't something I saw coming."

The denial sits on my tongue. But how can I explain without revealing everything? Including my job at the Envy Room?

"I know," I groan, peeking out from under the pillow. "But, please, I need coffee first. Then I'll answer all your questions."

She eyes me suspiciously. "Fine. But just so you know, I've already started planning double dates for us."

"You did *not* just say that."

"Oh, I absolutely did." A wicked smile lights up her face as she claps her hands. "I'm going to plan *so many* fun activities. The movies. Picnics. Roller-skating. Remember how much we used to love doing that?"

"I was right, this is a total nightmare."

She laughs before rising to her feet. "Come on, otherwise we're going to be late."

"Late? What time is it?" I ask, dragging a hand over my face.

"Almost eight. The guys left for practice a couple hours ago." She glances at the empty side of the bed. "Didn't Bridger tell you?"

"Of course he did," I mutter. "I must've forgotten."

She waggles her brows. "Or maybe you were too busy doing *other* things last night."

My mouth tumbles open before I swallow down my response and say the only thing I can. "Guilty."

Her eyes widen as she shakes her head. "It's like I've entered an alternate universe."

"That makes two of us." I toss off the covers and head for my bag in the corner where I pull out jeans and a sweater.

Willow's eyes dart to the duffel. "That's a lot of stuff. Kind of looks like you're planning to stay for a while."

"It's just for a couple of days," I say vaguely, shoving my feet into my Chucks.

Her expression says she doesn't buy it, but thankfully, she refrains from hurtling more questions at me. "All right, I guess that's a start, but you still owe me all the details. Don't think I'm going to forget."

My shoulders slump. "I know you won't. Let's get moving before we're late."

Twenty minutes later, we're on campus. My pace quickens as the Roasted Bean comes into view.

Thank fuck.

Coffee.

Is there a size bigger than extra large?

Is a shot or two of caffeine a thing?

If not, there's no guarantee I'll make it through the next couple of hours with my sanity intact. Plus, I have a test to study for.

"So, tell me exactly when this all started. Because the last I heard—"

Willow's voice comes to an abrupt halt when the *Jaws* theme music cuts through the chilly morning air.

And here I didn't think anything could make me smile.

Turns out I was wrong.

When she shoots a glare in my direction, my shoulders shake with laughter. "Come on, it's funny!"

She huffs, keeping her eyes on me as she answers. "Hey, Mom. What's up?"

I grin and point to the coffee shop. "I'm heading inside. I'll catch you later."

She covers the speaker with her hand. "We're not done talking about this!"

I cup my fingers around my ear. "What? Sorry, can't hear you. Bye!"

Before she can say anything else, I slip through the door. A little bell rings overhead, announcing my presence. Inside, the rich scent of coffee wraps around me like a comforting blanket, soothing my frayed edges.

It's a splurge I don't usually allow myself but today calls for reinforcements. I tossed and turned all night, unable to get comfortable. I couldn't stop thinking about the guy next to me.

Normally, I make a cup before leaving the townhouse in the morning. Unfortunately, that wasn't possible, especially after sniffing what the guys had lying around the house.

Um, no, thanks.

I choose life.

I slip my phone from my pocket and pull up the campus chat app, wanting to read *ColdAsIce17*'s message from last night. After my life went sideways, there was no time to do it.

COLDASICE17

> Exhausting is an understatement. People love to slap a label on you and call it a day. They don't care about the fine print.

ME

> Ugh, yes. It's like, "Sorry, I didn't realize my life was an open book for everyone to scribble in."

COLDASICE17

> Scribble? Nah, some people take a damn Sharpie to it.

A laugh bubbles out before I can stop it.

ME

> Talking with you is so easy. How do you get it?

COLDASICE17

> I'm annoyingly perceptive. It's one of my many talents.

ME

> Oh, many talents? Modest much?

COLDASICE17

> Never. But seriously, if someone's making your life harder, you don't owe them anything. You've got enough to deal with without carrying their bullshit too.

My chest constricts at his words.

ME

Easier said than done.

COLDASICE17

True. But you don't have to carry it alone.

I stare at his message, the sincerity in those simple words making my throat tighten. He doesn't even know who I am, yet somehow, he always knows exactly what I need to hear.

ME

Thanks. That means a lot.

COLDASICE17

Anytime. And hey, if you want me to send a strongly worded text or an army of angry emojis, just say the word.

ME

LOL. Tempting. I'll let you know.

COLDASICE17

I'll be here waiting.

For the first time all day, the tension in my shoulders loosens. Ice has no idea just how much his words steady me, but maybe that's okay. Some things are better left unsaid. For now, anyway.

I step up to the counter, ready to place my order, when a familiar voice catches my attention.

"Just the person I was hoping to run into."

I turn to find Garret, fresh from practice. His damp hair curls against his temples, and he's wearing a hoodie with sweatpants. It seems to be the unofficial uniform of college hockey players everywhere.

"Hey."

He steps closer, his expression troubled. "There's a rumor going around that you're seeing Sanderson." His sharp gaze searches mine as disbelief fills his voice. "Tell me it's not true."

I force myself to nod, knowing there's nothing else I can say. "Yeah, it is."

Garret's jaw tightens. "I don't understand. I thought you couldn't stand the guy."

My tongue darts out to lick my dry lips. "It's complicated. We were keeping things quiet." I retreat a small step, needing a little bit of distance. "Just kind of feeling out the situation."

"I was kind of hoping there might be something between us."

I blink, thrown off by his admittance. We've had a few classes together over the years and have always been friendly, but it was never anything more than that. At least, not on my end.

Awkwardness descends as I shift. "I'm sorry. I didn't realize. I thought we were just friends."

A mixture of hurt, disappointment, and anger swirls through his eyes. "Guess I was hoping we could be more," he says quietly.

Before I can figure out how to respond, a strong arm slides around my waist and hauls me against a very solid chest.

"Hey, babe," Bridger says, his voice hard.

When he rests his chin on my shoulder, I'm hit with the faint scent of sandalwood and cedar. My pulse skyrockets, and I don't know if it's because I want to slap him or because his proximity does funny things to my insides.

I'm really hoping it's not the latter.

Garret's eyes flash as his upper lip curls. "Sanderson."

"Akeman," Bridger acknowledges in a clipped tone, his grip tightening just enough to make my heart stutter. "Thanks for keeping my girl company."

"Strange, she never mentioned you," Garret says before glancing at me again. "Guess I'll see you around, Holland."

I open my mouth to respond, but nothing comes out. By the time I gather my thoughts, Garret's gone, leaving me alone with Bridger and the warmth of his body pressed against my backside.

"You're welcome," Bridger says, his lips brushing against my ear in a way that's way too intimate for my liking.

I whirl around and shove at his chest. "What the hell was that about?"

"That," he says with an infuriating smirk, "was me saving you from Garret Akeman's feeble attempts at flirting. The guy has zero game. You're welcome."

"You're the last person I need to save me."

He shrugs, clearly unbothered. "Could've fooled me. It looked like you were floundering."

"Floundering?" I glare up at him, ignoring the way my heart races at his proximity. "You're such a conceited—"

It's only when someone clears their throat that I bite back the rest of my comment.

We both turn toward the guy behind the counter.

"Sorry to interrupt," he mutters. "What can I get for you?"

"She'll take the McNichols Special."

"Excuse me? Exactly when did you start making decisions for me?"

"Since we became a couple. Remember, muffin?"

A growl builds low and deep, vibrating through me. It's so tempting to snap my teeth at him.

"Better make it extra grande," Bridger adds with a wink. "Someone didn't get enough sleep last night."

*Oh my God, he did not just say that!*

"Coming right up. Name on the order?"

"Muffin."

"Make sure you sleep with one eye open, Sanderson. Because I'm getting out of this relationship." I drop my voice before narrowing my eyes. "One way or another."

He flashes a grin. "You're adorable when you're all riled up."

With that, he tosses a few bills on the counter and presses a kiss against the tip of my nose. "This one's on me."

I release a frustrated groan as he saunters toward the exit, his confidence seemingly unshaken. There is no damn way I'll be able to put up with Bridger Sanderson for more than twenty-four hours straight.

Even that's pushing it.

# BRIDGER

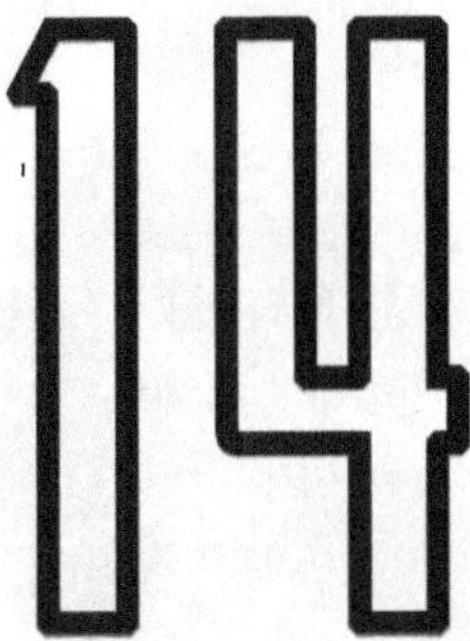

A smile quirks the corners of my lips as I push through the door of the Roasted Bean. Holland Tate is a live wire, always ready to spark. Riling her up has become something of a sport to me. One I'm starting to enjoy a little too much.

The way her eyes ignite with fire is addictive.

Added bonus—it takes my mind off all the other bullshit in my life.

My amusement fades when I find Garret waiting outside, his expression murderous as he closes the distance between us.

"What the hell do you want, Akeman?" I snap, all my good humor fading. He'd been up my ass all through practice this morning.

It's like everywhere I go, there he is.

The strange part is that we've been teammates for years and never had any issues.

Were we tight?

Not really, but our relationship was never contentious.

Now it feels like we're one wrong word away from throwing punches.

Instead of answering my question, he fires off one of his own. "What the hell are you doing with Holland Tate?"

Ah, there it is. I knew he had a thing for her.

I lift my chin, all the while holding his steady gaze. "That's none of your damn business, now is it?"

He scoffs, the sound sharp and bitter. "There's no fucking way she'd give you the time of day."

Something dark twists inside me, and the words shoot out of my mouth before I can stop them. "Actually, that's not true. She was in my bed last night, and it's exactly where you'll find her tonight."

His lips flatten as rage ignites in his eyes. "We'll see how long it lasts. I'll take her the same way I plan on taking your spot on the ice. And guess what? There's not a damn thing you or your daddy can do to stop it."

The way he spits out the word *daddy* stirs something ugly in my gut. His words echo the last message to screw with my life.

My fists clench. "What'd you say?"

Garret leans in, his smirk widening, as if realizing he just found a tender spot to sink his teeth into. "Oh, I think you heard me."

"Pretty sure I didn't. Why don't you say it again and let's see what happens?"

Holland bursts out of the coffee shop, freezing for half a second before marching over to plant a hand on my chest and pushing me back. Her touch burns even through my shirt.

"Are you two really doing this?" she seethes, looking between us with blazing eyes.

Garret's gaze stays locked on me as he snarls, "I'd like to know what you see in this guy. He's a fucking joke. A talentless hack."

Heat surges in my chest, and I open my mouth to snap back, but a sharp voice cuts through the tension.

"What's going on here?" My father strides toward us, suit immaculate and expression lethal. Tension thickens the air as his calculating gaze moves between me and Garret. "Is there an issue?"

Garret straightens. "No, sir."

"Good," Dick says, though his tone suggests he doesn't buy it for a second. His attention shifts to me, and his jaw tightens. "I'd like to see you in my office."

"Fine," I bite out, my fists still clenched as adrenaline pumps through my veins.

"Sooner rather than later." His gaze cuts to Holland, narrowing slightly before dismissing her entirely. "I'm sure all of you have somewhere to be."

The moment he walks away, Garret throws me one last glare before stalking off.

I force myself to breathe and relax muscles that are coiled for a fight. It's not easy after a run-in with the two people who get under my skin the most.

"So, that's your dad, huh?" Holland says, clearly trying to lighten the mood.

"Yeah."

"Seems like a real warm and fuzzy sort. Kind of like a big, squishy teddy bear."

The image tugs at my lips despite everything. "You nailed it."

"I figured as much." She adjusts her bag strap before glancing away. "I should probably get to class."

Before she can take two steps, phones buzz all around us. Dread pools in my gut as I pull mine out.

ANONYMOUS MESSAGE

Bridger Sanderson and Holland Tate—now there's an odd pairing. Betting pools are now open as to how long that situationship will last.

My face heats as I glance around. People have stopped in their tracks and are staring, their gazes darting between me and Holland as whispers spread like wildfire.

Holland stiffens beside me, her face paling as she stares at her phone. "Bridger..."

Her voice is oddly soft as her hand rises to touch my arm.

Instead of allowing her to comfort me, I take a hasty step in retreat. "I need to go," I say roughly, shoving my phone back into my pocket. "I'll see you in class."

"Bridger—" she tries again, but I'm already walking away.

My mind churns as I put distance between us.

That message wasn't as vicious as some of the others, but the implications are enough to make my skin crawl. Someone out there is watching us, stirring the pot.

Or is it her attempt to throw me off and turn my suspicions elsewhere?

I have no fucking idea.

And that's the problem.

The way she looked at me just now—like she was worried, like she actually cared—makes something inside me ache in a way I'm not used to.

Holland Tate isn't just tangled up in this mess, she's twisted up deep inside me.

And that might be the hardest knot to untangle.

What I do know is that I need to get my head on straight before I see her next.

HOLLAND

The moment I step out of the sciences building, the weight of curious stares and muffled whispers hits me like a tidal wave. Normally, I can blend into the flow of students on campus, but today is different.

Today everyone is staring.

At least that's the way it feels.

Maybe I'm capable of commanding this kind of attention on stage, but I'm not Holland Tate in those moments.

I'm Lavender Smoke.

"Holland! Wait up!" Ava's voice cuts through the noise on campus.

For a second, I consider ducking my head and running, but she's faster than me, weaving through the crowd until she falls into step beside me. Her expression is a mix of curiosity and amusement.

I know exactly what's coming.

"Did you see the message?" she asks, wide-eyed. "It's crazy. Every-one's talking about it."

I blow out a steady breath and keep my gaze focused straight ahead. "Yeah, I saw."

Ava tilts her head as she studies me. "I mean, it's obviously not true, right? Everyone knows you can't stand Bridger Sanderson."

I keep walking, my stride purposeful, as if it's possible to outrun this conversation.

When I remain silent, her voice dips, filling with confusion. "Holland?"

I glance at her, then at the path ahead. "It's not... untrue."

She stops dead in her tracks, forcing me to do the same. "What?" Her eyes go so wide I half-expect them to pop out of her head. "Are you saying—wait, no—you and Bridger? *Dating?*"

"Ava," I mutter, already regretting my choice of words.

"You're kidding. You *have* to be kidding," she says, crossing her arms. "Start talking, because I have *so many* questions."

I press my fingers to my temples, trying to come up with a response that will satisfy her without revealing too much. I fall back on the lame answer I gave Garret. "It's... complicated."

"Complicated?" she repeats, incredulous. "What does that even mean? When did this happen? Just last night you said there was nothing between you two."

Before I can reply, or more accurately, evade, her rapid-fire inquiries, the business building comes into view.

Thank God.

Even though I'll have to face Bridger for the second time this morning, I've never been so glad to see it.

"Look," I say, picking up my pace, "I'd love to explain, but we're going to be late for class."

"This conversation isn't over."

"Sure," I say, relieved to duck into the building and put some distance between us. Even after she walks away, her questions echo in my mind, stirring up things I'd rather not think about.

Inside the lecture hall, I head straight for a seat near the middle, hoping to disappear into the rows of students. I'm pulling out my notebook when the architect of my problems strides in and scans the room. That's when I do something I never would have before, and shrink back in my chair when his attention zeroes in on me.

I force my gaze away, hoping he'll do us both a favor and pick another spot, but no such luck. He drops into the seat next to me, his presence as overwhelming as ever.

"Hey," he says, glancing my way. "You doing all right?"

"Sure. Why wouldn't I be?" With a shrug, I lift a brow. "After all, I'm the one behind all the messages, right? Pretty clever to throw myself into the mix." I drop my voice and lean closer. His gaze dips to my mouth before flicking upward again. "And throw suspicion off myself."

His eyes narrow but he doesn't say a word.

I swivel toward the front of the room as Abbott dives into the lecture, talking about teamwork and communication. Us being paired up for this project feels more like an absurd joke.

We don't need to spend more time together.

We need to spend far less.

Midway through the class, Abbott pauses and looks directly at us. "Holland. Bridger. Why don't you share an update on your project."

I stiffen as every set of eyes in the room lands on us.

"Sure," Bridger says, jumping in and flashing an easy smile. "Holland and I have been making steady progress. She's a natural when it comes to organization."

I blink, caught off guard by the flattering remark. "And Bridger," I say, forcing a polite tone, "has been surprisingly good at brainstorming ideas."

"Surprisingly?" he murmurs, low enough that only I can hear. "Careful, Tate. That almost sounded like a compliment."

The professor nods in satisfaction before moving on. Bridger leans closer, his voice dripping with amusement. "Guess we really do make a great team."

I glare at him, but there's no real heat behind it. "Don't push your luck."

It's a blessing when the professor wraps up class and dismisses us. I shove my notebook into my bag and rise to my feet, ready to bolt from the room. But Bridger is already up, blocking my escape.

"Do you have another class after this?" he asks, falling into step beside me as I head toward the exit.

"Yup," I mutter. "That's what happens when you take eighteen credits a semester in order to graduate early."

"Six classes, huh? That's a heavy load." He gives me a bit of side-eye. "And you still have time to screw with my life? Impressive."

"Go fuck yourself, Sanderson." I give him a tight smile. "I'm sure you're used to that by now."

He snorts. "It's a real wonder that you don't have a boyfriend."

"Oh, but I do!" I raise my brows and feign innocence. "Remember?"

His lips curve into a smile. "How could I forget?"

"Well, I'm sure you have someplace to be that's not here." There's a pause before I add, so he'll get the hint, "With me."

"Actually, there's no other place I'd rather be than with you, my girlfriend."

"How lucky," I mutter, picking up my pace.

"And here I thought you'd want to spend a little quality time with your new BF."

"Turns out I like the idea of it more than I actually like having one."

His grin widens. "I'm just trying to be the best fake boyfriend I can be. You're welcome."

We bicker the entire way across campus. It's exhausting and exhilarating at the same time, like sparring with someone who knows all your best moves. I find myself having to level up my game.

When we reach the building, his movements stall as he clears his throat. "Look, I was serious when I asked how you were doing after this morning."

I blink, startled by the sincerity that fills his eyes. "I'm fine," I lie. "It wasn't a big deal."

"Well, if you're not actually the one behind the messages..." There's a pause as his tone softens even more. "Then I don't want you getting caught in the crosshairs."

The simple admittance has the rare ability to melt my irritation where Bridger is concerned. It takes effort to keep my walls firmly in place.

"I appreciate you looking out for me." I say the words before my brain catches up with my mouth. "I'll let you know if anything happens to change that."

He nods, his gaze steady. "Good."

And just like that, the tension between us shifts, softening into something quieter and far more complicated.

# WESTERN UNIVERSITY CHAT APP

BRIDGER
SANDERSON
17
17
17
WILDCATS

Every step that brings me closer to my father's office has my pulse thrumming with irritation. This is exactly what I didn't need today.

All right, let's be honest... I don't need an ass reaming from him any day of the week.

The eerie quiet of the hallway doesn't help dispel the dread pooling at the bottom of my gut. I can't remember a time when it wasn't like this between us. After Mom picked up and left, everything got a whole hell of a lot worse.

I glance around the outer sanctum and find his secretary's desk empty, which is unusual. Maybe luck is finally on my side and he's not here.

Nothing would thrill me more.

I knock once and hear a muffled thud from inside, followed by the faint sound of rustling papers and the low hum of conversation.

Is it possible the old man is stroking out?

Again, nothing would thrill me—

We'll just leave it at that.

My brow furrows, and I'm about to rap my knuckles for a second time when the door creaks open and his secretary slips out. A flush fills her cheeks and her blouse is buttoned wrong. She avoids eye contact as she tucks a stray strand of hair behind her ear.

*You've got to be kidding me.*

My stomach twists with a sick mix of disbelief and disgust.

She looks like she could be my age.

And Dick has the audacity to lecture *me* about propriety?

Un-fucking-believable.

"Go on in," she mumbles before scurrying to her desk.

With a shake of my head, I step inside and shut the door behind me. Dad is seated behind his massive mahogany desk, looking like the king of his little fiefdom. He glances up, his expression cool and unreadable. It's the tension in his jaw that gives him away.

The man is pissed.

Maybe even embarrassed to be caught in such a compromising situation.

Tough shit for him.

Here's an idea—don't fuck around at work.

"You're late," he says in a clipped tone. "I expected you an hour ago."

"Sorry. Didn't realize we'd set up an appointment," I shoot back before glancing at the door as if I can see his secretary seated out front. "Kind of seems like I interrupted something important."

Ignoring the comment, he points to the chair parked in front of the desk. "Sit your ass down."

Instead of following the command, I stay put. I just want to get this over with as quickly as possible and get on with my day.

His eyes narrow when I don't immediately fall into line, and he exhales slowly, as if trying to keep his temper in check. I'm surprised he's making the effort. Under normal circumstances, he wouldn't bother.

"Isn't it enough that your unsavory activities have become public fodder, now you're getting into fights on campus with your teammates? Is there no end to the humiliation you're hell-bent on causing me?"

My jaw tenses. "It wasn't a fight."

"It looked moments away from becoming one. And for what?" There's a beat of silence. "Some piece of ass?"

Anger surges inside me that he would refer to Holland that way. "She's not a piece of ass."

With a snort, he shakes his head. "Haven't you figured out by now that they all are? Your mother was a perfect example. Couldn't hack it and walked away, leaving me with a child to raise myself."

My hands clench at my sides. As much as I want to defend my mother, I can't. She wasn't mentally or emotionally equipped to handle life with Dick. So, she took the easy way out and ran away as fast as she could. I can't blame her for that. She should have taken me with her, though.

I remind myself that in a few months, I'll be able to leave him behind too. Some days, it's the only thing that gets me through.

"Have you forgotten that everything you do reflects on me? On this university? Perhaps you should give serious consideration to stepping away from the team. It's become a distraction. An embarrassment."

My eyes widen as his words whip around in my head.

Step away from the team?

They're more of a family to me than he'll ever be.

"No."

He lifts a brow. "Excuse me?"

I straighten as tension fills my shoulders. "I said no. I won't quit the team. Especially when we're in the middle of playoffs."

"Then maybe I'll have a conversation with the coach myself. I'm sure he'll see things my way."

A disbelieving laugh falls from my lips as I shake my head. "You'd actually do that to me?"

His icy glare never wavers. "Yes, I would."

My blood boils as the words shoot out of my mouth. "You do that, and I can't guarantee people won't find out that you're screwing your secretary. What is she? Twenty-five or six?" I pop a brow. "Possibly younger?"

The room goes deathly quiet. I tighten my hands again to stop them from shaking.

Dick's eyes darken and a muscle in his jaw tics as he rises from his chair with deliberate slowness. "Are you threatening me, you little shit? After everything I've done for you?"

The only thing he's done is beat me down.

And I'm fucking over it.

I lift my chin and hold his stare. "I won't quit the team."

"You'll do exactly what I tell you to do," he barks, slamming his fist on the desk. The sound echoes in the room.

"How about we cut the crap." I force out the words I've always secretly feared but hoped weren't true. "You don't give a damn about me. Only how I make you look."

Disgust twists his lips, and any hope that he'd correct the mistaken belief is snuffed out. I'm an idiot for hoping that deep down, he actually cared about me but didn't know how to express it. Turns out that's just another lie I've been telling myself.

"You've always been so fucking difficult, not to mention a disappointment. Just like your mother. She should have aborted you when she had the chance. God knows I offered her the money to take care of it."

The force of those words is like a punch to the gut, and air rushes from my lungs in a painful burst, making it impossible to breathe. Somewhere in the back of my mind, I always knew he felt this way. But hearing him say it cuts more than anticipated.

"I appreciate you letting me know how you feel," I say, trying to keep any emotion from bleeding into my voice. "It'll make walking away after graduation that much easier."

Without waiting for a dismissal, I turn and stalk out, closing the door behind me. My heart pounds a painful staccato as hurt and anger buzz through my veins. I fucking hate the sting of tears that prick the backs of my eyes.

He's never been so blunt about his feelings before.

As if he didn't care if the mask fell away and I caught a glimpse of the real Richard Sanderson along with the hatred that lives in his heart where I'm concerned.

My head is a mess as I slide behind the wheel of my BMW and start the engine before peeling out of the parking lot and into the flow of afternoon traffic. It doesn't take long before I'm going ten and then twenty miles over the speed limit. The sound of the engine roars in my ears, blotting out all the chaotic thoughts that fill my head. Instead of slowing, I press my foot harder on the gas pedal. My hands tighten around the steering wheel until my knuckles turn bone white.

Who knows?

Maybe the old man is right.

Maybe Mom should have gotten rid of me when she had the chance.

With my attention locked on the windshield, the town streaks by in a rush of color. The engine growls as I push the gas pedal harder than I should and the speedometer continues to steadily creep up until the road ahead blurs. My chest feels like it's caving in as my father's voice ricochets around in my head.

I grit my teeth, the weight of his words pressing harder with every mile. The faint glow of my phone catches my attention, a notification lighting up the screen where it rests on the passenger seat. My stomach clenches when I see the name.

*FragileLikeABomb.*

That's all it takes for my foot to ease off the gas. The thought of ignoring her feels wrong, but I can't text while driving like this. My hands are already trembling. I pull over to the side of the road, the tires crunching over gravel as I come to a stop.

The moment the car is in park, I rest my forehead against the steering wheel. My breath comes out in harsh, uneven bursts, and I fight the urge to punch something—*anything*—to rid myself of this frustration.

Inhale.

Exhale.

I repeat the pattern until the tightness in my chest starts to loosen. Slowly, I lift my head and reach for the phone, my thumb hovering over the screen.

FRAGILELIKEABOMB

Thanks for being there for me earlier. I really needed it.

Her message is like a balm over a raw wound, a reminder that not everything in my life is shit.

A reminder that someone, somewhere, gives a damn.

I take a deep breath and type back.

ME

> You never have to thank me for that. I'll always be here.

The response feels right, even though my hands are still shaking as I hit send. The reply comes quickly, like she was waiting for me to say something.

FRAGILELIKEABOMB

> I mean it. You're good people. How's your day been?

I hesitate, my fingers tightening around the phone. Lying would be easier, but I don't want to do that with her. Not when she's the only one who gets it.

ME

> Rough. Had an ugly run-in with my dad.

There.

It's out.

Poison released into the atmosphere.

I lean back in the seat and stare at the screen as I wait for her reply. My pulse thuds in my ears as anticipation and dread twist together.

The typing bubble pops up and then her message appears.

FRAGILELIKEABOMB

> I'm sorry. That sucks. Do you want to talk about it?

Her words stare back at me, offering a lifeline I didn't realize I needed. My chest tightens again, but this time it's different. It's less suffocating. More like the release of a valve.

I run a hand through my hair, trying to decide if I can even put it into words. If there's one person I can try to explain it to, though, it's her.

ME

It's just… him being him. He knows exactly where to hit me, and he never misses.

Her reply is immediate.

FRAGILELIKEABOMB

That's brutal. You don't deserve that.

The knot in my chest loosens a fraction more, her words cutting through the haze of anger and frustration. I don't respond right away. Instead, I stare at her message like it's something solid I can hold on to.

ME

Thanks. You're good at this, you know.

FRAGILELIKEABOMB

At what?

ME

Making me feel like I'm not completely falling apart.

The pause before her next message feels longer than it probably is.

FRAGILELIKEABOMB

That's because you're not. Falling apart, I mean. You're stronger than you think.

I let out a breath, some of the weight lifting from my shoulders.

ME

You're good people, Fragile. Don't let anyone tell you otherwise.

Her reply comes with a virtual eye roll.

FRAGILELIKEABOMB

Says the guy who is the definition of "good people." Don't even try to argue.

For the first time in hours, a smile tugs at the corners of my mouth. She always has a way of turning the worst days into something manageable.

Other than my cousin, she's the one person I can always count on to be there when shit goes south. She's become important to me. Ironically, I have no idea what she looks like or the sound of her voice. We could pass each other on campus and not even know it. Every so often, I find myself scanning the crowd, my gaze landing on a random girl before wondering—is that her?

Or is it the chick she's standing with?

ME

Fine. You win this one. But don't get used to it.

FRAGILELIKEABOMB

Too late. I'm already celebrating.

I chuckle under my breath, the sound foreign after the day I've had. For the first time since I left my father's office, I feel like I can breathe again.

ME

I should go. Talk soon?

FRAGILELIKEABOMB

Anytime you need.

I log off, a strange cocktail of emotions lingering in my mind. The hurt and anger have finally abated, and I know that has everything to do with this girl from the chat app. The one I don't even know in real life.

The one I wish I did.

Would meeting up ruin our relationship? Or make it that much better?

I have no idea.

As soon as that thought pops into my head, an auburn-haired spitfire with a sharp tongue forces her way back into my thoughts.

And suddenly, all I want to do is see her.

Touch her.

I really hope she's telling the truth and isn't involved in these messages.

Only time will tell because, one way or another, I'm going to get to the bottom of it.

I just hope Holland isn't the one I find there.

HOLLAND

The bass reverberates through the floor, pulsing up my legs and settling in my chest like a second heartbeat. The lights shift, casting a soft, golden glow across the stage, and I feel the crowd's attention sharpen, homing in on me. It's a high I've learned to control, a blend of power and vulnerability that keeps me balanced as I move.

My heels click softly against the polished stage as I take one final turn around the pole, the silk ribbons of my costume fluttering with the motion. My body follows the rhythm, every movement choreographed to leave an impression without revealing too much. It's all an illusion, a performance where confidence masks everything hiding beneath the surface.

I slide down to a graceful crouch, my fingertips brushing the stage as I arch my back in a deliberate tease. The applause swells, and the corner of my mouth lifts in a small smile. They love the act, the persona I've created, the woman who isn't afraid to demand their attention.

The music fades as I push to my feet, my chest rising and falling with a controlled exhale. I step to the edge of the stage, letting the golden light spill over me one last time. My final glance into the crowd catches the faint gleam of expensive watches, tailored suits, and top-shelf liquor in crystal tumblers.

I turn away before slipping backstage as the roar of the applause dulls and the adrenaline that carried me through the set begins to fade. It always feels like stepping from one world into another.

A huff escapes me as I slip my arms into a robe and drop onto my chair. The mirror is surrounded by soft, warm lights that make everything feel more glamorous than it actually is. My reflection stares back at me, framed by brushed gold edges. I focus on the smudge of mascara under my eye instead of the girl in the mirror.

I grab a makeup wipe and swipe it across my cheek, erasing the last traces of Lavender Smoke. Adrenaline still hums through my veins, making my hand tremble as I clean my face. I'm not sure if it's the aftermath of the performance or the fact that I spotted Bridger loitering near the bar, attention glued to me.

As much as I tried to ignore him in the crowd, that was impossible. After a handful of minutes, I stopped trying to pretend and kept my attention locked on him until it felt like I was dancing solely for him.

That's not something I ever imagined myself wanting to do.

The thought sends a prickle down my spine, and my gaze flicks to the side, realizing I'm no longer alone. In the reflection, I catch a glimpse of him leaning against the doorframe, his sharp jawline and broad shoulders unmistakable. He doesn't belong here. His presence clashes with the carefully curated elegance of the space.

I force my attention back to my reflection, and press the wipe harder against my skin, as if scrubbing away more than just makeup. My pulse quickens. I don't want him here. I don't want him to see me like this—stripped of the armor I wear outside this place. But more than that, I don't want to think about how his gaze feels like a physical caress, trailing over me even when I'm not looking.

Bridger doesn't speak or move.

He's just there, a steady presence I can't ignore.

The weight of his stare presses against my skin, making my hand shake as I dab at the stubborn eyeliner clinging to the corner of my eye. The makeup wipe slips, leaving a dark smudge across my temple.

I release a shuddering breath.

The shuffle of his footsteps makes me glance up, and suddenly, he's right behind me, close enough that his cologne, along with the scent of clean soap, fills my lungs. His eyes catch mine in the mirror, and for a moment, neither of us speak.

"You missed a spot," he says softly, his voice low and rough.

"I've got it." My hand trembles as I try to fix the smudge, but the wipe catches, smearing the black streak further.

"Clearly."

Before I can protest, he reaches forward and takes the makeup remover from my hand. His fingers graze mine, sending a jolt through me.

"Hey—" I start, but he's already tilting my chin upward, his touch surprisingly gentle as he wipes the smudge away.

My breath catches.

I should be annoyed, mortified even, but all I can do is stare at him. He's too close, his features more defined in the fluorescent light of the dressing room. The strong line of his jaw, the sharp angle of his cheekbones, the way his lips quirk ever so slightly as he concentrates.

He's ridiculously handsome.

The realization stirs emotions I've tried so hard to bury.

"There," he says, his voice softer now. "All clean."

Our eyes meet, and for a second, it feels like the room shrinks, leaving just the two of us. My heart pounds against my rib cage. I hate that he can affect me so easily. That he's always had this power over me. I tug my chin from his hand, needing to shatter the moment.

"Why don't you wait in the car," I say, my voice steadier than I feel. "I'll be out in a minute."

His mouth twitches, as if he's about to argue. Instead, he nods and takes a step in retreat. "Don't take too long."

The door closes behind him, and a puff of air escapes me as I turn to the mirror. My reflection stares back at me, flushed and wide-eyed. I pull my robe tighter around myself and shake my head, trying to snap out of the daze.

"You okay, hon?" Megan asks, walking past with a towel slung over her shoulder.

"Yeah," I mutter, fumbling for my clothes.

She glances toward the door Bridger disappeared through. "That guy yours? He's hot."

"No," I say quickly. "He's just someone I know from school."

She raises a brow but doesn't push. "Lucky you."

I roll my eyes and pull on my jeans, trying not to think about how ridiculous it is to associate the word *lucky* with Bridger Sanderson.

*Lucky* would be not feeling this weird pull toward him.

*Lucky* would be not sharing a house or a bed with him.

As I stuff my phone into my bag, a notification pops up from *ColdAsIce17*. My fingers hover over the screen for a moment before I open it.

COLDASICE17

Thanks for what you said earlier. You being there means a lot.

My heart constricts.

ME

Anytime.

I hit send and close the app before I get sucked into a conversation with him. Once we get started, it's difficult to stop. With a wave to a few of the girls, I grab my bag and head for the parking lot where Bridger is waiting. As soon as I slide into the passenger seat, the atmosphere turns suffocating. The silence between us is heavy, thick with things that remain unsaid. I rack my brain for something that will lighten the mood but there's nothing.

My mind is blank.

At this point, I'd take snarking back and forth like we usually do, over the explosive tension brewing between us like an impending storm. Any moment, it's going to break. I'm afraid of what will happen when it does.

It's a relief when we finally pull up to the hockey house. The windows are glowing with light, and the faint bass of music thumps through the walls. Inside, the living room is packed with his teammates and their girlfriends. Red Solo cups are scattered across every available surface. I recognize a few of the guys. Ryder McAdams and Wolf Westerville. They eye me with curiosity. Kind of like I'm a puzzle they're both trying to figure out.

"You want a drink?" Bridger asks, staring into the living room.

"Nah, it's not really my thing."

He tilts his head, studying me. "Huh. I didn't know that."

"Probably because we're not actually friends," I say with a pointed look.

"Yeah, that must be it."

I know he's teasing, but the words sting anyway. It's not like I don't have my reasons. I've watched my mom drink away her problems for years, stringing herself along from one bad decision after another. I love Vivienne, but I don't want to end up like her, hopping from man to man in hopes of finding my happily ever after.

I want to be the one in charge of my own destiny.

And that's difficult to do when you're intoxicated and your judgment is impaired.

"Should we head upstairs?" Bridger asks, interrupting the whirl of my thoughts. "It's quieter."

With a nod, I follow him up the staircase, grateful to leave the noise and watchful stares behind.

His footsteps are steady on the hardwood, the sound mixing in my ears with the echo of my pulse that seems a beat too fast. By the time we step into his room, I'm hyperaware of the silence that has fallen over us. He shuts the door, and for a moment, we stand there, awkwardly rooted in place.

He glances at me. "Should I step out while you change?"

The question takes me by surprise. It's thoughtful. Unexpectedly so. But probably unnecessary. The memory of his eyes on me during my performance flashes through my mind, and I push it aside, shaking my head.

"It's fine," I say, forcing my tone to be casual. "We can both just turn around."

He nods, and we move in unspoken agreement, our backs to each other as I drop down and sort through my bag. I pull out a pair of shorts and a tank top, my fingers fumbling slightly as I peel off my jeans. I remind myself that this is no different than getting ready for bed any other night.

Except for the fact that Bridger is only a couple feet away, changing in the same room.

I slip the tank on and glance over my shoulder, intending to grab my discarded clothes, but my eyes land on him instead. His back is turned toward me. He's stripped off both his hoodie and jeans, giving me an unobstructed view of his body. His broad shoulders taper into a trim waist, and his navy boxer briefs cling to him like a second skin. Heat rushes to my face, and I quickly look away, hoping he didn't notice.

"See something you like?" A teasing quality fills his voice.

I whip my head around to find him facing me, his brows raised and a smirk pulling at his lips.

My mouth opens, but nothing comes out.

After a few silent seconds, I manage a hasty, "No! I mean, I wasn't—"

"Relax, Tate," he says, clearly enjoying my flustered state. "I'm just messing with you."

I mutter something under my breath and busy myself with folding my jeans. It's only when he clears his throat that I force my attention back to him. His expression has softened, the smirk replaced by something that can only be described as uncertainty. It's an odd look on him. He usually seems so self-assured. And here I am, so discombobulated that I can't even enjoy it.

He clears his throat. "So, we've got a game tomorrow," he says, his tone deceptively casual as his eyes search mine.

I blink, unsure where he's going with this. "Okay?"

He scratches the back of his neck before shifting. "I, uh… got you something."

When I remain silent, he reaches into his backpack and pulls out a jersey before thrusting it in my direction.

I stare at it, the orange and black colors bright against his hands. "What's that for?"

"It's for you," he mumbles. "I picked it up at the school store today. You'll need it for the game. You know, since you're my girlfriend now."

The word *girlfriend* hangs in the air, heavy with the weight of everything it doesn't mean. I force myself to close the distance between us and take the jersey, running my fingers over the thick material.

"Fake girlfriend," I murmur, unable to help myself.

"Well, yeah," he says quickly. "That's what I meant."

Something tightens in my chest at the way he says it, like the words taste bitter in his mouth. I fold the jersey carefully and set it on his dresser before slipping beneath the covers of the bed. After turning off the light, he crawls in on the other side. The mattress dips slightly under his weight as he settles in beside me.

"Thanks," I say, my voice barely above a whisper.

He turns his head to look at me, his expression unreadable in the dim light that filters in through the window. "You're welcome."

The space between us feels charged, like it's holding something neither of us is ready to name.

"Why don't you drink?"

I glance at him, startled by the question. For a second, I consider brushing off the inquiry and lying, but I'm too tired to come up with something convincing. "My mom," I admit. "She's... not great with alcohol."

He nods, his expression unreadable. "I'm sorry. That sucks."

"Yeah." I pause, then ask, "How'd the meeting with your dad go?"

His jaw tightens as he stares at the ceiling. "The way it always does."

I shift onto my side, watching him. "Do you want to talk about it?"

His gaze slices to mine. And for a moment or two, it looks like he might say something else. "Nah. But thanks for the offer."

Then he rolls onto his back, and the silence stretches between us. Even though I close my eyes, sleep doesn't come easily.

Not with Bridger so close.

# BRIDGER

# 18

Rain patters against the window. It's a soft rhythm that pulls me from sleep. For a handful of seconds, I lie there and stare at the shadows that dance across the ceiling, listening to the steady sound of water hitting glass. It's calming, almost hypnotic, and I'm about to let it lull me back to sleep when I hear something else. It's a faint sound, sharp enough to stand out against the rain.

A whimper.

I blink, half-convinced I imagined it. But then it happens again, quiet and muffled. My pulse kicks up as I roll onto my side and glance toward Holland. She's facing away from me, her frame curled tight under the covers. The sound repeats, low and almost broken, and I realize with a jolt that it's coming from her.

She shifts slightly, her head turning toward me, her lips parting as a faint, shaky "No" slips out.

*Shit.*

I push myself up on one elbow and lean closer. Her brows are furrowed, her breathing quick and uneven. The sight has something clenching in my chest.

Holland Tate—sarcastic, sharp, and untouchable—is having a nightmare.

My hand hovers hesitantly over her arm. She's not exactly the kind of person who welcomes comfort, but seeing her so vulnerable and fragile pricks at me. Carefully, I lay my hand on her back. The heat of her skin seeps through the thin fabric of her tank top.

"Holland," I murmur. "Wake up."

She moves again, her features twisting as another whimper escapes from her. "Nooo," she whispers, her voice thick with fear.

"Holland," I say more firmly before shaking her arm. "You're all right. You're safe. Wake up."

Her eyes fly open, wild and unfocused, as a soft sob tears from her throat. The fear and confusion within that cry hit me like a punch to the gut. This isn't the Holland I've gotten to know over the past three years. It's not the girl who can slice me in half with a single look or leave me speechless with her sharp tongue.

This Holland is raw, exposed, and I really fucking hate that I'm seeing her like this.

Without thinking, I pull her into my arms. She stiffens for a heartbeat before collapsing against me. Her fingers clutch at my chest, as if I'm the only thing anchoring her to reality. I rest my chin on top of her head as my hand rubs soothing circles across her back.

"You're okay," I whisper, kissing the crown of her head. "I've got you."

Her breathing slows as her sobs quiet into shaky inhales. We lie like that for a long time. The rain outside is the only sound that fills the room.

"You want to talk about it?" I ask before tacking on, "They say it helps."

She releases a shuddering breath, her voice muffled against my chest. "Who's 'they'?"

"I have no idea. The experts, I guess?"

She shifts slightly, her head tilting to look at me. Her face is pale, her eyes red-rimmed, but there's a flicker of humor in her expression. "You don't strike me as the type to listen to experts."

I smirk. "Don't let it get around. I have a reputation to uphold."

There's a hint of a smile that tugs at her lips before it fades, leaving something softer in its place. "Do you think we could pretend for a little bit that we don't hate each other?"

Her words catch me off guard, but my response comes easily. "I don't hate you, Holland. I never hated you."

She snorts, but there's no real venom behind it. "Could've fooled me."

My fingers drift to her hair, sifting through the soft strands. "I'm sorry. I never meant to hurt you. I pushed you away after we slept together because I was scared."

It's so much easier to admit the truth in the darkness that blankets us.

She lifts her head again until her gaze can lock on mine. "Scared of what?"

"You," I admit, my voice barely above a whisper before forcing myself to say the rest. "What you made me feel. By the time I realized I'd made a mistake, it was too late. The damage was done."

Her eyes widen slightly, a vulnerability I've never seen in her, shining back at me. She resettles against me, and my nerves ratchet up with the passing of each silent second that ticks by.

"Holland?" My heartbeat thunders in my ears. "Are you still awake?"

"Yeah," she says, her voice quiet. "I'm not sure what to say."

The disappointment that crashes over me is heavy and unwelcome. I've never put myself out there like this or dropped my guard when it comes to women. And now, I wish I hadn't done it with her.

"You don't have to say anything," I mutter. "I just wanted you to know."

The air between us shifts, thickening with something I can't quite name. Slowly, almost hesitantly, she leans forward and brushes her lips against mine. It's a featherlight touch that sends a shockwave through my entire body.

Before I can sink into the caress, she pulls back, her cheeks flushing as she lays her head on my chest.

"Thank you," she whispers, her voice barely audible over the rain.

I wrap my arms around her and hold her close as the storm outside rages on.

Another silence falls over us, and after a while, her breathing evens out. My mind drifts with thoughts of her. Holland is the last person I expected to feel this way about. And yet, as I run my fingers absently through her hair, I realize the only other person I've ever been this honest with is *FragileLikeABomb*.

I'm not sure whether to be comforted or disturbed by the thought. Maybe that's why I feel so drawn to her. Somehow, in ways I can't explain, Holland makes me feel the same way Fragile does.

Like I'm seen.

Like I'm known.

And that terrifies me.

HOLLAND

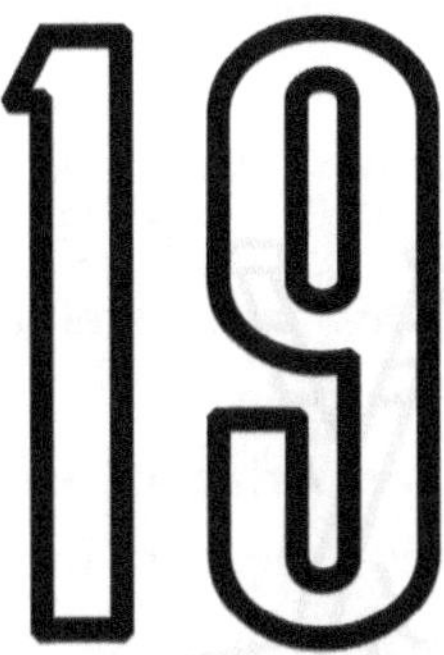

The first thing that hits me when I wake is the warmth.

The second is the hard, steady rise and fall beneath me, like I'm lying against a solid, living, breathing furnace. My brain is still foggy with sleep, and it takes a moment to play mental catch up and for the details to sharpen. There are strong arms wrapped around me, a hand resting possessively on my hip, and the faint scent of soap and something that is inherently *him.*

My eyes snap open to find Bridger Sanderson flat on his back, his annoyingly perfect jawline relaxed in sleep while I'm sprawled across his chest.

I should move before he wakes up.

Instead, I remain perfectly still.

As much as I hate to admit it, I've never felt so safe.

Safe in a way I can't explain.

Safe in a way I haven't allowed myself to feel in years.

Not since the last time I let my guard down with this guy and got burned for it.

But in the sliver of dawn where the world doesn't feel so sharp, I let myself indulge in the comfort I've found in his arms. My hand slides up his chest, fingers tracing the hard lines of muscle and the steady thrum of his heartbeat beneath them.

It's ridiculously soothing.

My fingers drift lower, brushing along the edge of his ribs, and—

"Enjoying yourself?"

His voice is gravelly, still thick with sleep, and I jerk my hand back, as if burned.

"Maybe." The response shoots out of my mouth before I can stuff it back inside.

Bridger stretches lazily, his arms extending above his head, and the movement makes his abs ripple.

I should look away but can't bring myself to do it.

His voice dips, growing even deeper. "Interesting. Go on."

I glance up at him and search his eyes. His mouth is closer than I realized. "What if we extended our truce? Maybe considered a cease-fire for the time being?"

He stills. "What exactly would that entail?"

The muscles of my belly spasm as thoughts circle through my brain. When I remain silent, unsure how to respond, he rolls us over until he's fully stretched out on top of me.

A gasp works its way free from me as his hard length nestles against the V between my thighs. That's all it takes for arousal to pool in my core. It's been so long since I've felt desire like this burn through my body. I don't realize that I've widened my legs until the blunt tip of his cock presses insistently against my center.

"Huh, Holland? What are you suggesting?"

He slides his erection against me, and every thought flies out of my head. It's impossible to think straight when he does that. The silveriness of his eyes deepens as he repeats the movement. A smirk curves his lips, as if he knows exactly how much he's able to affect me with the simple caress.

"That we..."

Another stroke.

When my voice trails off, he hikes a brow. "That we what?"

I stifle a groan as my teeth sink into my lower lip. His gaze drops to the movement as he holds himself steady. His biceps bulge as he cages me in. It's like the outside world, and maybe even our past, melts away into nothingness.

All I'm cognizant of is him.

And the moment we're teetering dangerously on.

It feels as sharp as a razor's edge.

He presses his pelvis against mine, and the pressure building in my core turns explosive.

"I can't think when you do that," I blurt in frustration.

"Is that such a terrible thing?"

Good question.

"I'm not sure," I say on another shuddering breath. It seems ridiculous that he's turned me on to this degree while barely touching me.

"Pretty sure thinking's overrated, you know?"

I blink as the comment echoes in my brain. It sounds strangely familiar. A different conversation maybe? It's on the tip of my tongue to ask what he means when he shifts his hips and his hard cock slides across my soaked shorts.

The pleasure is dizzying.

"So, about that ceasefire…"

As much as I want to blot out the past and start fresh, I'm not sure if it's that simple. There's a question that needs to be answered before we can move forward.

"Do you still believe I'm involved with the messages?"

He stills, and air leaks slowly from his lungs. "I'm not sure." There's a pause as he searches my eyes. "I really hope not."

I swallow down my disappointment and jerk my head into a nod. Before I can say anything, he rolls onto his back until I find myself stretched out on top of him. His morning wood is still nestled between my legs. When I wiggle, the head of his cock bumps my clit, sending my body into overdrive.

A whimper works its way up my throat as his fingers strum my sides before sliding past my waist until he's able to palm my ass cheeks.

If I were smart, I'd put an end to this.

"I suppose we could cuddle at night," I finally say.

"I'd be okay with that."

"Just okay?"

He presses me closer before flexing his hips. "Maybe a little more than okay."

The sensation reverberates throughout my entire being. It's almost a shock when my muscles tighten, clamping around nothingness. My brain clicks off, and I can't help but shift against him, chasing the delicious feeling.

His fingers dig into my flesh to keep me anchored in place.

"How close are you to coming?"

I'm almost ashamed to admit the way I'm tap dancing on the edge. It wouldn't take much to shove me over the precipice.

"Close." My eyelids feather shut.

"Eyes open, Holland. When you orgasm, I want you to see exactly who's getting you off."

Even though it feels like my eyelids weigh a thousand pounds, I force them open and hold his gaze. One long stroke upward is all it takes to make me shatter into a million pieces.

A muscle in his jaw tics as our gazes stay locked the entire time I moan out my orgasm. I masturbate regularly. The last thing I'm going to do is leave my pleasure in the hands of a man. If I'm horny or stressed, my trusty vibe always does the trick.

But this?

It's not even in the same ballpark.

It's so much bigger.

Brighter.

Like a burst of colorful fireworks that steals your breath away and holds it captive. He continues to grind against me the entire time until every last spasm has been wrung from my body.

I bury my face in his chest, feeling more exposed than I'm used to. What I'm most afraid of is that I'll find a smirk lifting his lips, followed up by enough gloating to make me regret everything that just happened. Only two nights spent in his bed, and I've already folded like a cheap house of cards.

It's demoralizing.

I thought I was better than this.

Stronger.

Turns out, I was wrong.

"Hey." His fingers slip beneath my chin to lift it. "Look at me."

I force myself to meet his gaze. Shock slides through me at the sincerity etched across every line of his face.

"Truce, right? Maybe we haven't hammered out the finer points, but I think this was a good start, don't you?"

I nibble my lip, surprised by how much I want to believe him. "Yeah."

It's only when his other hand squeezes the rounded curve of my ass that I realize it's still there, gripping me possessively.

"We should probably get moving. I've got class in thirty. Not that I've been stalking your schedule, but you do too, right?"

"Yup." I roll off him and onto my back, not needing to be told twice.

He raises himself up on one elbow to stare down at me. "Our game is tonight. You'll be there, right?"

It's tempting to tell him that I won't be able to make it. After what just happened between us, a little distance would do me some good. It would give me a chance to fortify my walls again. I don't like how quickly he was able to break them down.

"Yeah." I almost wince as the word slips free.

"And you'll wear the jersey?"

"It would be rude if I didn't after you bought it for me," I mumble as my cheeks heat under the intensity of his stare.

His expression relaxes as the corners of his lips quirk. "When have you ever been worried about being rude?"

I can't help but snort.

He's got me there.

Before I can come up with a snappy retort, he leans closer and brushes his lips across mine. Our gazes stay fastened until he pulls away and rises from the bed with a lazy stretch. It's only then that I notice the massive boner he's sporting.

*Damn.*

A thick shiver slides through me as I remember how good the stroke of his hard length felt. It takes a moment to realize that while I got off, he didn't.

After giving me a delicious orgasm, he asked for nothing in return.

"Am I free to go, or would you like to keep staring?" His tone drops, turning husky. "Because I certainly don't mind you eating me up with your eyes. In fact, I kind of like it."

I clear my throat. "Need a hand with that?"

"As tempting as the offer is, I don't think we have time. You stroking my cock isn't something I want to rush." He nods toward the door. "I'll take care of it in the shower."

My brows rise, and even though I just came, the mental image of Bridger stroking his hard length turns me on all over again.

There's no doubt about it, dropping my guard was a bad idea. And if I'm not careful, it's going to lead to problems.

If it hasn't already.

"Okay."

He pauses. "Can I take a rain check?"

I shrug, needing to shake off the disappointment that has settled over me. It doesn't make a damn bit of sense why I would feel this way. "We'll see."

A chuckle slips free from him as he steps into the hallway, leaving me alone in his room. I collapse against the pillows and stare at the ceiling, wondering exactly how I ended up in Bridger Sanderson's bed.

Even harder to believe... I just might be enjoying it.

BRIDGER
SANDERSON
17
17
WILDCATS

T he sharp slap of my stick against the ice reverberates in my ears as I dig in, chasing the puck down the boards. My pulse thunders, the stress of the playoff game pressing down on me.

This isn't just about winning.

It's about fighting for my place and proving to the team, and myself, that I deserve to be here. That I'm more than the sum of my screw-ups.

And then there's my father.

Even without looking, I can feel his disapproval radiating from the stands. It's the same suffocating presence I've been dealing with my entire life.

As my gaze flicks to the crowd, I don't focus on his scowl.

I focus my attention on something else.

Some*one* else entirely.

Holland.

She's sitting with the other girlfriends and wives, wearing my jersey.

*My number.*

Emotion wells inside me. It's a strange concoction of pride and confusion. She doesn't look like she wants to be here. Her back is straight and her face is unreadable.

But she came.

Honestly, I wasn't sure if she'd show.

The odds were fifty-fifty at best.

Even though I only falter for a fraction of a second, that's all it takes.

"Sanderson!" Coach's sharp voice cuts through the air.

But it's too late.

The puck slips past my stick before getting snapped up by the other team. I pivot hard and chase it down, but I'm behind the play. My gut twists as I watch them line up the shot and send the black disc sailing into our net.

The clang of the goal feels like a gunshot.

"Shit," I mutter under my breath, skating back to the line. The groans from the crowd hit me like a wave.

I don't look at my father. I don't want to see the disgust and anger that will be written across his face.

Coach catches my attention before motioning for me to come off the ice. My legs feel like lead as I make it to the bench.

"Akeman, you're in," Coach calls, barely sparing me a glance.

Garret knocks into my shoulder with his own. "You're making this too damn easy, Sanderson," he says, just loud enough for me to hear.

My jaw tightens as I grip my stick until my knuckles ache. The game continues, but I'm stuck in my head. My mistakes seem to multiply. Another fumbled play along with a turnover. It's like quicksand, and there's no way to get out of it.

By the time the buzzer sounds, we've managed to scrape out a win by one goal. My teammates are buzzing with relief and celebration, but I can't bring myself to join in. My stomach churns as I skate off the ice, my gaze darting toward the stands.

Holland's eyes find mine, and for a split second, it feels like everything slows. There's no scorn in her expression, no pity. Just something soft, something I don't deserve right now.

I look away before it can swallow me whole.

The locker room is chaos, filled with laughter and shouts. Ryder slaps me on the shoulder as I sink to the bench and stare sightlessly at my locker.

"Let it go, man. We all have off nights. That's all this was."

"Yeah," Steele adds, passing me a water bottle. "We won, and that's what matters."

Their words barely register as I nod. Coach gives a speech about keeping our momentum, reminding us that this is what we've been working for all season. The guys cheer and make plans to head to Slap Shotz to celebrate.

One by one, they shower before taking off, leaving me alone. I sit on the bench, staring at the floor, my brain going over every mistake.

How many of the goals the other team scored were on me?

At least two.

It's only when Coach clears his throat that I blink out of the thoughts circling around in my head. He pauses, eyebrows drawing together when I meet his gaze. His usual no-nonsense expression softens just a fraction.

"Sanderson." His voice is steady, not sharp like it was during the game. "What are you still doing here? I thought everyone had taken off."

With a shrug, I glance away. "Guess I just needed a minute."

Coach Philips walks over, his footsteps deliberate, the sound of his shoes against the tile echoing in the emptiness of the room.

He settles beside me on the bench. "You played a decent game, but I've seen you play better."

I let out a bitter laugh and shake my head. "Last I looked, decent didn't win championships."

"True," he admits. "I know when a player's head isn't in the game. And tonight, yours wasn't."

I grit my teeth and stare at the floor. As much as I want to argue, it's true. "I'll do better next time."

"Bridger." The way he says my name, not my last name like usual, makes me look up. His eyes meet mine, steady and unwavering. "I've been doing this a long time. I know what it looks like when someone's carrying more than just the weight of the game on their shoulders."

My chest tightens. "It's nothing," I say, forcing my voice to stay steady. "There's just a lot of pressure right now. That's all."

With a sigh, he drags a hand down his face before dropping it back to his side. "Pressure is part of the game. Whatever's going on outside the rink is bleeding in."

I straighten as my defenses snap into place. "I'm handling it."

"Maybe you are. But here's the thing, handling it alone isn't the same as handling it well. Just remember that my door's always open if you need to talk. Hell, it doesn't even have to be me. Find someone you trust and get it all out."

The words hit harder than expected and sit heavy in my chest.

I swallow hard. "Thanks, Coach."

He rises to his feet before clapping a firm hand on my shoulder. "You're a damn good player. But more than that, you're a good man. Don't forget that."

I nod, my throat too tight to respond. He doesn't linger, just gives my shoulder a squeeze before stepping back.

"Go home and rest up," he says as he heads for the exit. "And remember, nobody wins every game. You've got what it takes to bounce back. Prove it to me next time."

The door swings shut behind him, leaving me alone again. This time, the quiet doesn't feel so heavy. Everything he said stays with me, cutting through the noise in my brain.

Coach is right. I need to go home and get out of my own head.

Maybe the person to do that with is the girl sitting in the stands wearing the jersey I gave her last night. The very same one who I had my hands on this morning.

*Fuck.*

Just thinking about the way I rubbed my cock against her has the game fading to the background.

When the locker room door swings open again, I glance toward it, expecting Coach to walk back in. He probably forgot something in his office.

Instead, I find my father.

He strides in like he owns the place, his polished shoes clicking against the tiles. His suit is immaculate, and there's not a single hair out of place. He looks every bit the man in control, down to the frigidness in his eyes.

"You almost fucked that up," he says, his voice low and cutting, laced with barely suppressed fury. "You're lucky your teammates picked up your slack. Otherwise, they'd be blaming you for that loss. It would be the first time in ten years that this school didn't make it through the playoffs."

"My game was off tonight," I mutter. A conversation with him is the last thing I need right now. I'm well aware of my failures on the ice. I don't need him to point out each one before ramming them down my throat.

The one thing I can always count on is my father kicking me when I'm already down. It's his specialty.

"Your game was off?" he repeats with a laugh, but there's zero humor in the snapped-out question. "You were a goddamn embarrassment out there. I should have left after the first period instead of wasting my time watching that shitshow."

Even though his words cut deep, I keep my head down and focus on the tile beneath my feet. I don't trust myself to look at him.

"I don't need a lecture from you," I say, my voice low but firm.

"Excuse me?" he growls, stalking closer.

My head snaps up. That's when I remember just how dangerous it is to let my eyes stray from him. When he eats up the distance between us, I rise to my feet and straighten to my full height.

WESTERN UNIVERSITY CHAT APP
FragileLikeABomb
Okay, real talk. What's your go-to midnight snack?
ColdAsIce17
Peanut butter straight from the jar. You?
FragileLikeABomb
Gummy bears. I like to bite their heads off first.
ColdAsIce17
That's... mildly concerning.
FragileLikeABomb
Says the guy who eats peanut butter like it's soup.
ColdAsIce17
Fair point. Truce?
FragileLikeABomb
Truce. But I'm keeping an eye on you.

HOLLAND

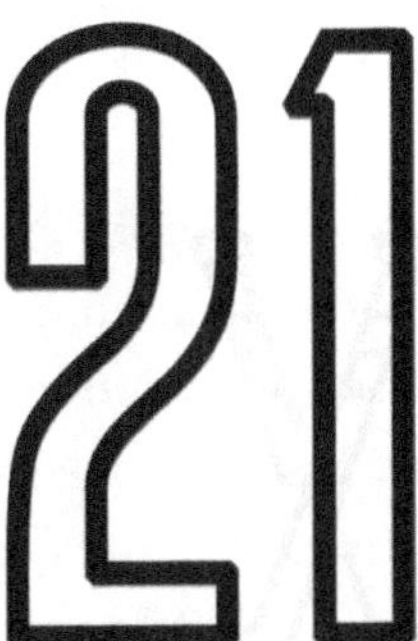

The lobby buzzes with post-game energy, a mix of excitement and relief that the Wildcats pulled off the win. The fact that I'm standing with the other girlfriends, their laughter and chatter flowing around me, feels a bit surreal.

This isn't a place I ever thought I belonged.

I'm not even sure I do now.

Especially wearing Bridger's jersey.

Carina nudges me, a knowing smile lifting her lips. "Can't say I ever expected you to be dating a hockey player."

I huff out a laugh. "It wasn't exactly on my bingo card for the year."

"Honestly?" Juliette chimes in, her tone light but thoughtful. "I like you and Bridger together. He needs someone. Sometimes he just seems so..." She hesitates, searching for the right word. "Lonely." She shrugs. "Anyway, it's nice to see."

My gaze gets snagged by Willow. When she beams like a Cheshire cat, I shake my head and roll my eyes.

I don't realize that the others have been listening to the conversation until they all murmur in agreement. My stomach twists into a series of painful knots. They'd be shocked to learn that this isn't the real deal.

He essentially blackmailed me to be here, pretending to be his girlfriend.

It doesn't escape me that these girls have gradually become my friends and I'm lying to them. I don't like the way it makes me feel.

Like a fraud.

My attention drifts across the lobby before landing on a trio of men near the far wall. Two of them are big, well-built, and impossibly good-looking. The third is the chancellor of the university, Richard Sanderson. Even from here, his presence feels sharp and cold, like a brittle winter wind slicing through a thin coat.

"Who are the two men with Bridger's father?" I ask, nodding toward the small group.

Juliette follows my gaze. "The one on the left is my dad," she says with a small smile, "and the other is Colby's father."

"They're both former NHL players," Britt adds, tossing her caramel-colored hair over her shoulder. "Gray McNichols now works for ESPN."

"No shit?" I nod, impressed despite myself. I've never been into athletes, but maybe I've been too hasty about that decision.

Carina leans closer, her voice low and teasing. "Almost makes you want a daddy, huh?"

My eyes widen as I choke on a laugh. "Jesus, Carina. What would Ford say if he heard that?"

Her expression turns sly. "Probably that he loves his baby girl more than anything."

I shake my head.

On second thought, I could totally see that.

The locker room doors finally open, and the guys start trickling out one by one. Each player greets their significant other with smiles, hugs, or kisses. Ford beelines straight to Carina before wrapping her up in his arms and smacking her lips with a kiss. A few of the other guys do the same with their partners. I've never been a girl who thought she was incomplete without a man in her life. I've never had the time for a relationship, and after allowing myself to get close to Bridger freshman year and getting burned, I didn't want to risk my heart again.

But...

Seeing all the other couples, especially Maverick and Willow, I can't help the loneliness that creeps in at the edges. Like maybe being on my own isn't all it's cracked up to be.

I scan the face of each player who joins the throng, looking for Bridger. A few more minutes tick by and there's still no sign of him.

I spent a lot of years at the hockey rink with Willow watching her twin brother, River, play. I wouldn't say I'm an avid fan. Although the fights that erupted were mildly entertaining. But I know enough about the game to understand that Bridger had a rough one.

After the way he held me in his arms and comforted me last night, the walls I normally keep in place where he's concerned have started to crumble.

My attention drifts back to Richard Sanderson. He exchanges a few more words with the two former NHL players before striding purposefully down the hallway that leads to the locker room. Something about him sets my teeth on edge. It's not just his aloof demeanor. It's the way he carries himself, like we should all be thankful he decided to grace us with his esteemed presence.

Say what you want about my mother and her parenting style, but deep down I know she loves me. Maybe not the way I want, but I've never questioned it.

"I'll be right back," I say, forcing a casual tone as I step away from the group. "I'm going to use the bathroom before we head out."

"Want me to come with?" Ava asks as Hayes wraps his arms around her from behind and presses a kiss against the side of her face.

"Nah, I'm good." Instead of waiting for a reply, I swing away and follow Richard, making sure to keep a careful distance.

The hallway is quiet, the hum of fluorescent lights amplifying the sound of my Chucks against the polished floor. My pulse quickens when he pushes through the heavy door and disappears inside the locker room.

I hesitate as my hand hovers over the metal handle.

If I had any brains whatsoever, I'd return to the lobby and wait for

Bridger there instead of eavesdropping on a private conversation. For a handful of seconds, curiosity wars with common sense.

I take a deep breath and cautiously ease the door open before slipping inside, trying to make as little noise as possible. The last thing I want is to alert either of them to my presence.

My nose scrunches at the heavy scent of sweat and humidity that permeates the air. It's enough to knock me on my ass. I duck behind a row of lockers as my heart picks up tempo, pounding a harsh beat in my ears.

"You almost fucked that up." Richard's sharp voice cuts through the space, making me jump. "You're lucky your teammates picked up your slack. Otherwise, they'd be blaming you for that loss. It would be the first time in ten years that this school didn't make it through the playoffs."

My breath catches.

*What the hell?*

*Is his father really berating him about what happened on the ice?*

"My game was off tonight," Bridger mutters, his voice barely discernible.

"Your game was off?" the older man repeats with a disbelieving laugh. "You were a goddamn embarrassment out there. I should have left after the first period instead of wasting my time watching that shitshow."

"I don't need a lecture from you," Bridger says in a clipped tone.

"Excuse me?" his father growls.

My chest constricts at the heavy footsteps that strike the tile. Any second, my heart is going to explode from my chest.

"Why don't you just admit that the only thing you care about is how this reflects on you?"

"Watch your damn tone," Richard snaps.

"Or what?" Bridger's voice grows stronger, defiance bursting from it. "You'll bench me? Oh wait, you don't make those decisions, do you?"

Even though I can't see what's happening, the suffocating tension is enough to choke on. The sound of the slap slices through the air, stopping me cold. My mouth drops open, and my eyes widen in stunned disbelief.

*Oh my God.*

Did that just happen?

The silence that follows is deafening.

"You'll regret that attitude, boy," Richard hisses.

My heart pounds a painful tattoo as I press my back against the locker and scoot around the corner until I'm out of sight. Richard's footsteps echo throughout the room, each sharp click a countdown to when I can finally breathe again. It's only when the door swings shut behind him that I force out the shaky exhale and step out from my hiding spot.

I find Bridger sitting on the bench with his elbows braced on his knees and his head hanging between his shoulders. The red mark on his cheek stands out against his skin, evidence of what I heard. The sight of him like this, so beaten down and vulnerable, has something uncomfortable thrashing deep in my chest.

For a second or two, I wonder if it might be best for me to slink away and let him lick his wounds in private. If the situation were reversed, that's exactly what I'd want.

But how can I do that?

Especially after he was there for me last night.

That thought only solidifies my decision. Even though I know he won't be happy to see me, I take a deep breath, summoning courage I'm not sure I have, before stepping forward and making my presence known.

"Hey."

His head snaps up, and his eyes narrow when they land on me. For a painful heartbeat, he only stares before asking, "What are you doing here?"

"I..." I hesitate, biting down on my lip. "I wanted to make sure you were all right. You had a rough game."

He blinks, like he's not used to anyone checking in on him. "Yeah, it was definitely shitty." His voice is low. He leans back, rubbing a hand over his jaw. "The old man wasn't very happy about it." A beat of silence stretches between us as his eyes harden. "I suppose you saw that."

It's tempting to lie so he can save face. Instead, I nod. My throat is tight as I force out the words. "Yeah. I'm sorry. Your father is an asshole."

"Guess we found something else we can agree on." He glances away as his shoulders stiffen. "You should go, Holland."

Rather than follow the directive, I step closer until all the distance between us has been swallowed up. Only then do I slip my fingers beneath his chin and gently turn his face toward me. His gaze flickers with surprise as I study the red mark. My stomach clenches as a wave of anger and disgust crashes over me. I'm tempted to stomp out of the locker room and find Richard Sanderson so I can give him a taste of his own medicine.

Even more than that, I want to comfort Bridger. Without thinking, I lean in and press a soft kiss against the handprint. "I'm sorry."

For a moment, he doesn't say anything, just looks at me with an unreadable expression before releasing a long, slow breath. "It's not the first time, and it won't be the last."

The surety in his tone reignites my anger.

Before I can respond, he rises to his feet and locks his fingers around the hem of his jersey. "I should hit the showers."

"Okay," I say, forcing a small smile. "After that, we can get out of here."

"Yeah, I don't feel up to going to Slap Shotz," he mutters, his voice quiet.

"What a coincidence, neither do I," I reply, trying to keep my tone light.

With a nod, he pulls the material over his head. My breath catches as he strips off his chest pad, revealing lean muscle. The rest of his gear gets removed until he's completely naked. That's all it takes for air to clog in my throat. When he turns and walks toward the showers, I can't stop my eyes from lingering.

His ass is seriously impressive.

Once he disappears around the corner, I shake my head to clear it. It takes effort to get my runaway thoughts back under control, not to mention the arousal that has sprung to life.

Bridger Sanderson might drive me crazy, but right now, he's also reminding me why pretending not to care about him is getting harder with the passing of every second.

# BRIDGER

Even when the water scalds my skin, I don't bother adjusting the temperature. I let the hot spray pound against my shoulders before turning so it can do the same to my chest. With any luck, it'll wash away the sting of Dick's words. My jaw aches from being so tightly clenched, and my lungs burn, like I'm still holding my breath, waiting for the world around me to explode.

Then there's Holland.

I press my forehead against the cool tile and squeeze my eyes closed. Of all the people who could have witnessed that train wreck, it had to be her.

The girl I can't stop thinking about.

The one who ignites my temper.

The one I can't bring myself to trust.

She saw something I would have preferred to keep hidden away in the dark, and she didn't flinch.

Another wave of embarrassment rolls through me, sharp and unforgiving.

Holland already thinks I'm an asshole. Tonight she discovered that the apple doesn't fall far from the tree.

And yet, she stayed.

My feelings for her have always been complicated.

A tangled mess.

I used to tell myself it was nothing more than the hum of attraction, but it's not that simple.

Not with Holland.

She's a problem without a solution.

I'm startled out of those thoughts when a curvy body brushes against mine from behind and hands stroke their way across my pecs.

"What are you doing in here?" I croak.

"I thought that would be obvious." There's a beat of silence. "I'm helping you clean up."

For just a second or two, the warmth pressed against my back disappears, and with the steam filling the room, I almost wonder if I hallucinated that she was here with me.

Touching me the way I've dreamed of for two years.

She returns before rubbing soapy hands up and down my back with measured movements.

*Fuck.*

Her touch feels so damn good.

No. It's way better than that.

It's the exact balm I need.

All the tension from the game and the confrontation with my father gradually dissolves, leaving a clawing need in its place. No one has ever turned me on the way this girl does.

She sparks something deep inside me.

If I'm being completely honest with myself, it's what scares me most about her.

I can't help but lean into her touch, my body betraying me even as my mind screams for me to pull away and put some distance between us. Her fingers trace the sculpted lines of my muscles. Her touch sends shivers cascading down my spine despite the scalding water.

"Holland," I groan, my voice barely audible over the pounding spray. "Are you sure this is a good idea?"

"Shh," she murmurs, her lips sweeping over my shoulder blade. "Let me take care of you."

I want to protest, to push her away and maintain the walls I've carefully erected around myself where she's concerned, but the brush of her skin against mine is intoxicating.

Her hands glide downward, fingertips grazing my ass. She soaps the taut muscles before dropping down and running her hands along the backs of my thighs and calves. A groan rumbles up from my chest before echoing off the tile.

I've never been taken care of this way.

She straightens, wrapping her arms around my rib cage and pressing a kiss against my spine. Her fingers strum the ridges of my abdomen before sinking to my groin. My breath catches as one hand wraps around my shaft. I'm hard as steel. Her grip tightens as she strokes my cock from the tip to the root and then back again. She repeats the movement until my balls tighten, drawing up against my body.

I sink my teeth into my lower lip, suppressing the sound building in my throat. This girl already has me in the palm of her hand in more ways than one. And there's a part of me that's cautious about dropping the last of my barriers.

No matter how fragile they might be.

I'm still not sure if she's telling me the truth.

Or if I can trust her.

Just when I think I might explode, her touch disappears. Air rushes from my lungs when she cups my balls before massaging them. My head tips back. This time, keeping the pleasure trapped inside is impossible, and a long groan breaks loose from me.

She presses another kiss against my skin. "Do you like that?"

"Fuck yeah."

"Mmmm. You're so long and thick."

"Is that a compliment?"

"Maybe." Her teeth scrape against my shoulder. "I might have thought about you once or twice after we had sex."

"You want the truth?" The question is out of my mouth before I can stop it.

She continues to squeeze and release my soft flesh. "The truth is the only thing I want from you."

"I might have thought about it more than once or twice." Even that's a lie. I thought about her way more than that. I've had a difficult time staying away.

I turn in her arms until I can drink in the sight of her wet hair clinging to her face. She's so damn beautiful.

Sexy.

The way her eyes have darkened with arousal only intensifies my own desire.

For a long moment, we stare at each other as the air crackles with electricity.

Her hand rises to cup my cheek as her thumb traces my jawline. The tenderness of her touch is my undoing, and I lean in, capturing her lips with my own in a desperate, hungry kiss.

She responds instantly, pressing her naked body flush against mine as her arms wind around my neck and pull me closer. I groan into her mouth as my hands roam down her sides to grip her hips. The kiss deepens and our tongues tangle as two years of pent-up longing and frustration pour out of me.

Everything else falls away. The embarrassment of how I played tonight, my father and what Holland witnessed, along with the reasons I've been careful to keep her at arm's length.

There's only her soft skin and eager mouth.

She breaks away to nip at my lips and then chin before trailing down the column of my neck, licking and sucking her way along my chest until arriving at my nipple. Her tongue darts out to stroke over the little nub until it stiffens beneath her touch. The scrape of her teeth sets off every nerve ending in my body, making me feel more alive than ever before. She turns her attention to the other one before sliding lower. Her vibrant green eyes spark with a life all their own as they stay fastened to mine and she drops to her knees.

My erection bobs inches from her pouty lips.

"You don't have to do this," I force myself to say.

She leans in, pressing a kiss against the tip. "I want to," she murmurs, her breath hot against my sensitive skin. "Let me make you feel good."

Before I can offer up one last protest, she takes me into her mouth, and a delicious warmth surrounds me. The velvety softness of her tongue swirls around me, drawing me in deeper until I nudge the back of her throat.

Already, I'm close.

My hands find their way into her wet hair, not guiding, just needing something to hold on to as pleasure floods my system.

Holland slides up and down my shaft with expert precision, her tongue swirling around the head before taking me even deeper. As tempting as it is to close my eyes and enjoy the sweet torment, I can't bring myself to look away from the expression on her face as her eyes hold mine captive. The way she looks as her cheeks hollow and water runs down her face is so damn erotic.

The sight is almost enough to make me come on the spot.

What I love most is that she's not tiny and waif-like.

Holland is strong and sexy.

Her confidence on stage turns me on so much.

"Fuck," I groan, my fingers tightening in her hair.

She hums in response. The vibrations send shockwaves of pleasure through my body. Her hand caresses what she can't fit in her mouth, twisting on the upstroke in a way that has my toes curling against the shower floor.

She must sense how close I am, because she doubles her efforts, bobbing her head faster as her free hand cups my balls. The coil of tension in my lower abdomen tightens as my release continues to build. When I try to warn her to pull away, she grips my hips firmly to keep me in place.

"Holland, I'm gonna—" I rasp, my voice strained.

She looks up at me through spiky lashes, her eyes dark with intensity. The sight of her, combined with the relentless suction of her mouth, pushes me over the edge. I come with a strangled cry, my body shuddering as waves of pleasure crash over me. The thought of her taking my release deep inside only makes my orgasm more powerful.

Holland swallows down every drop I give her, continuing to work me gently with her tongue until I'm spent. Only then does she press a kiss against my softening cock before rising to her feet.

I pull her against me, claiming her mouth in a searing kiss. The fact that I can taste myself on her tongue only fuels the fire burning inside me.

I pull away long enough to murmur, "That was—"

"Pretty fucking fantastic?"

I snort out a laugh as the edges of my lips curl. "Sure, we can go with that."

Humor dances in her sparkling eyes.

I like it.

More than that...

I like *her*.

That thought is all it takes to break down the last of my barriers.

HOLLAND

# 23

After the impromptu shower in the locker room, hunger wins out, and we go in search of food. Bridger takes me to a place called Harvey's Eats and Treats. It's a diner that looks like it was ripped straight out of a 1950s postcard. The red vinyl booths gleam under the soft glow of hanging lights, and the walls are plastered with Coca-Cola memorabilia and black-and-white photos of old Hollywood stars. A retro jukebox hums in the corner, its colorful lights twinkling to some old-school rock song I vaguely recognize.

Willow has mentioned this place before, but I've never been here. As I take it in, I have to admit that it lives up to the hype.

"Pretty cool place, huh?" Bridger says, holding the door open for me.

"Yeah, it is," I agree, stepping inside. The smell of sizzling burgers and fried onions wraps around me like a hug and makes me realize just how famished I am. "Although, I'll reserve judgment until after I eat."

A waitress wearing a pink uniform approaches with menus tucked under her arm. "Looking for a table or booth?"

"Booth," we say at the same time before glancing at each other with small smiles.

"Aren't you two adorable," she says. "Follow me."

I don't look at Bridger as we trail after her. I'm pretty sure my face is a dead giveaway.

*Adorable?*

That's not exactly the word I'd use to describe us.

More like complicated.

Or maybe combustible.

The waitress slides two menus onto the table, her pencil poised over a notepad. "Would you like drinks to start out with?"

"Root beer float," Bridger and I echo simultaneously.

When I glance up from my menu, he smirks. "Wow, just add it to the growing list of what we have in common," he says, leaning back and stretching an arm along the top of the booth.

"Like I said—adorable," the waitress chirps.

I clear my throat. "I'll also have a bacon cheeseburger with the works, and onion rings."

Bridger's gaze stays pinned to mine. "Same."

The older woman jots down our order before taking off.

"Seems like we're a match made in fake dating heaven," I force myself to say, needing the reminder.

Especially after what happened in the locker room.

He flashes a slow grin that arrows to the heart of me before exploding on impact.

I don't like it.

I don't like what he does to me.

And I certainly don't like the sensations running rampant beneath my skin, trying to claw their way to the surface.

It's dangerous.

We need to steer this conversation to safer terrain.

"So," I say, folding my arms on the table. "What's the story with this place? Sentimental favorite, or do you bring all your fake girl-friends here?"

His smirk deepens. "Wouldn't you like to know?"

"Not really."

Maybe.

His eyes narrow. "Liar."

The banter flows easily between us, like it's second nature, and I hate how much I enjoy it. The guy definitely keeps me on my toes.

Before I can come up with a biting response, a small voice interrupts.

"Excuse me?"

We both turn to see a little boy standing at the edge of our booth. He can't be older than nine, and his face is lit up like Christmas morning. The waitress drops off two glasses of water before beelining to another table.

"Are you Bridger Sanderson?" he asks, his voice quivering with nerves.

Bridger sits up a little straighter, his brows lifting in surprise. "Yeah, that's me."

The boy's eyes go wide as he bounces on the tips of his toes. "I knew it! You play for the Wildcats, right?"

"That's right," Bridger says, his tone warm and easy.

"Could you... could you sign something for me?" He holds out a crumpled napkin along with a pen, his expression hopeful.

With a chuckle, Bridger takes both items. "Sure thing. What's your name?"

"Charlie," the boy says, his voice barely above a whisper.

As Bridger scribbles on the napkin, I sit back and watch. There's something about the way he interacts with the kid that throws me off balance and has everything softening inside me. He's kind and genuine, without a trace of his usual cockiness.

Charlie practically vibrates with excitement when Bridger hands back the napkin. "Are you gonna play in the NHL next year?"

The question hangs in the air for a second too long.

Bridger leans back, his smile dimming just a bit. "As much as I'd like to do that, it's not in the cards for me, bud."

Charlie's face falls, and I feel a pang in my chest.

Bridger reaches out and taps the boy's shoulder gently. "But who knows? Maybe someday. Are you gonna keep cheering on the Wildcats through the playoffs? We could sure use the support."

The boy nods and his grin returns. "I just know the team is going to make it to the Frozen Four!"

"That's the plan."

As Charlie rushes back to his table, clutching the napkin like it's a prized possession, my attention returns to Bridger. He's staring down at the table, his fingers tracing the condensation on his water glass. For the first time, I realize there's so much more to him than I allowed myself to believe.

I lean back in the booth before picking up the paper straw wrapper and folding it accordion style.

Bridger's quiet, his gaze far away as he absently taps a finger against the edge of his glass. For a guy who's usually so quick with a sarcastic comment, his silence feels heavy.

"If you're not playing hockey next year," I ask, breaking the stillness, "what are you going to do?"

With an exhale, he runs a hand through his short, dark hair. "My uncle owns a marketing firm in Chicago. He offered me a job last summer after I interned with him. I actually enjoyed the work, and being around family will be nice."

"That makes sense," I say softly. "You're creative and pretty good at coming up with ideas."

"Careful, Tate—two compliments in one night? People might start thinking you actually like me," he says wryly.

I shrug. "Don't let it go to your head."

His lips quirk, but the humor doesn't quite reach his eyes. "It's not my dream job, but I need to get the hell away from my father. And that's one way to do it."

The heaviness of his words sinks deep into my chest and reminds me of what I witnessed in the locker room. On impulse, I reach across the table and clasp his hand in mine. His gaze drops to where we're now connected, and for a moment, I wonder if he'll pull away.

It's almost a surprise when he doesn't.

The warmth of his fingers permeates mine, making me aware of the intimate gesture.

"What about you?" he asks, his voice quieter. "You've got another year left, right?"

I shake my head. "No, I'll graduate after my summer courses are complete."

His brows lift. "That's impressive."

"The heavy course load has been a killer, but I need to graduate and get a job." The corner of my mouth lifts slightly. "A different job."

He leans forward, closing some of the distance between us. "You don't like working at the Envy Room?"

"It's not that," I say quickly. "I actually don't mind it. The money's good, and Randi's a great boss. We're like a family there. And I've never really had that." My fingers tighten slightly around his. "It's always been just me and my mom, so it's kind of nice to have a group of people looking out for me."

His chin dips once as his gaze remains fixed on me. "Yeah, I get that. It's what the team has always felt like for me." His brow furrows. "At least, it used to. Before all this bullshit with the messages started. Now, I don't know who to trust. I look at some of the guys in the locker room and I can't help but wonder if they're behind it."

The pain in his voice slices through the very heart of me. I chew my bottom lip before blurting, "Can I tell you something?"

His gaze sharpens, his attention fully locked on me. "Sure."

I suck in a deep breath as my pulse picks up speed. "At first, seeing those messages made me happy." When his brow arches, I rush on, the words tumbling out in a jumble. "It felt like karma, you know? But now I feel like shit for taking pleasure in your pain. Trust me, that's not something I thought I'd ever say."

For a second, he doesn't respond, and I brace for whatever sharp, cutting remark he'll make.

Instead, he snorts as a faint smile tugs at the corners of his lips, and he slides his hand out from beneath mine, only to cover it with his own. His palm is warm, and it grounds us in the moment.

"I don't blame you. The way I dropped you was shitty and immature. I meant every word of my apology last night. I'm sorry for hurting you. If I could go back and make different decisions," he continues, his voice low and steady, "I would."

I blink, stunned into silence. My breath catches, his unexpected honesty throwing me for a loop. It's one thing to apologize under the cover of darkness and quite another to do it while sitting across from me at the diner.

As we stare at each other, the air between us turns charged with something I can't quite name. Or maybe I'm afraid to label it.

"I think I missed out on something really great."

His words are so quiet I almost miss them.

A knot forms deep inside me, and I have to look away before he sees the emotion threatening to spill over. I wasn't prepared for him to crack open the door to his feelings and let me peek inside. I'm unsure what to do with everything careening around within me.

Before I can figure out how to respond to Bridger's quiet confession, the waitress appears at the edge of the table, balancing two plates stacked with food.

"Here we go!" she chirps, setting the dishes down with practiced efficiency. "Two bacon cheeseburgers with the works, extra onion rings, and root beer floats to keep those sweet teeth happy."

That's all it takes for the tension between us to snap like a rubber band. I sit back, grateful for the interruption, as the waitress tops off our waters and leaves us alone with a wink.

"Perfect timing," Bridger mutters, his lips lifting into something that resembles a smirk, though I can tell he's still unsettled.

"Yeah," I reply, picking up an onion ring and dipping it into the tangy sauce on the side. "Can't let these babies get cold."

He raises a brow, clearly amused by my attempt to steer the conversation into safer terrain. "Let me guess, onion rings are your weakness?"

I shrug, taking a bite and savoring the crunch. "I prefer to think of them as my love language."

When he laughs, it's a low, genuine sound that sends a flutter through my chest. "So, other than threatening bodily harm, onion rings are your love language? Good to know. I'll keep that in mind for when I'm trying to get on your good side."

"Don't bother, Sanderson. I don't have one."

We settle into a comfortable rhythm, the seriousness of our earlier conversation fading as we dig into our food. Bridger talks about the playoffs, describing the team's strategies and rivalries with an enthusiasm that makes me smile.

It's easy to forget how much I used to dislike him. Sitting here with him now, sharing burgers and banter, I almost feel like I'm getting to know an entirely different person. One who's kinder, funnier, and far more vulnerable than I allowed myself to believe.

And damn if that doesn't scare me just a little.

"Hey," Bridger says, breaking into my thoughts. "You okay?"

I blink, realizing I've been staring at him, my burger frozen halfway to my mouth. "Uh, yeah. Just distracted."

His lips hitch as his eyes twinkle with mischief. "By me? Guess I can't really blame you for that."

With a groan, I throw an onion ring at him. "You were doing so well. Don't ruin it now."

He catches the onion ring midair before it can hit him, then pops it into his mouth with a wink. "Admit it, that was impressive."

"You're ridiculous," I mutter, but I can't stop the chuckle from slipping free.

For the rest of the meal, we trade snarky comments and easy smiles. By the time we've polished off the last of our dinner, I realize that I'm not ready for the tentative peace and camaraderie we found to end.

It's actually nice.

As Bridger leans back in the booth, stretching his long legs out beneath the table, the vulnerability from earlier creeps back into his expression.

"Thanks for coming here with me tonight," he says quietly, his gaze locked on mine. "I needed this more than I realized."

My throat tightens, and for once, I don't deflect. "Me too."

And just like that, the unspoken tension between us settles into something softer, something that feels a lot like understanding.

BRIDGER
SANDERSON
17
17
WILDCATS

The house is buzzing when I step through the front door. Ryder and Ford are battling it out on *NHL 24* in the living room, the sound of buttons clicking rapid-fire and their trash talk spilling into the hallway. Steele lounges on the couch, a textbook open on his lap. I have no idea how he's able to tune out the chaos that surrounds him. In the kitchen, Hayes and Riggs are deep in an argument about which protein powder reigns supreme.

Steele glances up as I stop in the living room. "Hey. What happened to you earlier? I thought we were grabbing lunch this afternoon."

"Sorry," I mutter, rubbing a hand over the back of my neck. "I got caught up talking to the tech department, hoping there was something else they could do. Maybe give me some insight."

Steele closes his textbook with a snap before jerking a brow. "And?"

I shake my head. "Nothing."

He straightens, irritation flashing in his eyes. "Are you kidding me? We're just supposed to let this keep happening?"

"Apparently," I say, my jaw tightening. It feels like I'm hitting a brick wall at every turn.

My phone buzzes, and my pulse kicks up as I yank it out of my pocket. Holland hasn't responded to any of my texts this afternoon. After everything that's gone down between us lately, I thought things were slowly changing. That we were... Hell, I don't even know what I thought. Clearly it was wrong. Her silence has me feeling like we're right back to square one.

Instead of Holland's name flashing across the screen, it's my father's.

Great. Just what I need.

I shove the phone back in my pocket and exhale sharply. "Have you seen Holland?"

"Nope, not since this morning." Steele stretches his legs out and crosses them at the ankles. "Should we slap her face on a milk carton?"

I level him with a look. "You're hilarious."

He smirks, unfazed, but before I can press him for more, there's a knock at the door. It swings open before anyone can answer, and Lilah steps inside. She flashes me a smile before her attention shifts to my cousin.

The second he sees her, he sits up straighter. "Hey," he says, his tone softer. "What are you doing here? I thought you had a date with that basketball guy."

"Cameron," she corrects.

"Whatever," Steele mutters, looking thoroughly unimpressed.

"My plans fell through at the last moment."

Steele's gaze sharpens as he tries to play it cool. "Huh. That's too bad."

I snort. "Is it, Steele? Is it too bad that her date didn't work out?"

He shoots a glare at me. "Don't you have somewhere to be? Weren't you looking for Holland? Maybe you should continue your search somewhere else."

Well, shit. He's got a point.

"Right." I roll my shoulders. "Maybe I'll stop by her place." Then, looking at Lilah, I smirk. "Tell Cameron I say hello."

She grins. "Will do."

As I climb the stairs, I glance over my shoulder to find Steele flipping me the bird. With a chuckle, I shake my head. That guy is in so deep with Lilah, he can't see straight.

Once I reach the landing to the second floor, I pull out my phone and hit Holland's number. Just as it rings, a muffled chime comes from inside my room.

That's weird.

I push open the door and freeze when I find Holland curled up in my bed, cocooned in my comforter like a burrito. Her normally bright skin is pale as her lashes rest against her cheeks. Her hair is a mess around her face, and she looks so damn vulnerable that it sends all my protective instincts surging to the surface.

I carefully step closer. "Holland?"

She stirs slightly as her eyes crack open. "Yeah?" Her voice is hoarse, barely above a whisper.

"What's going on?" I crouch beside the bed, brushing my fingers over her forehead. Her skin is hot to the touch. "Jesus. You're burning up."

With a shift, she tries to wave me off. "I feel shitty," she mumbles.

I let out a harsh breath, frustration mingling with something heavier in my chest. "Why didn't you text me?

"It's not that big of a deal, and I didn't want to bother you."

"Bother me?" I bark, trying to rein in my temper. "You're lying in my bed, looking like you've been run over by a truck. You should've told me what was going on."

She blinks, her expression dazed. "You had a test."

I drag a hand through my hair. "And? I probably could have emailed the professor and taken it tomorrow."

A weak smirk ghosts over her lips. "Now you don't have to worry about it."

I huff, torn between wanting to comfort her and wanting to wring her neck for feeling that she always has to be so damn strong.

"Stay put," I finally say. "I'll be right back."

"Okay," she murmurs, burrowing deeper into the covers.

I practically jog downstairs and head straight for the kitchen.

Riggs looks up from his phone. "Hey. What's going on?"

"Holland's sick," I mutter, rummaging through the pantry. "She's upstairs in bed."

Ryder raises a brow. "Want me to run to the store and grab anything?"

"Nah, I got it," I reply, grabbing a can of chicken soup.

After heating it up, I pour a glass of water, scoop up the pain meds, and start back up the stairs.

When I return, Holland has kicked off the comforter and turned her face toward the pillow. I set the tray on the nightstand and settle beside her, spooning up a small amount of soup. "All right, you're going to need to sit up if this is going to work."

She groans but slowly pushes herself up. "I'm not hungry."

"Yeah, well, tough. You need to eat." I hold the spoon out to her.

Her glare is weak at best. "I can do it myself. I'm not a child."

I raise a brow. "You sure about that? You kind of look like one at the moment."

She swats at my arm, but there's no real strength behind it. "Shut up."

"When's the last time you ate?"

She jerks her shoulders. "This morning. I had a handful of gummy bears."

My jaw clenches. "Just have a little bit. It'll make you feel better."

Her eyelids droop as she murmurs, "You're really bossy, know that?"

Something tightens in my gut. "Please, Tate. You haven't seen anything yet."

Once she manages a few bites and takes the meds, I shift beside her, resting against the headboard. It's a surprise when she leans her head on my shoulder.

"You don't have to stay," she says softly. "I know you have practice."

"It'll be fine. I'm not going anywhere," I tell her. "Someone's gotta stay and make sure you don't pass out."

She chuckles weakly, the sound barely audible. "Thanks. I think you were right about the soup. It helped."

My lips brush the top of her head. "Hey, what are fake boyfriends for?"

Her lips curve into a small smile as her eyes flutter shut.

It's always a surprise when she drops her guard. Even if it's not entirely purposeful.

Holland is tough.

Fiercely independent.

It's one of the things I like most about her. The girl can give just as good as she gets.

But right now, she's letting me take care of her.

The strangest part of all this is that there's nowhere else I'd rather be.

HOLLAND

The sunlight streaming through the blinds is what wakes me. It's soft and warm against my face. I blink, momentarily disoriented, until memories from the previous day come rushing back.

The fever.

The soup.

The feeling of Bridger's steady presence after he discovered me curled up in his bed. My cheeks heat as I roll onto my side and pull the blanket tighter around me. I feel a million times better than I did yesterday, though a dull ache still lingers in my muscles. Only then does my stomach rumble, reminding me that I barely ate anything in the last twenty-four hours.

Movement beside me draws my attention, and I glance over to see Bridger sprawled out on top of the comforter, one arm slung over his eyes. His chest rises and falls steadily as the soft sound of his breathing fills the quiet room. It's comforting in a way I can't explain.

I swallow hard, my gaze lingering on him longer than it should.

I hate to admit just how great he was yesterday.

After finding me in his bed, he didn't hesitate to jump in and take care of me. He made sure I ate, stayed by my side, and didn't so much as complain once. My mind reels as a confusing mix of gratitude and fear swirls inside me.

Because as much as I liked it, as much as I liked him taking care of me... it terrifies the hell out of me.

This isn't real.

Not in the way it feels like it is.

What I've learned is that relying on someone like this opens you up to all kinds of hurt.

Bridger stirs, his arm shifting as he cracks one eye open. "Caught you staring, Tate," he says, his voice rough with sleep.

I scoff, sitting up and tucking my legs beneath me. "Don't flatter yourself, Sanderson. I was actually thinking about breakfast."

With a grin, he sits up against the headboard. His hair sticks out in every direction, and the scruff on his jaw is more pronounced than usual.

He looks... good.

*Too good.*

"Liar. You were totally staring."

"Only because you're taking up most of the bed," I shoot back, narrowing my eyes.

With a chuckle, he stretches his arms over his head before letting them fall. "Are you feeling better?"

"Much," I admit. "Must've been a twenty-four-hour thing. I'm fine now."

"Good. Because you looked like death warmed over yesterday."

I grab a pillow and smack him with it. "You should probably stop with all the flattery or it'll go straight to my head."

He laughs, catching the pillow before it can hit him again. "Hey, I'm just saying it's nice to see some color in your cheeks. You had me worried."

My laughter fades at the genuine concern in his voice, and I hesitate before admitting, "No one's ever taken care of me like that."

His brow furrows. "What do you mean?"

"I mean exactly what I said." I pick at the edge of the blanket, avoiding his gaze. "When I got sick as a kid, I had to deal with it myself. There wasn't anyone to... do what you did."

The room goes quiet, and when I finally force myself to look up, his gray eyes are steady and unwavering. "That's messed up," he says, his voice low. "No kid should have to take care of themselves like that."

I shrug, trying to brush it off. "It's just how it was. I got used to it."

"Well, you don't have to do that when I'm around," he says firmly.

I blink, and my heart stutters. "Bridger, this isn't—"

"Real?" he cuts in as his expression grows serious. "Yeah, I know. But that doesn't mean I can't take care of you if you need it. That's all."

Instead of responding, I grab the pillow again and toss it at his face. He catches it easily, laughing as he pulls me down onto the bed beside him.

"Admit it," he says, his voice teasing. "Little Miss Independent liked being taken care of."

I glare at him, but my lips twitch, betraying me. "Maybe. Just a little."

He grins, his hand brushing a strand of hair from my face. "Good. Because you're stuck with me for the time being, Tate."

I swallow hard, the weight of his words settling over me. I should argue or push him away. At the very least, remind him that whatever this is doesn't mean there's anything between us.

But as his gaze holds mine, I can't bring myself to say anything at all.

WESTERN UNIVERSITY CHAT APP

FragileLikeABomb
Hypothetical question: You're stranded on a desert island. What three things do you bring?
ColdAsIce17
Easy. A multi-tool, a water filter, and a boat.
FragileLikeABomb
A boat? Isn't that cheating?
ColdAsIce17
Says the person who probably just thought "Wi-Fi."
FragileLikeABomb
Touché. But let's not pretend you wouldn't miss messaging me.
ColdAsIce17
Miss? You overestimate yourself.
FragileLikeABomb
Keep telling yourself that, Cold.

# BRIDGER

# 26

I slouch in one of the library's oversized chairs, scrolling through my phone. Steele sits across from me, leaning back with his hands folded behind his head.

"You doing okay, bro?" he asks, breaking the quiet hum around us. "That last message was brutal."

With a shrug, I keep my eyes focused on the screen. "I'm fine."

Even though the messages have been relentless, blowing up phones on a daily basis, the sting has dulled. Or maybe I've just gotten better at pretending they don't bother me. Either way, I'm not giving whoever's behind this the satisfaction of knowing they've burrowed deep beneath my skin.

The only thing I can control in this situation is my response.

Steele studies me like he's trying to crack a secret code. After a long pause, he leans forward. "You know what? Strangely enough, I actually believe you. You no longer look seconds away from committing homicide."

I glance up. "What's so strange about that?"

"I don't know. I was kind of expecting that you'd be going off the rails by now." He smirks. "Maybe having a fake girlfriend suits you."

A huff of laughter slips free from me. "You might be right about that."

"Crazy, huh?"

"Yeah, I guess it is."

He raises a brow, clearly enjoying himself, before dropping his voice. His expression shifts to something more serious. "So, do you still think she's the one behind the messages?"

"No," I say without hesitation.

Steele tilts his head, clearly skeptical at how I've reversed course so quickly. "Is it because she said so? Or because she said so after sucking your dick?"

The anger that whips through me is sharp and takes me by surprise. My shoulders tense as I shoot him a glare. "Shut the fuck up, Steele. You don't know what you're talking about."

He raises his hands in mock surrender as concern floods his eyes. "Hey, I'm just saying. At this point, everyone's still a suspect. Even Holland." There's a pause. "Or maybe I should say *especially* Holland. And less than a week ago, you thought the same damn thing."

I open my mouth to fire back when my phone chimes with an incoming message, cutting me off. I glance at the screen, and my heart does a weird little flip when I see the notification is from the campus chat app.

*FragileLikeABomb.*

It's the first time in days I've thought about her. Normally, she's the first person I turn to when things go sideways.

But now it's Holland.

Steele pushes to his feet, stretching like he's been sitting there for hours. "I'm gonna take off. I'll see you back at the house."

"Yeah," I mutter, distracted by my phone.

He hesitates, and I wonder if he'll say more about Holland. I brace myself for an argument. But it never happens. In the end, he walks away, and I breathe a sigh of relief.

He's the one person I hate being at odds with.

Not wanting to think about my cousin, I tap the message and open the chat.

FRAGILELIKEABOMB

Hey, how've you been? We haven't talked much lately.

Guilt presses down on me as I stare at the screen. She's right. I've been MIA, and it's not fair to her.

ME

Yeah, sorry about that. Things have been busy.

Her reply is quick.

FRAGILELIKEABOMB

No worries. Just glad you're okay.

Our conversation feels off. Stilted in a way it never has before. Usually, our chats flow effortlessly, like we've known each other forever. But that's not the case this evening.

Even though my response isn't exactly a lie, that's what it feels like I'm doing.

Lying to her.

Maybe I should end it.

The thought makes my stomach churn. Fragile has always been there for me, and now I'm just going to ditch her because things with Holland have become complicated?

What kind of person does that make me?

I'm still staring at the screen, lost in thought, when Holland appears out of nowhere.

"Hey," she says, her voice soft but steady.

I glance up, and just like that, everything in me eases. Seeing her does that to me, and I'm still trying to wrap my head around why. My gaze drifts over her outfit, and I sit up straighter, the tension in my shoulders momentarily forgotten.

*Holy fuck.*

Holland looks more like a walking distraction. She's rocking a black band T-shirt that clings to her curves in all the right ways, and a leather jacket that's just a touch too big, giving her an effortlessly cool vibe. But it's the rest of her outfit that nearly derails me. My gaze slides over her short plaid skirt that's paired with black fishnet tights. If that wasn't enough, her socks have tiny pink lip prints stamped on them. The look is finished off with platform sneakers that somehow make her legs look even longer.

In all the time I've known Holland, I've never seen her wear a skirt.

I like it.

Too damn much.

She drops into the seat across from me, pulling me out of my daze.

"Hey," I manage to reply, shoving my phone into my pocket and trying not to blatantly stare. My voice falters as my brain scrambles for words. "You look..."

Her brow quirks, a hint of amusement playing on her lips. "Nice?"

"Better than that." The word tumbles off my tongue before I can stop it. "Hot."

Her cheeks flush, and she ducks her head, a small, self-conscious smile tugging at her mouth. "Thanks," she murmurs before meeting my gaze again. "Have you been waiting long?"

"Not really." I lean forward and rest my elbows on the table. "Although, I'm not sure how you expect me to get any work done when you look like that."

"You'll figure it out," she says with a snort.

I narrow my eyes playfully, the corner of my mouth tugging upward. "We'll see."

"Yes, we will," she counters, her smile growing as she pulls out her laptop. The easy banter between us settles something inside me, like a knot loosening after being pulled too tight.

For the first time all day, I finally feel like I can breathe again.

And that has everything to do with the girl sitting across from me.

HOLLAND

I sneak another peek at Bridger from across the table. This newfound friendship that has sprung up between us is seriously disturbing.

And yet, I like it.

The more time I spend with him, the more I find myself falling.

My heart skips a beat as everything inside me freezes.

No way.

Falling is the last thing I'm doing.

So maybe he's turning out to be different from what I originally thought.

He's deeper.

Softer.

Kinder.

*Fuck.*

It's almost a relief when the chime of my phone pulls my attention away from him. I scoop up my cell and glance at the screen.

A muffled groan rises in my chest.

MOM

Amazing idea! Let's double date this weekend! Me and Jigsaw with you and his club buddy, Hammer! It should be fun! Let me know if you're in.

Jigsaw.

Hammer.

Double date.

I blink at the message, half-expecting it to morph into something less insane. My guess is that he wasn't dubbed Jigsaw because he enjoys putting puzzles together.

And Hammer?

I don't even want to know how he got that nickname.

Mom's pop-up romances normally fizzle after a few days. It's a little disconcerting that this one is still going strong.

"Okay, I'll bite. Who was that from?" Bridger's voice cuts through my thoughts as he glances at me from above the laptop open in front of him. "Usually that kind of scowl is reserved solely for me. Should I be jealous?"

"Hardly." Instead of explaining, I tilt the screen toward him. His eyes scan the message, and before I can pull it back, his fingers wrap around mine, taking the phone.

"Hey! What are you doing?"

His lips curve as his thumbs move across the mini keyboard. "Solving your problem."

Doubtful.

"Bridger—"

Before I have the chance to threaten him, he passes the slim device back to me, looking entirely too pleased with himself. "You're welcome."

I read his message, and my jaw drops.

"Oh my God." I scan it for a second time just to be sure I didn't misread it as heat creeps up my neck. "You told her that I would bring my own date and—" My eyes narrow as I process his words. "And that I'm really into him?" I glare. "Are you being serious right now?"

He grins as his shoulders shake with laughter. "What? I'm just helping maintain our cover."

"By telling my mother I'm *really into* you?"

"Would you prefer if I said that you find me irresistible? Because I can send another—"

I swivel on the chair and hold the cell away so he can't grab it again. "Don't you dare."

My phone chimes immediately.

MOM

OMG!!! You're dating someone?? Why didn't you tell me? THIS IS INCREDIBLE! I need details! SEND PICS ASAP!!

I don't realize that Bridger has walked around the table and is now standing behind me, reading over my shoulder until his warm breath stirs my hair. "She seems super excited at the prospect of meeting me."

"Shut up." I elbow him, but he doesn't move away. "Now she's going to be impossible, and I'll never hear the end of it. You have no idea the can of worms you've just opened."

"Can of worms? Really? Should I grab you a rocking chair and some hard candy, gam-gam?"

I press my lips together until they feel bloodless. This situation is spiraling out of control, and there doesn't seem to be anything I can do to stop it.

Another text appears.

MOM

Is he hot? Please tell me he's hot.

"Obviously, you should answer yes." He makes a swipe for the phone. "Here, just give it to me. I'll field that question."

With a groan, I shove him away. "You better sleep with one eye open from now on, Sanderson. Because I'm going to murder you."

His smile intensifies. "Ahhh, there's the threat of bodily harm again." He waggles his brows in the most ridiculous way. "If I recall correctly, that's one of your love languages."

"It'll be a pleasure to take you out. I can put both of us out of our misery."

"I'm starting to understand that you jest because you love."

Somehow he manages to pluck the phone from my hands again. "I think we both know you'd miss me way too much if you did that."

"What are you—" I catch a glimpse of what he's typing and try to snatch the cell away. "Don't you dare tell her that!"

When he lifts it just out of my reach, I pop to my feet and make a last-ditch effort to take it from him. He uses his free hand to keep me at bay. I slip beneath his arm and redouble my efforts, but he thwarts me by lifting the cell above his head. I'm tall, but not that tall. The way he grins down at me is maddening.

"Bridger." My voice comes out sounding ridiculously breathy. "Give me my phone."

His eyes darken as we stare at each other, neither of us daring to move a muscle.

It's only when my phone chimes that the moment is shattered.

I jerk his bicep down and grab my cell before swinging away to read the message.

> MOM
>
> He sounds dreamy!! I can't wait to meet him. Although, Hammer will be disappointed. I really talked you up.

"Well, would you look at that?" His voice is rougher than usual. "Guess I'm meeting Mama Tate after all."

I throw an irritated glance over my shoulder, trying to ignore how scattered his proximity makes me. "This is going to be a disaster."

"Nah." When he steps closer, it becomes necessary to tilt my chin upward to meet his gaze. "Added bonus, you won't be going on a blind date with some guy named Hammer."

"Hmm. It almost sounds like you're worried about me, Sanderson."

He shrugs. "Just looking out for my fake girlfriend." But there's an edge to his voice that makes my pulse skip. "Can't have you getting dismembered during playoffs. It would be a bad look for the team."

"That is so thoughtful of you. I didn't know you cared so much."

"Hey, what can I say? I'm a giver." He flashes a grin. "I think you found that out for yourself the other morning."

The memory of him grinding against me until I orgasmed rushes in, and heat explodes in my core. I've been thinking about that moment way more than I should. And it's not like I packed my trusty vibe with me to take care of business.

Although, who knew I'd need it?

"Penny for your thoughts, Tate." He cocks his head. "Actually, I'd be willing to pay a lot more than that."

I'm not a girl who blushes easily, but I can feel the heat rising in my cheeks.

Before I can wrap my lips around a response, he says, "And don't tell me nothing." There's a pause. "Or maybe you're just chickenshit? Cause I didn't take you for that either."

Well, hell.

Now I'm trapped.

He's right. I've never been scared to voice my opinions or tell someone exactly how I feel. And I don't want to start now.

My gaze stays locked on his as I lift my chin. "I was just thinking about how good that morning felt."

His eyes darken, turning gunmetal in hue, as he steps closer until the broad expanse of his chest presses against the steady rise and fall of my breasts. The delicious contact is enough to have my nipples peaking. The way his pupils dilate, the black swallowing up the varying shades of gray, tells me that he feels them.

"It did feel good," he whispers before walking me backward until my ass hits the edge of the table. "I can't stop wondering what your pussy tastes like. Makes me wish I'd taken the time to find out."

My breath catches as more liquid heat pools in my core and dampens my panties. I shift as my thighs clench with need.

When was the last time a guy turned me on this much?

One whose name wasn't Bridger Sanderson?

It's pretty revealing that I can't recall.

He's certainly not the only guy I've slept with, but he's the only one who left an indelible mark.

I brace my palms on the smooth surface and tilt my face upward to meet Bridger's eyes. The heat in his gaze makes my breath catch. The instant his lips crash into mine, the world narrows until there's nothing but the press of his mouth, the warmth of his body caging mine. Bridger has this infuriating ability to make me forget everything.

Where we are.

The reason we're pretending.

Why I shouldn't want this.

His tongue sweeps across the seam of my lips, demanding entry, and I open without hesitation. The kiss is all-consuming. A heady rush of sensation that leaves me dizzy and unmoored. He tastes like mint and something darker, more addictive. His hands slide into my hair, angling my head to deepen the kiss, and I forget all the reasons this is a bad idea just waiting to explode in my face.

I'm pulled from those thoughts when someone clears their throat.

Once.

Then twice.

On the third time, my eyes crack open, and I pull back slightly, craning my neck to find an older woman standing stiffly next to our table. Judging by the tight set of her lips, she's less than pleased about making the journey from the circulation desk.

"Uh..." My hands fly to Bridger's chest, pushing him back.

He growls—actually growls—at the interruption. "What's wrong?"

I jerk my chin toward our audience. "We have company."

His head swings around, and his expression shifts to something boyishly sheepish that shouldn't be as charming as it is. "Oh. Hey, Mrs. Greeny."

"Bridger." Her voice could freeze hell itself as her eyes dart between us. "The library is no place for shenanigans."

He wipes at his mouth with his thumb, looking entirely too pleased with himself. "You're absolutely right," he says smoothly, turning on that charm that probably got him out of trouble his whole life. "It won't happen again."

I bite my lip to stifle a laugh, though whether from his obvious lie or the whole ridiculous situation, I'm not sure.

Her frown deepens. "See that it doesn't." With a spin, she marches back to her desk.

I clear my throat, running fingers through my thoroughly mussed hair. "Well, that was mortifying. Maybe we should get back to—"

"Not a chance," Bridger interrupts, his eyes dark with intent. "I'm nowhere near done with you yet. Pack your bag."

My brows shoot up. "Excuse me? Are you always this demanding?"

His lips curve into that dangerous smirk that makes my stomach flip. "Oh, Tate. You have no idea how demanding I can be."

The promise in his voice shorts out my brain. I blink, for once without a sharp comeback.

He takes advantage of my silence, efficiently packing our laptops into our bags and slinging both over his shoulder. His fingers wrap around my wrist as he tugs me toward the staircase. He doesn't spare Mrs. Greeny another glance as we pass.

The cool evening air hits my flushed skin as we burst through the library doors. Campus is unusually quiet, the normal buzz of students replaced by an almost eerie stillness. Instead of heading for the parking lot like I expect, Bridger leads me around the corner of the building.

My pulse thunders beneath his fingers, excitement and something darker rushing through my veins.

This is a terrible idea.

But I'm starting to think those are my favorite kind.

The moment we're hidden from view, Bridger spins me against the brick wall. Our bags hit the ground with a thud as his hands bracket my face. He pauses, his breath mingling with mine.

"You drive me crazy, you know that?" His voice comes out rough. "I can't think straight when you're around."

"That's not my problem," I say, but the words lack their usual bite. It's difficult to maintain my prickly demeanor when he's looking at me like this.

"No?" His thumb traces my bottom lip. "Because from where I'm standing, you seem just as affected."

I should deny it.

I should push him away and remind him this is all pretend.

Instead, I fist my hands in his shirt and pull him closer. "How about you just shut up and kiss me?"

His laugh rumbles against my lips before he claims them. This kiss is different from the one in the library. It's deeper, hungrier, like he's trying to devour me whole. His body presses mine into the wall, one hand sliding into my hair while the other grips my hip.

I arch into him, drawing a groan from deep in his chest. Every point of contact between us burns, and I can't get enough. His lips trail down my neck, finding that spot just below my ear that makes me gasp.

"God, the sounds you make," he murmurs against my skin. "Do you have any idea what you do to me?"

"Bridger…" His name comes out somewhere between a warning and a plea.

He pulls back just enough to meet my eyes, and what I see there makes my heart stumble. There's desire, yes, but something else too. Something that looks dangerously close to—

"No," he cuts me off, his voice low and raw. "No more interruptions."

He leans in, and the rest of my protest melts away the moment his lips claim mine again. Our tongues tangle and teeth scrape. A groan works its way free from him as my arms slip around his neck to pull him closer.

One hand falls from my cheek before drifting down my breasts and rib cage.

He pulls away long enough to mutter, "Have I mentioned how fucking hot you look in that outfit?"

"I think—"

He swallows up the rest of my response as his hand slips beneath the band of my skirt and into my panties. I whimper when he grazes my clit before sliding two fingers deep inside my core.

"Already wet for me, huh?"

He nips my lower lip as he pumps in and out of my pussy. His eyes remain locked on mine, intent and hungry, as if he's determined to catch every fleeting emotion that crosses my face. The intensity of his gaze only deepens the intimacy we're sharing.

We don't break eye contact as I find my release. He continues to stroke me the entire time. It's only when he's wrung every drop that my knees weaken.

His fingers are still buried deep inside me when he says, "I'm willing to bet your pussy tastes just as sweet as your mouth."

"There's only one way to find out."

His teeth flash in the darkness that has fallen as he withdraws from my body before bringing his fingers to his lips and sucking them deep into his mouth. Arousal floods his eyes as more wetness leaks from me.

It's only when he licks them clean that he says, "I was right. Just as sweet."

Before I can come up with a pithy response, my phone buzzes with an incoming message. I groan, remembering that Bridger invited himself on a double date with Mom and her new boyfriend.

"Think it's Mama Tate?"

"Stop calling her that," I say with a snort. "But, yeah, it probably is."

"Should we check to see what she has to say?"

"Just so you know, you've officially ruined this moment."

His lips tremble with a smile as he smacks another kiss against my mouth and slips his hand into the pocket of my jacket before pulling out my phone and glancing at the screen.

"You're right, it's Mama Tate."

"Pretty sure she doesn't want you calling her that," I can't help but point out.

He refocuses on my cell. Maybe if I still weren't in an orgasmic haze, I'd swipe it away from him.

"Hmmm. You're not password protected? That's surprising. I would have expected a higher level of security from you."

"Maybe that's because nosy fake boyfriends have never been a problem in the past."

His gaze dips to my lips. "In case you haven't noticed, muffin, things have changed."

"Apparently so."

When he continues to stare, I clear my throat. "What does Mom have to say? Has she taken pity on me and decided to cancel? Something came up with Jigsaw? Puzzle night at the club trumps dinner with her only kid?"

"You wish."

"Truth."

He glances at the screen and sums up the message. "Your mom wants to know if she can finally post about her baby girl and her new boyfriend."

"Oh God." I drop my head into my hands. "Look what you started."

His laugh is warm. "Want me to field that one too? I don't mind."

"Haven't you done enough damage for one day?"

"Please, Tate. I haven't even started yet." There's a pause. "Think she'll regale me with embarrassing childhood stories?"

"I really fucking hope not."

His grin turns wicked. "Or how about baby pictures? Think I'll get to *ooh* and *aah* over some of those?"

"This is going to be a disaster."

"Probably." He leans closer before brushing his lips across mine. "But at least it'll be entertaining."

Mom's texts keep flooding in, each one more excited than the last. Bridger continues to read them, his quiet laughter washing over me, making my lips twitch. I can't help but wonder exactly what I've gotten myself into.

But as I stare into his eyes, I'm finding it harder to remember why that's necessarily a bad thing.

BRIDGER
SANDERSON
17
17
WILDCATS

# 28

If someone had told me a month ago that I'd be sitting on a wobbly diner stool in a podunk bar in the middle of nowhere, waiting to meet Holland Tate's mother and her biker boyfriend, I'd have laughed them out of the room.

And yet, here I am, scanning the laminated menu in front of me while trying not to focus on how Holland's knee keeps brushing mine under the counter, each touch sending jolts of electricity through my veins.

It's the oddest sensation.

One I haven't quite come to grips with.

"Having second thoughts about forcing your way into this?" Holland's voice is low and teasing, but I catch the underlying tension woven throughout it. She shifts on her stool, her thigh pressing against mine before she catches herself and moves away. "You don't seem nearly as smug as earlier."

"Please." I lean closer, drawn to her warmth. "I can't wait to meet Mama Tate. I've been looking forward to it for days."

"Is that so?" She arches a brow, and damn if that doesn't do things to me. "Because you're gripping that menu like it's a shield."

I force my fingers to relax. "Just trying to decide between the heart attack special and the cholesterol bomb. Thoughts?"

Holland shakes her head. "Ah, yes, the famous hockey player appetite. I'm just as impressed by how much you can put away as I am revolted by it."

"I seem to remember someone joining me for that midnight study break feast last night. There weren't any complaints when I fried us up a couple eggs and turkey bacon." The memory of her laughing over the impromptu breakfast, more relaxed than I'd ever seen her, makes my chest tighten. Her guard had dropped, and it had been nice to joke around and learn more about her life.

Her lips curve into a genuine smile. "That was different. Late-night study sessions require sustenance."

"Is that what we're calling it?"

"Better than calling it the truth, which was avoiding my marketing project."

The bell above the diner door jingles, and Holland stills beside me. A woman with auburn hair sweeps in like a hurricane in leather, wearing what appears to be a motorcycle jacket two sizes too big, and sporting a smile that's equal parts mischief and mayhem. I take a closer look and realize there's a gap in her smile.

Beside her is a burly man, who looks exactly like someone named Jigsaw should look. All beard, bulging biceps, and tattoos inked across every inch of available skin.

"Buckle up, buttercup," Holland mumbles. "Shit's about to get real."

Without thinking, my hand drops to her knee under the table, and I give it a gentle squeeze. She tenses for a moment before relaxing beneath my touch.

"Holland!" Her mom's voice carries across the diner and people turn to stare. "I missed you, baby girl!"

"Hey, Mom." Holland's voice is steady, but her knee presses harder against my palm.

The older woman's gaze lands on me. The wattage of her smile intensifies as her eyes dance with speculation. "And this must be Bridger! You weren't kidding, Holland. This man is handsome with a capital H."

A low groan rumbles up from Holland's chest as I suppress my laughter before standing to offer my hand. "It's nice to meet you, ma'am."

She holds on to me a little longer than necessary as her eyes twinkle. "And he's polite too? You might want to keep this one." She sends a wink my way. "Or maybe I will."

"Mom," Holland warns, her cheeks turning a pretty shade of pink.

"I'm Vivienne, by the way."

The man besides her takes the opportunity to step forward and extend a hand that could probably crush concrete. "Jigsaw," he says simply. His grip is firm but not challenging. It's undoubtedly the best I could hope for from a guy named after a power tool.

"Bridger," I reply, matching his tone.

The waitress appears, notepad in hand, and Holland's mom orders a Bloody Mary without missing a beat. I glance at the girl beside me, who looks like she's mapping out an escape route through the kitchen.

I'll admit that I would be quick on her heels.

"So," her mom starts, resting her chin in her hand. "How long have you two been dating? Holland tells me nothing." She casts a glance in her daughter's direction. "She's so secretive about everything."

"A couple weeks," I answer quickly.

"Oh, I don't know, has it really been that long?" Holland's tone is honey-sweet but loaded with warning. "We're still pretty new and taking things slow. Just one day at a time." She side-eyes me. "Not really sure if it'll work out in the long run."

"Now, muffin," I say, resurrecting my pet name for her, "I told you that we'll deal with whatever life throws our way."

Her eyes narrow as Vivienne sighs and leans forward. "I just love a man who's all in."

The tension filling my muscles eases as I flash a smile, making a big show of patting Holland's hand. "When you find the right one, you need to hang on for dear life."

"Oh, I wouldn't say that I'm necessarily the right one," Holland mutters between clenched teeth.

I tap her gently on the chin. "My girl here still needs a little more convincing. Don't worry, I'm up to the task."

Her mother nods. "Holland's always been cautious when it came to relationships. She's not like me at all." Her mother grins, and I try not to focus on her gap-toothed smile. "I tell her all the time that she just needs to lighten up and have some fun. If you can't do that at your age, when can you?" She glances at Jigsaw. "Right, baby?"

He nods before his stare returns to me. "Viv says you play hockey?"

"Yup," I confirm, my gaze drawn to Holland like a magnet. "But she's the impressive one here."

Holland blinks, caught off guard by my response. Her mom coos, clearly eating up the moment, but I'm not doing this for show. It's the truth. "Balancing eighteen credits a semester, working part-time, and still managing to keep her GPA nearly perfect while dealing with..." I pause, wanting to choose my words carefully. "Everything else. She's pretty incredible."

The words come out more honestly than I intended. Holland's fingers find mine under the table, squeezing them once before letting go.

"I'm not surprised. Holland's always been the responsible one," she says with a smile that's filled with pride. "I can be a bit flighty."

Holland stares at her glass of water. "It's fine, Mom."

"I'm just being honest." Vivienne takes a long sip of her Bloody Mary. "Remember that time in high school when I forgot to pay the electric bill, and you had to study by candlelight for your AP exams? Or when—"

Holland goes rigid beside me. "I don't think we need a trip down memory lane."

"She still passed with flying colors," her mom continues, oblivious to Holland's discomfort. "No matter what happens, my baby girl always figures out a way to succeed."

My chest tightens at the pride in her voice, mixed with something that feels too much like absolution. Like her daughter's resilience somehow makes up for everything she put her through.

I watch the interaction, feeling like an outsider to a private war. That's when it hits me that Holland's had to be the adult in this relationship for a long time. Every sharp edge, every wall she's built, makes so much more sense now. This girl has been carrying more weight than anyone should have to, and her mom's carefree attitude only underscores it.

"She shouldn't have had to figure it out," I say before I can stop myself. Holland's head snaps toward me, shock written across her expression.

Her mother's smile falters. "Excuse me?"

"Bridger," Holland warns softly, but I can't let this go.

"She was a kid," I say, keeping my voice level, even though it feels like an impossible task. "Kids shouldn't have to figure out how to study in the dark."

The silence that follows that comment is thick enough to cut through. Jigsaw shifts in his seat while Holland's mom stares at me, her earlier warmth cooling by several degrees.

"You're right," she admits in a softer tone. "She shouldn't have had to do that."

"Mom, he didn't mean it like—"

Vivienne's brow furrows. "No, it's true. I thank my lucky stars that Holland turned out the way she did. She's so put together and driven. So..." There's a pause before she adds softly, "Not like me."

"Mom," Holland murmurs, "there's nothing wrong with you."

Vivienne dabs at the corners of her eyes with a napkin. "We both know that I'm a mess. But I'm trying." She glances at Jigsaw. "For the first time in my life, I finally feel like I have a true partner in crime."

The burly man wraps an arm around her shoulders before tugging her close and pressing a kiss against the crown of her forehead. "We're in this together, babe."

She casts a watery smile toward her daughter. "I'll be the first to admit, I've made my share of mistakes." Her expression turns sheepish. "Okay, more than my share. But Holland? She's a fighter. Despite having me as a mother, she turned out pretty damn amazing, don't you think?"

"Yeah," I say softly, looking at the girl next to me with fresh eyes. "I do."

Holland's face is a study in conflicting emotions. Embarrassment, anger, and something else I can't quite read. Under the table, her knee presses against mine, but I can't tell if it's a warning or a thank you.

"Your dinners will be out in just a few. Anyone need a refill?" The waitress appears like a gift from the awkward conversation gods.

"Please," Holland and I say in unison.

Her mom laughs, breaking the tension just a bit. "Oh, look how in sync these two already are. I love it."

"So, Bridger," Jigsaw speaks up, clearly trying to steer us toward safer waters. "What are your plans after college? Looking to play hockey?"

"No, I'll probably get into marketing," I say, grateful for the change in topic. "My cousin Steele's family owns a marketing firm and I've already been offered a position."

"Your cousin's name is Steele?" Her mom perks up. "Do all your family members have such unique names?"

"Mom," Holland groans, but I catch her fighting a smile.

"Actually," I lean forward and say with a straight face, "my real name is Chad. I just thought Bridger was more interesting."

Holland nearly chokes on the sip of water she just took. "I'm sorry, what did you say?"

I raise my brows. "What? You can't see yourself with someone named Chad?"

Her mouth falls open as her brows shoot up her forehead. "I..."

"Just kidding." I grin, nudging her shoulder. "The look on your face was priceless, though."

"I really hate you," she says with a small laugh, all her previous tension dissolving, which is exactly what I wanted.

One side of my mouth rises in a smirk. "No, you don't."

There's a beat of silence. "No," she murmurs, something in her expression making my heart stumble. "I don't."

Her mom watches our exchange with a soft expression. "Didn't I tell you that one day you'd meet someone who would change everything? I think Bridger just might be that guy."

It's almost a surprise when Holland doesn't immediately refute her mother's comment.

"Hey, babe," Jigsaw rumbles from beside her, "why don't you tell them about the rally last weekend."

As her mom launches into a story about leather-clad mayhem and questionable decision-making, Holland gradually relaxes beside me. Her shoulder presses against mine, and it takes effort to resist the urge to wrap my arm around her.

By the time the food arrives, the conversation has turned to lighter topics, mostly led by Jigsaw recounting some of his glory days with his "brothers."

Holland picks at her fries as she stares at her food. Her brows pinch, as if she's trying to solve an equation. I nudge her under the table with my knee to catch her eye.

"You good?" I ask quietly.

She nods but doesn't look at me. "Yeah, fine. I'm just thinking about the work I still need to get through tonight." The way she avoids eye contact makes me wonder if she's telling me the truth.

An unexpected surge of protectiveness rushes through me. "We can take off whenever you're ready. Just say the word."

Her mom notices our exchange and smiles. "He really is perfect for you, Holland. Don't let all my mistakes frighten you away from taking a chance when the right one comes along."

Holland scoffs, but her cheeks flush. "It's a little early to be thinking long term." Her gaze flickers to mine. "Like I said before, we're taking this relationship one day at a time."

Jigsaw nods. "Nothing wrong with that. Plus, Hammer wouldn't mind getting a shot with you. He's a real fan of fiery redheads."

I slip my arm around Holland before tugging her close. "Tell Hammer to find his own woman. This one is taken."

Jigsaw shrugs before raising his glass. "To new faces and old friends."

"To getting out of here as fast as humanly possible," Holland mutters, loud enough for only me to hear.

I grin, my chest tightening in a way that feels alarmingly perma-nent. It's the moment I realize that whatever this is between us isn't so fake after all.

HOLLAND

# 29

The door to Bridger's room closes softly behind me, the quiet click somehow louder than my heartbeat pounding in my ears. His space is an odd mix of disarray and organization. There's a stack of books and papers on his desk, hockey gear tossed haphazardly in the corner, his bed neatly made. It smells like him, clean and woodsy with a hint of something darker, and it settles over me like a weighted blanket.

"Well, the good news is that we both made it out alive," he says, pulling his hoodie over his head and tossing it onto the chair. His voice is casual, but there's an edge of something else buried beneath.

Nerves, maybe?

It's oddly comforting to know I'm not the only one experiencing them.

"Kind of feels like it was by the skin of our teeth." I settle on the edge of his bed, the soft mattress sinking beneath me. My fingers toy with the hem of my shirt as he grabs two bottles of water from the mini fridge tucked beside his desk.

"Here," he says, passing one over before dropping into the chair across from me. His legs sprawl out, brushing against mine, and he looks so at ease, it makes me want to fidget.

"Thanks," I mumble, twisting off the cap.

Silence stretches between us. It's heavy but not uncomfortable, like we're both waiting for the other one to speak first.

Finally, he leans forward, resting his elbows on his knees. "So, your mom and Jigsaw…"

I groan and cover my face with my hands. "Please, can we not?"

"What? I'm just saying, he's… interesting." His lips twitch, and I know he's trying not to laugh.

"He's not her usual type," I admit, peeking through my fingers. "But she seems to really like him, so what can I do?"

"Try to talk her out of it?" he suggests, his smile widening.

"Yeah, I'm sure that'll go over well. She's not exactly the listening type."

He leans back, studying me with those piercing gray eyes that seem to see more than I want them to. "Seems like you've been looking out for her a long time."

The comment catches me off guard, and I blink. "Someone has to."

His jaw tightens, and he nods in understanding, which somehow makes it worse. The last thing I need is his pity.

Even though it's not a conscious decision, my muscles tense and I brace for the worst.

Instead, he surprises me.

"It's a lot to carry," he murmurs. "I hate that you've had to do it alone all these years."

I don't know what to say to that.

The sincerity filling his voice is almost too much for me to take.

I look down at my water bottle, twisting the cap back and forth. "It's not like I had a choice in the matter."

"You always have a choice," he says, his voice firm. "Let someone help you for once."

"There's never been anyone else to lean on. I wouldn't even know how."

"Well," he says, a teasing note creeping back into his tone, "maybe we should practice. I promise that it's not as difficult as you think it is."

My throat tightens, and I shake my head. "The last time I trusted someone to help, they walked away. It's easier to handle everything by myself."

"Life doesn't have to be a battle you fight alone, Holland." He searches my eyes. "Sometimes letting someone else take control can be a relief."

"Sure, I'll just give it all over to you."

He grins. "Hmmm. I like the sound of that."

I roll my eyes, but the corner of my mouth quirks up despite myself.

The room feels lighter now, the tension of the previous few hours easing. He gets up and moves to the bed before sitting beside me. His shoulder brushes against mine and his warmth seeps through the fabric of my shirt.

"Can I ask you something?" he says, his voice quieter now.

"Sure."

"What's it like?" He tilts his head. "Dancing."

The sudden change in topic surprises me. "You mean at the club?"

He nods, his gaze steady. "Yeah. You seem so in control up there. Like nothing can touch you."

I let out a short laugh and shake my head. "It's all an act. A really good one."

"That's funny, because it doesn't look like an act. It looks like you're owning it. Like you're unattainable."

I chew my lower lip as my fingers twist in my lap. "Maybe that's part of the reason why I do it. For those few minutes, I feel powerful. More in control than at any other time." There's a pause as I think about it. "But it's not real."

"It feels real," he says, his tone steady. "At least, it looks real from the outside."

I glance at him, and my defenses slip. "It's all part of the illusion."

He reaches out and brushes a strand of hair behind my ear. The touch is so gentle, so intimate, it makes my heart stutter.

"I like watching you up there. Everything around me fades away and it feels like you're dancing just for me."

My breath catches, and for a moment, I don't know what to say. I find myself leaning into him instead, resting my head on his shoulder. His arm wraps around me, pulling me closer, and for the first time in a while, I feel like I don't have to carry everything on my own.

"It's the same for me," I whisper, my voice barely audible. "I forget about everyone else."

"Would you..." His voice trails off.

"What?"

"Would you dance for me?"

My pulse stutters, a wild, unsteady beat as I meet his gaze. "Here? Now?"

His eyes darken. "Yeah. For me."

The room feels smaller suddenly, charged with electricity. This is different from the club. There aren't any lights or a stage. There's no way to put distance between us. It's just his bedroom, the soft glow of a lamp, and two years of unfinished business hanging in the air.

It feels dangerous.

"I don't have music." But I'm already rising to my feet.

He reaches for his phone. "What do you want?"

"Something slow." My voice comes out huskier than intended. "Something you can feel."

He takes a moment to pick a song. It's something with a deep bass line that vibrates through the floor. I close my eyes and let the rhythm sink into my bones. When I open them again, his gaze is locked on me. The intensity in it is enough to burn the house down.

I start moving, but not like I do at the club. It's slower, more intimate. My hips sway to the beat as I run my fingers through my hair. There's no costume to shed, just my T-shirt and leggings. The strangest part is that I feel more exposed than when I'm nearly naked on stage.

"Holland," he breathes.

The way he says my name makes my skin tingle.

I turn slowly, looking over my shoulder. He's sitting on the edge of his bed, hands gripping his thighs as if he's physically restraining himself from reaching out.

Longing floods through every inch of me.

"You can touch me," I whisper, moving closer. "If you want."

His hands find my hips, pulling me between his legs. I roll my body to the music, and his fingers glide over my skin, holding me in place.

"Pretty sure there's a no touching rule in place at the club," he says roughly.

"You're right," I agree, reaching back to tangle my fingers in his hair. "There is."

His forehead rests against my back as the heat of his breath seeps through my shirt. "I'd fucking kill anyone who laid their hands on you."

The possessiveness of his words stirs something deep in my core, making my stomach flip.

"Good thing Rocco's there to take care of any problems." I turn in his arms, still moving to the music. "I don't really want to visit you in prison."

His hands slide up my sides as I straddle his lap, still dancing, still keeping that last bit of distance between us. His eyes darken with desire, but there's something else there too. Something that makes my blood boil in a way it never has before.

I reach down, gripping the hem of my shirt and dragging it over my head before tossing it to the floor. His attention remains riveted to me as I continue to sway and move my body just like Randi taught me. The bra is the next article of clothing to be shed.

He squeezes his eyes tightly closed.

"Look at me," I whisper. Our mouths are inches apart as I cradle his face in my hands. "Right now, I'm dancing just for you."

"You're so damn sexy."

I grind my hips against him, coaxing a rough groan that resonates from deep within. His hands rise to my chest and his callused fingers trace patterns on my skin before cupping the softness.

"Holland…" My name comes out sounding like a tortured prayer.

I barely notice when the music fades into another song. All I can focus on is the way he's staring at me. Almost like I'm something precious and dangerous all at once. Like he's afraid I'll disappear if he blinks.

"I'm here," I whisper, though I'm not sure which one of us I'm trying to convince.

His hands tangle in my hair, pulling me closer until our foreheads touch. We stay fused together, breathing the same air, my body moving slowly against his.

This isn't like the club at all.

It's not an act or a performance.

It's real.

The press of his thick erection against me has heat exploding in my core. His breathing picks up tempo, turning heavy every time I shift against him.

He rolls my nipples between his thumbs and forefingers until both stiffen up. Only then does he slip his hands beneath my breasts, lifting them until he can suck one bud between his lips. The heat of his mouth envelops me, and I arch, wanting more of the delicious sensations that are rushing through me. He licks the tip before giving the same attention to the other side. My fingers tunnel through his hair, only wanting to pull him closer.

Once he releases me, he lifts his head until his mouth can find mine. His tongue sweeps across my lips. As soon as I open, he plunges inside. There's nothing gentle about the caress, and I don't want there to be. Our relationship has always been explosive.

I'm starting to understand that our combativeness over the years has been a kind of foreplay that was always going to end here.

His hands slide around my rib cage to my back before dipping lower until he's able to cup each ass cheek before squeezing. I love the feel of his hands on me, palming me, making me come alive in ways I never imagined.

Before I realize what's happening, his grip tightens as he rises to his feet and swings around before lowering me to the mattress. Our mouths remain fused as his tongue lashes mine. It's all too easy to lose myself in the feel and taste of him.

He eases away, straightening so he can look down at me. His gaze roves over my face and then down to my chest before he reaches out, his knuckles grazing the outsides of my breasts.

"You're so fucking gorgeous. I've never been able to get you out of my head. I've never been able to forget."

Men have watched me dance on stage for more than a year, but none have ever made me feel more beautiful than the way Bridger stares at me now. His eyes are full of adoration. Something I never thought I'd see in them.

One hand wanders along my ribs and across my abdomen before arriving at the waistband of my leggings. His fingertips slip beneath the elastic band, strumming from one hip bone to the other. The way his fingers tease my skin but never dip lower to the part of me that throbs with need only heightens the tension building within me.

When he remains silent, I force myself to say, "Take them off."

"Are you sure? We don't have to. That's not what I had in mind when I asked you to dance for me."

"I want to."

I've wanted to for years.

Only now am I able to fully admit that to myself.

His fingers lock around the black leggings before dragging the stretchy material down my hips and thighs. It's a surprise when he leaves the panties in place.

He must see the question in my eyes because one side of his mouth hitches even as more heat gathers in his gray depths. "You're like unwrapping a Christmas present. I'm going to take my time and savor the anticipation."

His hands drift from my ankles along the delicate skin hidden behind my knee

before meandering upward to the V between my thighs. I inhale a sharp breath when he drags his knuckles across my slit. I can't help but shift beneath his touch, needing more.

It's heady and addictive.

His gaze stays fastened to my core, and there's something so sexy about the expression on his face. The longing that floods his eyes. The way his breath catches.

"You're already wet for me."

"I want you," I say simply. The way he touched me at the library has been playing on repeat in my head for days. Instead of doing something about it, I've let it slowly build until it's become more of a clawing need beneath my skin.

"How much do you want me, baby?"

My gaze dips to the thick erection pressing against the fly of his jeans as I turn the question on him instead. "How much do *you* want *me*?"

There's a beat of silence, and my heart clenches.

"I never stopped wanting you, Holland."

My muscles loosen as he drops down between my legs so that he's eye level with my center. His attention stays locked there as his fingers glide over me. Up and down until I can't stand another moment. Just when I think I'll scream, he hooks one finger in the band of my panties before tugging down the material until the top of my slit is revealed. He leans close enough for his warm breath to stir across my flesh before pressing his lips against me.

A whimper works its way up my throat. "Don't stop."

He draws the material down my legs until I'm totally bare. Music from his phone still hums in the background, but the only thing I'm aware of is Bridger and the way he eats me up with his eyes.

He presses my thighs farther apart. Flexibility has never come naturally to me. It's something I've had to train my body for, pushing myself to move with fluidity and grace while dancing.

He forces my knees to the mattress until I'm spread wide.

Totally vulnerable.

Air gets trapped in my lungs as my heart pounds a steady beat.

"I don't think I've ever seen anything as beautiful as your pussy spread so that every pink inch is on display for me." He squeezes my thighs before his hands slide to my core. His fingers drift across my lips before massaging them, spreading them apart with his thumbs.

I can almost feel the heat of his stare scorching me alive. My skin hums with warmth as tiny sparks of sensation dance along my nerves.

"Bridger."

His gaze flicks to mine. "Yeah, baby?"

"I want your mouth on me."

His eyes darken as heat sparks within them. "You need your pussy eaten?"

"Yes."

He lowers his face to my core and takes a long lap of my flesh. A wave of pleasure crashes over me as my muscles loosen and I sink deeper into the mattress.

He raises his head just enough to ask, "Like that?"

My fingers tunnel through his hair, locking him in place. "Exactly like that."

He swipes at me again before stabbing his tongue deep inside my center. I press my pelvis forward, craving more of what only he can give me. He nibbles at my clit, and more sensation crashes over me until it becomes dizzying. My muscles tighten as arousal gathers in my core. It doesn't take long before I'm falling to pieces. The warmth of his mouth disappears as he slaps my clit with the tips of his fingers.

I didn't think it was possible for more pleasure to crash over me.

I was wrong.

A scream tears from my throat as my orgasm intensifies, shattering everything inside me. And then his mouth is back, feasting on me, prolonging the pleasure until every last drop has been wrung from my body.

I stare at the ceiling, still riding a euphoric high. "That was..." My voice trails off, trying to find an adequate description of what just transpired.

"Amazing? Fantastic? Incredible?"

A gurgle of laughter escapes from me. "How about D. All of the above."

He nods. "I'll take it."

"Know what I need now?"

"Tell me."

"Your cock."

His fingers wrap around the hem of his T-shirt before dragging it over his head. "You don't have to ask twice."

I lift myself up on my forearms and allow my thighs to fall open as I watch him shed his clothing in record speed. All those rippling muscles are sexy as fuck. I never thought I'd be a girl who was into chiseled athletes.

It's just another thing I was wrong about.

I could stare at his hard body for hours.

With a flick of the button on his jeans, he shoves the material down his legs until it puddles at his feet and he's standing before me in black boxer briefs. His cock presses against the material as his gaze roves over me before settling at my core.

He groans before yanking down his underwear until his thick erection can spring free.

Just like the rest of him, his dick is perfection.

A shiver slides through me, and even though I just came, I'm desperate to be filled by him. One knee settles on the mattress before he pauses.

"I need a condom."

Thank fuck he thought about it because I sure didn't.

And that's saying a lot, considering I've always been a safety girl.

He yanks open the drawer of the nightstand next to the bed and pulls out a square packet before tearing it open with his teeth and sliding the latex over his hard length.

Then he's back, crawling onto the bed. Midway up my body, he presses a kiss against my pussy before slowly making his way upward until he can stare into my eyes.

"Are you sure about this?" He searches them carefully. "I don't want anything else to happen between us that you'll regret."

"I'm sure. I want this."

He nods before shifting until the head of his cock nudges my entrance. I widen my legs and angle my hips, only wanting him to sink deep inside me. Instead, he remains still.

When I can't stand another second of the torture, I shift. "Bridger!"

"You're so damn greedy, aren't you?"

"More like horny."

His mouth lifts into a smile. "Maybe I want to torment you just a bit."

As if to emphasize his words, he slides an inch inside before retreating again.

A groan works its way free from me. "Tease."

"You don't have to worry, baby. I'm a sure thing."

My eyelids feather shut.

"Uh-uh. I want those pretty green depths locked on me the entire time we fuck so you see exactly who's cock you're getting off on."

As soon as my eyelashes flutter open, he eases in another inch. I squirm, trying to draw him deeper into my body.

He seems to understand exactly what I'm up to and flashes a tight smile. "I'm the one in control now. Understand?"

My teeth sink into my lower lip as I force my muscles to relax. It's almost a shock when I hear myself say, "Okay."

Heat leaps to life in his gray depths as he retreats before sliding back inside my body, deeper than before. Slowly, he rocks against me. With every tilt of his hips, I meet the movement until our bodies move as one. Almost as if we've been doing this for years.

Our gazes stay locked as he rouses my body all over again. Pleasure mounts, gradually building as he maintains a steady rhythm. It's the tight hold on his self-control that allows me to surrender and give myself over to him.

"You feel so fucking good. So soft and wet. I just want to stay buried in you forever."

I arch as sensation continues to mount and my muscles coil tight with anticipation.

"Are you ready to come for me?" he asks, his pace quickening. The orgasm I'm chasing feels like a wave being pulled out to sea only so it can regroup and crash on shore with a vengeance.

"Please." It's the only thing I can focus on.

"Mmmm. I love that word on your lips. Holland Tate begging for my cock. Is there anything better than that?"

Before I can come back with a response, he bottoms out, hitting that spot deep within. The one that makes my eyes nearly cross. His pelvis grinds against mine, hitting my clit at the perfect angle to set off a chain reaction.

And just like that, I fall apart.

Bridger groans, and the deep scrape of his voice only amplifies my own pleasure. My pussy clenches around him, milking the last of his release before he collapses on top of me, burying his face against my neck, his warm breath feathering across my skin.

In this moment, a strange sense of completion settles over me.

It's not something I've ever experienced before, and it doesn't take much to realize just how easy it would be to sink into the sensation.

To get used to it.

To crave it.

And if that's not frightening, I'm not sure what is.

HOLLAND

he moment I step out of the lecture hall, my phone buzzes in my pocket. I don't need to look to know who it's from.

T he moment I step out of the lecture hall, my phone buzzes in my pocket. I don't need to look to know who it's from.

*ColdAsIce17.*

My steps falter, and I veer off to the side of the building, letting the flow of students sweep past me. The preview of his message flashes on the screen, sending a ripple of something familiar and unsettling through me.

He's been my secret lifeline for months. The one person I can talk to about anything without fear or judgment.

But now?

Now there's Bridger.

My chest tightens as I tap the screen and open the message, bracing myself for whatever comes next.

> **COLDASICE17**
>
> Hey, stranger. Just checking in to make sure everything's good.

The text stares back at me, and my thumbs hesitate over the keyboard. For the first time since we started this back-and-forth, I don't know how to respond. It feels... complicated.

Everything in my life is complicated.

Bridger and I are a tangled mess of secrets, trust issues, and a chemistry so intense it burns. Yet here I am, holding on to something with Ice that feels simpler.

Or at least it used to.
I type out a response before deleting it.
Then another.

COLDASICE17

You there?

My pulse skitters, and before I can talk myself out of it, I type back.

ME

Yeah, I'm here. Everything has been a grind.
You know how it is.

His response comes instantly.

COLDASICE17

I get it. Just know I'm here if you need me.

A familiar warmth seeps through my body. What doesn't make sense is that it feels like I'm betraying Bridger.
But how can I betray something when it's never been defined?
Bridger still doesn't trust me.

ME

Thanks. That means a lot.

COLDASICE17

Sure you're okay? You sound off.

The weight of his words presses down on me. I pause, trying to come up with what to say. I could brush him off and keep it casual or I could admit the truth.

ME

I'm just trying to figure things out.

COLDASICE17

Ah, one of those phases.

ME

You have no idea.

COLDASICE17

Try me.

I stare at the screen, my throat tightening. There's no way I can tell him what's really going on. That I've been falling for Bridger in real life while growing closer to *ColdAsIce17* online. That it's starting to feel like I'm being split in two.

ME

Just the usual. Life. School. People being people.

COLDASICE17

Hmmm. Sounds suspiciously vague. Want to get specific, or should I start guessing?

I huff out a laugh despite myself. He always knows how to cut through my BS. It might be the reason this feels so hard.

Instead of coming clean, I turn the question around on him.

ME

What about you? You've been awfully quiet.

It's only after typing the comment that I realize how true it is. He's been just as MIA. But I haven't noticed because I've been spending so much time with Bridger.

It makes me wonder...

The dots appear, then disappear, and my stomach knots as I wait.

COLDASICE17

There's just been a lot of shit to figure out.

It's cautiously that I type out my reply.

ME

Kind of sounds like we're in the same place.

COLDASICE17

Maybe we are.

I grip my phone tighter, my thumbs moving before I can think.

ME

Anything you want to bring to the circle of trust?

COLDASICE17

That's a loaded question.

ME

How so?

COLDASICE17

I think I'll save it for another day.

I bite my lip, deciding not to push it any further. That's never been our relationship.

ME

Just know I'm here for you if or when you need it.

COLDASICE17

Thanks. It's exactly what I needed to hear.

ME

Whatever is going on, you'll make the right decision.

When the dots appear again, I hold my breath.

COLDASICE17

Have I mentioned that you're good people?

ME

Maybe once or twice. I'll try not to let the compliment go to my head.

COLDASICE17

You should. It's the truth. Thanks for being you.

The words hit like a punch to the gut, and I stare at them, my emotions spinning. How ironic is it that Ice and I are both confused and opting to pull back just a bit to get some perspective?

ME

It's easy when you're the one on the other side.

As I stare at the message, I have to wonder if I actually miss *him* or the simplicity of our conversations, the anonymity of them. The freedom to be honest in a way I can't be with most people. With Ice, there were no complicated feelings. No walls to break through or awkward silences to fill.

I hate how tangled everything now feels.

As soon as I hit send, a familiar voice cuts through my thoughts, and my head snaps up to find Garret, his expression carefully guarded. I shove my phone into my pocket and force a small smile.

"Hey, Garret. What's up?"

"I was hoping we'd run into each other." He stops in front of me, dragging a hand through his hair. "Do you have a moment to talk?"

"Umm." I hitch my backpack higher on my shoulder. "I was just headed to the library to study for a test. Could we find a different time to meet up?"

His face falls in disappointment as he shifts. "Oh." There's a pause as he tilts his head. "It seems like you've been avoiding me lately."

I glance away. The last thing I want to do is lie. "I'm sorry. You're right, I have been. With everything going on, it just felt easier."

He steps closer. "You mean because you're with Bridger?"

"Yeah."

His shoulders fall. "I'd really like the chance to explain some things to you. I promise, I won't take up too much of your time."

As much as I don't want to sit down with Garret, maybe it's better to get it over with. Even if Bridger weren't in the picture, I don't see Garret as anything more than a friend.

And that's not going to change.

Against my better judgment, I nod. "Fine. Lead the way."

His lips lift into a smile that doesn't quite reach his eyes. "Let's take my car."

# WESTERN UNIVERSITY CHAT APP

FragileLikeABomb

Quick poll: Are pineapple toppings on pizza a culinary masterpiece or an abomination?

ColdAsIce17

Bold of you to assume there's even a debate. Abomination, obviously.

FragileLikeABomb

Wrong answer. Pineapple on pizza is elite.

ColdAsIce17

That explains your gummy bear habits.

FragileLikeABomb

And your peanut butter habits explain your terrible taste.

ColdAsIce17

It's official. We're at war.

FragileLikeABomb

Bring it, Cold

# BRIDGER

The quad buzzes with activity as students hurry between classes. Their laughter and chatter blends with the faint strains of music carried on the brisk spring breeze. I lean against a bench near Holland's building, the coffee in my hand starting to lose its warmth. I scan the steady stream of people spilling out the doors, searching for a familiar flash of auburn hair.

I want Holland to understand that what I feel for her is genuine. I meant what I said about regretting the way I ghosted her two years ago. After last night, I don't want to do anything that makes her think I'm pulling away.

The past few weeks have been a whirlwind of unexpected shifts. Fake dating has morphed into late-night talks, quiet confessions, and moments I can't bring myself to overanalyze.

Moments that feel disarmingly real.

Like last night, curled up in my bed, Holland's sharp edges softened as we talked about everything and nothing. It's enough to make me think we're both moving in the same direction.

Most times in life, you don't get a do-over. There isn't a chance to go back and correct a mistake.

But I'm really hoping that's what's happening between us now.

An opportunity to undo the choice I made out of fear.

"Dude, your behavior is really starting to freak me out. Maybe the guys are right and you need an intervention." Steele's voice breaks into the chaotic whirl of my thoughts.

It's not like I don't get where he's coming from. This entire thing with Holland started out as a way to keep her close so I could watch her every move until she either fucked up or came clean.

Instead, I'm the one who's done a complete one-eighty.

My fingers tighten around the coffee as I glance over my shoulder to meet his eyes. "You can hold off on the intervention for the time being. I haven't started scrolling through the Humane Society's adoption pages yet."

"You sure about that?" he asks, shoving his hands into his pockets. "Just curious why you're hanging around, looking for your fake girlfriend like a lovesick puppy." He glances at the cup. "Don't tell me that's for her."

"Yeah, it is." I pull it out of his reach when he makes a grab for it. "And, no, you can't have it."

His brows shoot up. "Why do I get the feeling this relationship is no longer fake?"

I roll my eyes as heat floods my cheeks. "It's coffee," I grumble. "Don't make a bigger deal out of it than it is."

He leans against the bench beside me, his concern fading into something more thoughtful. "You actually believe her?"

It's on the tip of my tongue to lie.

At the last moment, I decide against it. "Yeah, I do. And if I hadn't been such a chickenshit two years ago, we wouldn't be in this place now. I wouldn't have spent all this time wondering if we could have been something more." My shoulders loosen. "I don't want to continue wondering."

I brace for an argument.

For my cousin to lose his shit and make a last-ditch effort to talk some sense into me.

But that's not what happens.

He presses his lips together and is silent for a long stretch of moments. "Okay."

I blink. "Okay?"

He shrugs. "Yeah. If you truly believe she's not the one behind the messages, then I'll support you. Hell, dude, I'll even root for you two crazy kids. If that's what you want."

I snort out a laugh as my muscles lose their rigidity. "I appreciate it."

"That's what cousins are for, right? I'll always be on your side and want what's best for you. If anyone deserves it, it's you. Seriously."

His words hit me hard. Steele has always been more like a brother to me, and I have no idea what I'd do without him.

Thank fuck, I'll never have to find out.

"One last question."

I almost groan. I should have realized that he capitulated way too easily. "Shoot."

"Do you trust her?" There's a pause. "I mean *really* trust her?"

I don't even have to think about it. "Yeah, I do."

"Okay," he drawls, his tone loaded. "Then explain why she's deep in conversation with Garret Akeman."

My head whips around so fast that the coffee cup nearly slips from my hand.

There's no damn way.

The moment my gaze lands on them, it's like the air gets knocked from my lungs.

Sure enough, they're standing off to the side of the walkway. My jaw locks at the way Garret sidles closer to her. Holland's expression is unreadable.

But here's the thing, she hasn't moved away from him.

"What the hell?" I mutter.

"She knows you two have an issue, right?"

"Yeah."

"So, why are they together, then?" There's not a single drop of smugness in Steele's voice.

"I don't know." My pulse spikes, a mixture of confusion and something darker twisting in my chest.

Holland never glances in my direction. Her attention stays focused on my teammate. The one who has continued to fuck with me every chance he gets.

Garret says something, and she nods.

That's all it takes for my stomach to churn.

"Look, man. I know you want to trust her." Steele's voice is quieter now. "I'm just not sure if you can. I'm worried that he's the one feeding info to someone. The very same someone who's been sleeping in your bed at night."

*Fuck.*

I turn back to Steele, but the words are stuck in my throat. The doubts he's just resurrected are taking root, tangling with the flicker of unease that's been buried in the back of my brain since the start of all this.

Before I can respond, my phone vibrates in my pocket. I yank it out, hoping for a distraction, but what I see only makes everything worse.

Another anonymous message.

ANONYMOUS MESSAGE

Bridger Sanderson thinks he's untouchable, but I know the truth. It won't be long before all the dark secrets get dragged into the light.

The words hit like a physical blow, and my hand tightens on the phone. Steele grabs my cell and stares at the screen before swearing under his breath.

He glares in the direction of Garret and Holland. "If it turns out they're working together, I'll bury both of them alive."

"Yeah," I mutter, rage bubbling under my skin. I feel like I'm drowning in a storm I can't control.

The messages.

My father.

The creeping doubts when I was so fucking sure I could trust her.

My phone vibrates again.

This time, it's a notification from the chat app.

FRAGILELIKEABOMB

What do you do when you want to trust the one person you shouldn't?

Her message feels too fitting, too timely.

My thumbs hover over the keyboard as I stare at her question. Anger and frustration swirl in my chest.

For the first time, I realize that I have no idea how to respond.

I don't stop Steele when he grabs the coffee out of my hand and tosses it into the nearest trash can. "Sorry, bro. As much as you wanted to believe whatever this is between you two is real, I just don't think it is."

Instead of replying, I shove my phone back into my pocket and stare across the quad, watching as Holland and Garret fall in line together before heading toward one of the parking lots on campus.

My throat constricts until it becomes hard to breathe.

I'm at a loss.

I don't know if Steele's right, but it sure as hell feels like he might be.

HOLLAND

We slip into Garret's beat-up Ford Escape and the door groans as I close it. The faint, cloying sweetness of a pine air freshener clings to the air. The seats are worn, with a couple of tears in the fabric revealing the foam beneath. My fingers skim the edge of the cracked dashboard, and a small part of me softens at the sight. Like me, it's obvious that Garret doesn't come from money.

As we pull out of the parking lot and head south, I glance around, watching the scenery blur past the window. The fraternity and sorority houses near campus morph into the small shops and boutiques of downtown, the streets lined with brick façades and empty flower planters. It doesn't take long before we turn into a residential area where the houses are compact and a little run-down. Paint peels from porches, and yards look a little unkempt.

That's when it hits me that I haven't asked the most obvious question.

"Where are we headed?"

Garret flicks a look in my direction, his hands tight on the steering wheel. "Just a place I like to go when I need to think."

"Oh." I shift in my seat. The unease I've been feeling since I agreed to this rises another notch. "Okay."

The silence stretches between us, broken only by the hum of the engine. My fingers drum against my thigh as my instincts scream that this was a bad idea.

We come to a stop at a small park. It's the kind you'd miss if you weren't looking for it. A couple of trees dot the landscape, their branches casting thin shadows over the cracked basketball court and rusting jungle gym. A single picnic table sits off to the side, its once-red paint faded to a dull brown.

Garret parks and turns off the engine, and I swivel toward him, just wanting to get this over with. The sudden silence feels heavy, thick with tension.

A strange pit has taken up residence in my gut. Garret has never scared me, and he doesn't necessarily now, but I'm getting a weird vibe from him. My instincts have always been sharp, and at the moment, they're practically screaming at me.

"Would you mind if we sat over there?" He nods toward the picnic table.

I hesitate. My gut tells me to decline, to stay in the safety of the car or, better yet, to leave entirely. Instead, I nod. "Sure. I just... can't stay long."

He jerks the handle and pushes the door open before climbing out. "Yeah, no problem."

The chilly air nips at my skin as I follow him, careful to avoid the muddy puddles scattered across the grass. Once we reach the table, I settle across from him, lacing my fingers together and resting them on the scarred wood.

"So, what's on your mind?" I ask, my voice steady despite the nervous energy bubbling inside me.

Garret shifts, his knee bouncing like a jackhammer under the table. His gaze flits around the park before landing on me. "I've always liked you, Holland."

The bluntness of his words knocks me off balance, and my brain spins, unsure how to respond.

"I guess I was hoping that, at some point, you might feel the same. I think we have a lot in common."

I shift in my seat as unease prickles across my skin. "You're right, we do have some things in common, and I've always liked you too," I admit carefully. "As a friend."

He nods, his expression tightening. "Yeah, I get that. It just sucks. Sanderson isn't the right guy for you. In the end, he'll just hurt you. And I don't want to see that happen."

"I appreciate you looking out for me, but I didn't come here to discuss my relationship with Bridger. Even if I weren't with him, it wouldn't have changed anything between us." I keep my tone gentle but firm, hoping to defuse the situation without wounding him further.

His jaw works as he nods again, the continuous bouncing of his knee betraying his agitation.

"Garret?" I prompt when the silence stretches too long. "Is there something else?"

"This is hard," he mutters, dragging a hand through his hair.

I watch him closely, the uneasy pit in my stomach growing. "Sometimes it helps to just get it off your chest."

Before he can respond, his gaze shifts over my shoulder and his features harden. I turn, following his line of sight. My stomach twists when I spot a middle-aged man in a suit stepping out of one of the nearby houses. The man's tie hangs loose, and he straightens his jacket, as if he's in a rush or maybe leaving somewhere he shouldn't have been.

My pulse quickens as recognition slams into me. "Wait a minute, isn't that Bridger's father?"

Garret's glare sharpens. "Yeah."

I blink, my brain struggling to process what I'm seeing. "What's he doing here?"

Garret exhales sharply, his hands curling into fists on the table. "He stops by once a week and stays for about forty-five minutes. An hour, if Mom's lucky."

The world tilts as the pieces start to fall into place. "Are you saying this is your house? That Bridger's father is seeing your mom?"

Garret's lips press into a thin line as his nostrils flare. For a moment, I wonder if he'll deny it, but then he nods.

And then everything clicks—the sharp cheekbones, the similar jawline, the tension that always simmers just beneath Garret's surface. I suck in a breath as the realization slams into me.

"Is he... your father?"

Garret's eyes slice to mine, cold and unforgiving. "Yes."

For a moment, all I can do is stare at him as my mind cartwheels. The pieces are all snapping into place, but I don't like the picture they're forming. The texts, the personal details only someone close to Bridger would know, the bitterness in Garret's tone whenever his teammate's name comes up.

*Oh shit.*

"It's you, isn't it?" My voice is barely above a whisper. "You're the one behind the messages."

Instead of denying it, he leans back on the bench, his posture almost defiant. "Yeah. It's me."

My jaw drops, and for a second, I can't find the words. Then anger surges up, hot and sharp. "Do you have any idea how much damage you've caused? To Bridger? He's one of your team—" I stop myself and shake my head, trying to get a mental grasp on it all. "He's your brother?"

"Half-brother," he bites out. "And Mr. Perfect will be just fine."

"Don't do that. You don't get to play the victim here. Whatever issues you have with your dad or Bridger, you don't get to hurt him like this. He doesn't even know!"

*Oh my God, he doesn't even know he has a brother.*

*Half-brother.*

Garret's expression hardens, and I catch a flicker of something behind his eyes.

Guilt?

Regret?

The emotion disappears before I'm able to decipher it.

"He deserves to know the truth," I say firmly. "About your dad. About everything."

Garret shakes his head before dragging a hand through his windswept hair. "No. You're not telling him."

I cross my arms and hold his gaze. "If you think I'm just going to sit on this—"

"You will," he interrupts, his tone icy. "Because if you care about Bridger, you won't throw this at him during playoffs. I'll handle it in my own time."

I narrow my eyes. "And when exactly are you planning on doing that? When it's convenient for you? After you've hurt him with more humiliating messages?"

"I'll tell him when I'm ready," he says through gritted teeth. "And the messages are done. I'm over it."

"You're damn right they are," I snap, rising to my feet and staring down at him. "Because if they aren't, I'll make sure everyone on this campus knows who's behind them."

His jaw clenches, but he doesn't argue.

Without waiting for a response, I turn and walk away, my heart thundering. My thoughts are a chaotic swirl, but one thing is clear—Bridger deserves to know the truth.

I'm not going to let anyone else hurt him.

Not even his own family.

# BRIDGER

# 33

The house buzzes with activity as I sit on the couch, staring at my cell like it holds all the answers to the universe. It doesn't, but my fingers itch to open the campus chat app anyway. My thoughts are a jumbled mess of Holland, the messages, and the scene with Garret earlier.

Steele drops onto the armchair across from me with a bottle of beer. He takes a slow swig of his drink before speaking.

"So," he says, his voice hushed so no one overhears our conversation. "You make any decisions about what we saw earlier?"

I force my gaze to his. "Nope."

He arches a brow when I don't elaborate. "Okay then. Let's hear what she had to say about it."

"She didn't say anything."

A faint scowl creeps onto his face, but it's more bewildered than angry. "What do you mean she didn't say anything? Like, exactly what were the words that came out of her mouth? Sheesh. This is like pulling teeth."

With a huffed breath, I admit, "I didn't ask."

His body jolts upright. "Are you shitting me, right now? Please tell me you're not just going to bury your head in the sand and ignore what we both saw this afternoon."

Unsure how to respond, my hand rises to rub the tightness at the nape of my neck as I focus on the video game playing out across the screen, wishing it were possible to get lost in it. Even for a few mindless minutes. "I don't want to talk about it. Can we just drop it for tonight?"

He shakes his head before guzzling down half the bottle.

"You do realize that you're sleeping with the enemy, right?" There's a pause before he continues. "You need to point-blank ask what the hell she was doing with Garret fucking Akeman."

My jaw tightens. Even though I don't necessarily believe it, I mumble, "You're making a big deal out of nothing."

"Sure, I am." Steele leans forward so his elbows can rest on his knees. "Somehow I must have forgotten that Garret is a stand-up guy with nothing shady going on."

I shoot him a glare. "What are you getting at?"

Steele shrugs, but his eyes remain sharp. "I'm just saying this entire thing with Holland started because you suspected her of being behind the messages. You spend a little time with this girl and now you think she has nothing to do with it even though she's hanging around with Garret Akeman. Know what I think?" He doesn't give me time to respond. "I think they're both in on it."

After everything Holland and I have shared, I don't want to believe it. I don't want to believe that her hatred for me could run that deep.

That she's been lying to me this entire time.

Or worse, that I've been played.

"You don't know what you're talking about," I mutter.

"Don't I?" Steele leans back, taking another sip of his beer. "Look, man, I get it. She's hot. She's got that whole *I hate the world* vibe going on that you apparently find irresistible. But you're not thinking straight. The messages, Holland Tate, and Garret Akeman are all connected. That girl is a bigger part of it than you want to admit."

Sadness and anger twist together inside me, tightening like a painful knot. "She's not behind the messages."

"How do you know?" Steele presses, refusing to let it go. "Because she said so? Or because you want to believe her?"

My phone digs in my palm as I clench my fist. "Because I know her, okay? She's not like that."

Steele snorts. "You force her to spend a little time with you, and your attitude where she's concerned does a total turn around. I don't know if that girl has a unicorn pussy or what, but you're blinded by whatever this thing is between you two."

Unable to sit here for another minute and listen to him, I rise to my feet. "You don't know her like I do."

"And you don't know her like you *think* you do," Steele counters, his tone softer but still pointed. "I'm just saying, don't let your feelings for her blind you to the facts in front of your damn face. Hell, I'd love for her to be innocent. But if she's not, you're gonna be the one left picking up the pieces. You need to think about that."

Instead of responding, I head to the front door.

"Hey, where are you going?" he calls after me.

"I need some fresh air." My chest is so tight, there's no way I can stay here.

"Want me to come with?"

"No. I just want to be alone so I can think."

Just as I reach for the door handle, Steele's voice stops me in my tracks. "Bridger?"

I force myself to turn and meet his eyes.

There's a solemn expression on his face. "Don't do anything stupid."

"I won't."

His head dips in a stiff nod as I make my escape. The moment I step foot onto the porch, I stumble to a halt before sucking a big breath into my lungs. The chill of the night air is enough to banish the suffocating sensation that grips me. My mind races, every doubt and insecurity bubbling up to the surface.

Once inside the BMW, I press the start button. The engine's growl fills the quiet street. Instead of pulling away from the curb, I grab my phone, open the chat app, and fire off a quick message to Fragile.

ME

How do you let yourself trust someone when every instinct screams not to?

I hit send before I can second-guess myself.

The reply comes quickly, as if she's been waiting for me.

FRAGILELIKEABOMB

That's a heavy one to start with. Sure you want to go there?

ME

I don't have a choice. There's someone… but she's different.

FRAGILELIKEABOMB

Different in a good way or a bad way?

I hesitate as Steele's words echo in my head.

ME:

Both. Good, because she's important. Bad, because that's what makes her so dangerous.

Fragile's typing bubble appears, then vanishes before reappearing. Finally, her message comes through.

FRAGILELIKEABOMB

Trust is always a risk. That's kind of the deal, isn't it? You put yourself out there and hope to hell it's not a mistake.

ME

Yeah, but what if it is? What if it blows up in your face?

FRAGILELIKEABOMB

Then you pick up the pieces and move on. You're stronger than you think.

ME

That's easy to say until you're the one staring at the wreckage.

FRAGILELIKEABOMB

True. But what if it doesn't blow up? What if it's the best thing that ever happens to you?

The best thing.

Her words pluck at something in my chest, and I rub a hand over my face. My throat feels tight as I stare at the message, the possibility of it gnawing at the edges of my resistance.

ME

You really think it's worth the risk?

FRAGILELIKEABOMB

I think some people are worth the risk. And if you're asking this, maybe they are.

Damn her.

She has a way of slicing to the heart of the matter like no one else. It's equal parts infuriating and comforting. It's the reason I needed to get her perspective before doing anything else.

My fingers tremble slightly as I type my next response.

ME

You make it sound so simple.

FRAGILELIKEABOMB

It's not. Trust me, I know. But sometimes you have to take the leap and figure out the landing later.

ME

You always know what to say.

FRAGILELIKEABOMB

Not always. But I know what it's like to be scared to trust. I'm still figuring it out myself.

ME

Maybe we both need to take a leap.

FRAGILELIKEABOMB

Maybe we do.

I stare at her words, my thoughts swirling in a chaotic mess. She's right. Maybe we both need to close our eyes and take that leap of faith.

ME

Thanks, Fragile.

FRAGILELIKEABOMB:

Anytime, Ice. That's what I'm here for.

I sit back and stare at the screen, allowing her words to settle inside me. Only then do I pull away from the curb and into traffic.

BRIDGER
SANDERSON
17
WILDCATS

*uck.*

I shouldn't be here.

The rational part of me knows this is a terrible idea, but my vehicle still ends up in the Envy Room parking lot. I sit behind the wheel for what feels like forever, my fingers gripping the steering wheel so tightly they ache. The sign overhead casts a soft glow over the lot.

I tell myself I just need to see her.

That's all.

Just to...

Confirm what I already know?

Prove myself wrong?

I have no idea.

The fact that I can't answer my own question pisses me off even more.

With a frustrated exhale, I climb out of the car and head for the door.

The music hits me first. It's a deep bass that reverberates through my body as soon as I step inside. I keep my head down, avoiding eye contact, and stick to the shadows along the back wall. The place is packed, and the thought of any of these guys looking at her the way I do makes my stomach burn with jealousy.

Because I can't lie to myself anymore.

I don't just *look* at Holland.

I feel her.

In my chest.

Under my skin.

In the spaces of my life that used to be empty but are now charged whenever she's near.

And that terrifies the hell out of me.

The lights dim and the crowd quiets for a beat before erupting as the next dancer takes the stage. My heart slams against my rib cage because I know before I even see her who it'll be.

The air in the room shifts and the low hum of conversation dulls to a hush as all eyes turn to her. She's wearing something black and strappy, the fabric hugging her curves in a way that's both artful and provocative. The spotlight cuts through the dark, framing her body.

She looks like a goddess.

My throat goes dry. I try to swallow, but it's useless as my pulse kicks into overdrive. She moves to the rhythm of the music, her body a perfect blend of grace and seduction. Each sway of her hips, every languid roll of her shoulders, pulls me under like a riptide.

Her gaze scans the room, and for a second, I think I'm safe. Just another face blending in the crowd.

But then it locks on mine.

That moment of connection is like a punch to the gut.

My vision tunnels, locking on her as everything else fades away. She looks at me like she knew I was here the moment she stepped onto that stage. Like she could feel my stare before she ever saw me.

Her lips curve into a small, knowing smile, and something inside me unravels. That smile isn't for the crowd.

It's for me.

The music swells, low and throbbing, as she moves in time with it, her body fluid and hypnotic. Her hands slide up her sides, grazing over her bare shoulders before trailing back down to her thighs. She dips low, her hair cascading forward as her fingers trace the curve of her legs. The soft, warm light of the spotlight catches on her skin, making her glow.

My breath hitches, frozen in my lungs.

She rises slowly, her back arching as she spins, her movements seamless and deliberate. It's not just a dance. It's a performance. And every move feels like it's meant for me. The way her gaze flicks back to mine, the way her lips part as she undulates her body. It's like she's daring me to break as she continues to dance.

When her hands reach for the ties of her top, my fists clench at my sides. Part of me wants to storm the stage and drag her away, out of the spotlight, away from every leering set of eyes.

But the other part?

The one that's captivated and helpless to do anything but watch?

That part knows she's doing this for me.

Her top falls to the stage, and the crowd roars, but her focus stays locked on me. Jealousy and desire tangle into something darker, something primal.

The song builds to its climax, and she twirls once more before dropping low again, her hands skimming the stage as she tosses her hair back. When the music fades, she straightens, retrieving her top from the floor, her gaze never leaving mine.

The applause is deafening, but she barely acknowledges it. She holds my stare for one more beat, her lips curling into a smirk that sets my skin on fire, and then she slips behind the curtain, leaving the crowd in a frenzy.

I don't remember moving.

One second, I'm rooted to the spot, and the next, I'm weaving through the crowd, pushing past patrons and dodging bouncers. My heart races, each beat echoing louder as I slip backstage.

The air is cooler, quieter, but it's charged with her presence. The faint scent of rosemary and mint lingers, and I know it's hers. My feet move of their own accord, leading me down the narrow hallway toward the dressing rooms.

I find Holland leaning against the wall near one of the doors, her top hanging from her fingers. She doesn't look surprised to see me.

"Couldn't stay away, huh?" she says, her voice low and teasing.

"No," I admit. "I couldn't."

Her smile softens, but there's something guarded in her eyes. "What are you doing here, Bridger?"

I step closer, eating up the space between us. "I don't know. I just needed to see you."

Her head tilts to the side, and there's a flicker of something in her eyes. Something I don't want to inspect too closely.

"Are you all right?"

I shake my head.

I have no idea how to voice all the questions and doubts that continue to circle through my mind. Anything I say will only send us tumbling backward, and that's the last thing I want to do.

Tonight, I just want *her*.

I want to forget everything that happened today.

I want to erase the image of her and Garret from my mind.

She pushes away from the wall, closing the distance between us. With her gaze pinned to mine, her palms drift to my cheeks. "Do you want to talk about it?"

"No, I don't." Unable to help myself, my hands rise until I can cup the heavy weight of her breasts. My fingers tighten, and a soft moan slides from her lips. That's all it takes for her eyes to darken and arousal to crash over me.

I roll the stiff little peaks, playing with them, tugging and teasing them. Her lips part as she presses against me.

How the fuck am I ever going to get enough of this girl?

"Mmmm. I love the way you touch me," she whispers.

The heavy beat of the music vibrates through my bones as it wraps around us, insulating us in a world of our own.

"I need you." The admission slips out before I can stop it.

Her eyes soften as she leans up and brushes her lips across mine. Before I'm able to sink into the caress, she pulls away and glances around the dressing room. For the first time, I realize that we're alone, but it won't stay that way for long. The couple times I've slipped back here, there's been a bevy of girls getting dressed for a performance or stripping off their makeup.

The lull of activity feels odd.

Holland grabs my hand. "Come on."

I don't question where she's taking me. I just follow. That's the moment I realize I'd follow her anywhere. I just want to be close to her. Near her. Soak in her presence. She's the one person who anchors me in reality even when it feels like it's being blown apart.

With our hands clasped, we head to the back of the dressing room before escaping through a door that leads to a small office. The lock clicks shut behind us so that we're alone.

The air between us feels thick, charged with unspoken words and feelings.

Before I can say anything, she fists the sweatshirt I'm wearing and draws me closer. Her lips slam into mine. The kiss is fierce, all fire and frustration. My hands move to her waist, gripping her as if she'll slip through my fingers if I'm not careful. She tastes like vanilla and something I can't name but never want to forget. When she pulls away, her forehead rests against mine, our breaths mingling together in the small space.

"You drive me insane," she whispers.

"Good," I say, my voice low. "Because you've been doing the same thing to me for years."

She laughs softly, and the sound is enough to unravel me. But there's something else buried beneath it.

Something vulnerable and fragile.

Our tongues tangle and our teeth scrape. Her fingers settle on the waistband of my jeans before popping open the button and lowering the zipper. Seconds later, her hand delves into the cotton of my boxers and wraps around my cock. A groan works its way up from my chest as she slides her palm along my hard length.

"As much as I love that, you're going to make me come."

"Isn't that the name of the game?"

"I'd like to enjoy this for more than two minutes, if you don't mind."

With that, I gently pull her hand out of my jeans. Before she can make her next move, I grip her shoulders and force her backward until her ass hits the desk. Desire blazes in her eyes as her breathing quickens.

Unable to resist, I nip at her pouty lips. It's so tempting to press her onto the flat surface, but that's not how I want to take her.

Not this time.

I twist her around until her backside is turned to me. My gaze slides down the length of her spine to her nipped-in waist and flare of her hips before arriving at the lushness of her ass.

Holland is all curves.

I slip my hands around her rib cage, the fingertips trailing along her naked flesh until I can cup her breasts, massaging them as I draw closer. What can't be denied is that we fit together perfectly. Her head falls back until it can rest against my chest, and a sigh of contentment slips free as I press my lips against the slender column of her neck.

"Ready to get fucked?"

Instead of answering, she fires off a question of her own. "Are you ready to fuck me?"

"More than ready."

"Good. My pussy is so achy for you."

*Fuck.*

"And wet?"

"Maybe you should find out for yourself."

The need to do that thrums through me as one hand stays wrapped possessively around her breast while the other skims along her bare skin until it reaches the scrap of material that barely covers her ass.

My fingers delve beneath the black fabric before dipping lower to her smooth mound. As soon as I brush the sensitive flesh, she widens her stance, giving me room to maneuver. Moisture gathers on my fingertips as they stroke the seam of her lips. Another whimper works its way free from her as she presses her hips into my touch.

"Always so needy."

"Do you blame me?"

"Not at all. But I do love it."

With that, I slide two fingers inside her until they're buried deep within her heat. From this angle, I'm able to rub soft circles against her clit with my thumb as I tweak her nipple with the other hand. It's only when she shifts that I pump my fingers in and out of her body.

"Looks like the tables have turned. If you're not careful, you'll make me come."

"No way," I whisper against her ear. "I'm just getting you ready for me."

"Mission accomplished. I'm ready."

I withdraw from her pussy and tap her clit with my fingertips. "I'll tell you when you're ready to be fucked. Not the other way around."

When she squirms, I tweak her nipple before one hand settles on the area between her shoulder blades. "Now, bend over, baby. Show me that pretty little ass."

With a groan, she drapes herself across the desk. Her arms stretch above her head as her palms flatten against the hard surface.

My hungry gaze roves over her as another wave of need crashes over me.

A tiny scrap of thin material is the only thing that bars her naked body from me. The bottom piece of her costume is more of a glorified thong. The ribbon sits prettily in the cleft between her rounded cheeks. All I have to do is rip it away and I'd get an eyeful.

As desperate as I am to fuck her, I want to draw out this moment until we're both tap dancing on the edge. I reach out and trail my finger along the silky fabric from the top where it meets the elastic band that encircles her waist before grazing her rosebud until finally making my way to her soaked pussy. The place where the ribbon meets the cloth is nestled between her plump lips.

I'm not sure if I've ever seen a sight as stunning as Holland bent over.

I drop down until I'm eye level with her backside.

My hands settle on her ass cheeks before gently spreading them.

She's so fucking drenched.

*Is this what I do to her?*

As tempted as I am to yank the thong to the side and fuck her with it on, I want her totally bare.

I want Holland Tate at her most vulnerable.

For me.

And only me.

My fingers slip beneath the band at her waist before sliding it over the generous curve of her hips and thighs before it puddles on the floor at her feet. I lift one foot and then the other before picking up the thong and straightening. Her palms are still flattened against the desk. As much as I like them there, I want her completely at my mercy.

I shackle one wrist with my fingers, careful to bend her arm in a sweeping motion until I can fold it against the small of her back. It's a surprise when she remains silent, not questioning what I'm doing. That little bit of trust she's handing over means everything, and it makes me want to be even more gentle with her.

It's the balm I didn't realize I needed, and manages to soothe everything that had been raging inside me.

I repeat the process with her other arm, until one wrist is crossed over the other, before using the thong to bind them together. Her breathing hitches as she stares at the far wall in silence.

I take a step back and admire the way she looks draped across the desk, her gorgeous ass on display. In the stilettos that lengthen her legs even more, she's a fucking sight to behold.

I don't even want to fuck her.

I just want to stand here and eat her up with my eyes.

All right, that's a lie.

I want to fuck this girl hard.

I want to fuck all the doubts I have regarding Holland Tate out of my head until we're both satisfied.

When a punch of arousal hits me, I blink out of those thoughts and step closer. I press her thighs farther apart before laying my hands on her smooth flesh, squeezing the taut muscles of her ass. She makes a humming noise deep in her throat, and I take that as the green light to proceed before dropping down for a second time, needing her sweet honey on my tongue. The taste I had the other night wasn't nearly enough and has only whet my appetite for more. I nibble at her, making sure to lap up all her cream.

"Bridger, please."

I press my lips against the rounded curve of her ass. "Please what?"

"I need you."

"How much, baby?"

"I want you to fuck me. Now."

The sound that rips from my throat is low and raw.

I slowly slide one finger deep inside her body. "Is that what you needed?"

With a whimper, she shifts, attempting to wiggle closer. "No."

I pump it a few times. "How about that? Is that better?"

"Stop teasing." The words come out sounding more like a groan. "We both know I need something thicker."

With my other hand, I give her ass a little smack. "I know you do. Something meatier. Something that will fill you up and satisfy you."

"Yes."

Unable to wait a second longer, I yank down my boxers and free my cock. I'm so damn hard. Seeing Holland like this has me teetering on the edge.

I've never craved anyone the way I do her. The bitch of it is that I have no idea if I'll ever feel this way about anyone else. I want to fuck the all-consuming need right out of me, but I have the sneaking suspicion it's not possible.

Unwilling to dwell on the prospect, I shove that thought from my head and focus on the way she's stretched out before me with her ass in the air.

She's fucking perfection.

I pump my dick a few times until pre-cum leaks from the tip. Only then do I step close enough to smack the bulbous head against her crevice. A shiver slides through her as I do it for a second time in a different spot. Clear fluid trails across her skin. And I fucking love it.

I want to mark this girl as my own.

Even though I have no idea if that will ever be the case.

But for this sliver of a moment, that's exactly what she is.

*Mine.*

"Stop playing around and fuck me hard." She arches, tipping her backside so I can see even more of her glistening pussy. "I think it's what we both need."

She's right about that.

It's exactly what we need.

I pull a condom from my back pocket before sliding the rubber over my hard length. As soon as I'm covered, I press the head of my cock into her entrance and lock my fingers around her bound wrists, holding them tight as I slide deep inside her, filling her to the brim. We both groan as I hold myself perfectly still.

She's so damn wet.

And warm.

The way her inner muscles clench around my shaft makes it difficult to maintain control.

I withdraw before thrusting back inside. Over and over, I grind against her, feeling the slap of my balls against her pussy.

"God, that feels so good. Please don't stop."

I pick up my pace, giving her more of what she asked for. Wanting to give her every damn thing she needs.

When my balls draw up against my body, I know it won't be long before I find my release. What I won't do is get there before her. One hand skims from her hip around to her clit, where my fingers begin rubbing circles over the sensitive nub. A few soft caresses are all it takes for her to come undone and me to follow her right over the edge and into oblivion.

I come so hard that stars dance behind my eyelids, and I nearly black out.

The last spasm racks my body as my muscles turn slack and I collapse on top of Holland. My teeth scrape across her shoulder blade. The last thing I want to do is leave the comforting warmth of her pussy, but as I glance around, I realize we're in someone's office. And who knows if that person will make an unexpected appearance.

I press my lips to the delicate skin at the nape of her neck before straightening. As soon as I slip free, I remove the condom and toss it in the trash can. After tucking myself back inside my boxers, I pull up my jeans and zip the fly. Holland doesn't move a muscle. I unwind the thong from her wrists before massaging the fragile flesh and checking for marks. Her skin is a little red from the fabric sliding against it but nothing more. After helping her to straighten up, I grab a few tissues to wipe up the mess.

As I stare at her naked body, I can't help but take in her disheveled appearance. Her auburn hair is a tumbled mess around her face and her makeup is a little smudged. It's almost as if the mask she normally wears has fallen away, leaving her completely exposed. The vulnerable picture she makes tugs at my heart in a way I couldn't have imagined months ago.

I don't want her to be the one behind the messages.

The one out to ruin me.

"What are you thinking about?" The question is tentative, as if she's able to read me. Or has a sixth sense about the direction my thoughts have turned.

I close the distance between us before wrapping my fingers around her chin and lifting it so I can stare into her eyes. "Did you see the message today?"

Emotion flickers across her face. It's there and gone before I can fully decipher what it means. "I did. I'm sorry."

"What are you sorry for? You're not the one behind it, right?"

Her posture stiffens, but she doesn't move. "You still don't believe me?"

I press my lips together before jerking my shoulders. "I don't know what to believe anymore." When she tries to pull away, I blurt, "It would fucking kill me to find out you were behind this. Or involved in any way. No one has ever made me feel the way you do."

Her palm settles on my chest before fisting the material. "Like what?"

The last thing I should do is drop my guard and allow her to peek inside. But that knowledge doesn't stop the words from tumbling out of me. "Like I'm seconds away from unraveling. Like you're the only one who calms the chaos raging inside me."

Her gaze drops to the floor, and for a moment, I think she's going to shut me out. But then she looks up, and there's something raw in her expression. "I don't have all the answers. And even if I did, I'm not sure you'd want to hear them."

"That's the thing." I lower my mouth until it can ghost over hers. "I don't know if I can trust you. Every time I think I've got you figured out, something happens that makes me question everything."

Her jaw clenches as guilt clouds her features. "I see the way you watch me," she says, voice breaking. "Like you're just waiting for me to confess. But I won't admit to something I haven't done."

"The problem is, I think you know more than what you're telling me."

Her shoulders slump, and for the first time, she looks... almost fragile. It's so un-Holland-like that I want to gather her into my arms and press her close. "It's not that simple."

"Why not?" I argue, my frustration mounting. "You should trust me enough to just say whatever it is."

She shakes her head, her hair tumbling around her face. "This has nothing to do with trust. It's about—" She stops herself, pressing her lips together like she's afraid to let the truth out. When she speaks again, her voice is quieter, back under control. "It's about trying to protect people. And that includes you."

"That's bullshit," I snap. "You're not protecting me. You're keeping me in the dark. And it's driving me insane because I can't stop wanting you, even when I'm not sure if I can trust you."

Her eyes widen slightly, and for a moment, the tension shifts. There's a trace of something softer in her gaze, something that makes my chest ache.

"Do you think this is any easier for me?" she asks, her voice barely above a whisper. "I'm afraid you might not forgive me once you find out the truth."

Her words hit like a punch to the gut, and I take a step back, trying to process what she's saying. "Then why not just tell me now? Let's get everything out in the open."

"Because sometimes the truth does more damage than the lies," she says quietly, her eyes glistening with unshed tears. "And I don't want to hurt you."

I shake my head, the frustration and helplessness bubbling over. "You're already hurting me. Every time I see you, every time I feel whatever this thing is between us, it hurts. Because I want to trust you. I want to believe in whatever this is. But you're not giving me a choice in the matter."

For a moment, she looks like she might crumble before she sucks in a deep breath and straightens. Her expression hardens into something almost defiant. "You're right," she says softly. "You don't have a choice."

"That's not good enough," I fire back, my voice cracking. "Not for me."

Her eyes fill with something I'm unable to name as she takes a step in retreat. Her palm falls away from my chest, drifting back to her side. "You want the truth?" she whispers, her voice trembling. "Here it is. I care about you. More than I ever thought I would. And that scares the shit out of me because I don't know how to make this better without breaking both of us in the process."

The honesty in her words hits me like a freight train, and for a moment, I can't speak. My hands itch to reach for her, to pull her close and erase the space between us, but I hold back. "I don't know how to do this," I admit. "But I know I don't want to walk away from you."

"Then don't." There's a pause as she pleads with me. "Just... don't."

Her words linger in the air between us, tenuous and full of unspoken promises. I reach out, my hand brushing against hers, and for the first time, she doesn't pull away.

It's in no way a resolution.

But it's something.

And for now, it has to be enough.

HOLLAND

The sun filters through the tree branches as Willow and I stroll across campus. Students mill about, rushing to classes or lingering in groups on the lawn. Even though it's a beautiful day, my mind remains clouded, burdened by the secrets I'm carrying.

Ones I never asked to know.

Ones that have made my relationship with Bridger even more complicated than before.

"I have some news." Willow's voice breaks through the turmoil of my thoughts. "Maverick asked me to move in with him next year."

I stumble and nearly trip over my own feet. If I was looking for a distraction to pull me out of my head, that bomb does the trick. "You're kidding."

Her grin widens as a touch of nervousness flashes in her eyes. "Nope. He brought it up last night. Since you'll be graduating in the summer, I think I'm going to do it."

"Wow." I blink, still trying to process this new phase of their relationship. "Things are really moving quickly between you two."

She glances at me. "Too quickly?"

I shake my head and give her a small smile. "For most people? Maybe. But you two have this thing... like you've known each other forever. Maybe I was skeptical of your hotshot hockey player at first, but Maverick has proven himself. He's solid. He gets my official stamp of approval."

The tension in her shoulders eases and her smile turns softer. "I love him."

"I know you do," I say, looping my arm through hers and pulling her close. "It's written all over your face when you're together. After everything you've been through, you deserve all the happiness he can offer. And, hey, even Becks has backed off. I didn't think that was going to happen during our lifetime."

"Speaking of Mom, she stopped over the other day to do a surprise deep clean and opened all the windows to get a little fresh air in the townhouse now that the weather has turned warmer."

"Damn, I'm sorry I missed her."

She smirks. "I'm sure you are."

"Did you break the big news?"

"No, I'm going to need a little more time to ease her into that situation." Willow gives me a bit of side-eye. "Not to mention River. I'm not sure who will flip out more."

"Actually, if you don't mind, I'd like to be there when you share the good news. Because if I know your brother, he's gonna lose his proverbial shit." When a mixture of anxiety and fear flares across her expression, I bump her shoulder with my own. "I'm just kidding. Your twin will be fine. I thought he and Mav hashed out most of their shit."

"They did," she says. "Sort of."

"At the end of the day, they both want the best for you. That's all that matters."

Willow nods, but her silence on the subject says she's still mulling it over. "You and Bridger seem to be going strong."

"Yeah." I force a smile, not wanting to dwell on our conversation last night.

"I still can't believe you two are an item."

"Same," I mutter.

She gives me a sidelong glance. "But you like him, right?"

"Yeah, I do," I admit. I actually like him a lot. The worst part is, I have no idea how everything will shake out. There might be too much standing between us.

Too many secrets.

Too many lies.

Too much baggage.

And then there are the trust issues that plague both of us.

It's a relief when she doesn't press for more. My life feels complicated enough without trying to explain it to someone else.

"Holland."

I glance up only to find Steele Sanderson approaching. His attention stays locked on me.

"Hey, Steele," Willow greets. "I saw Lilah in the tutoring lab the other day. We're going to get together later this week for coffee."

His expression softens when he glances at her. I'd think there was something wrong with him if it didn't. Willow is the sweetest, kindest person on the face of the planet. I'm lucky she befriended me way back in elementary school and that we've stayed close ever since.

"Oh yeah? Make sure she orders decaf. Otherwise, she'll be a total squirrel," he replies before turning back to me. "Got a minute, Holland?"

I hesitate before glancing at my bestie. She gives me a questioning look. "Go ahead," I say quietly. "I'll catch up with you later."

Willow takes off, but not before throwing a curious glance over her shoulder.

When Steele gestures toward a patch of grass just off the walkway, I follow.

Even though I have a sneaking suspicion, I ask once we're clear of the crowd, "What's this about?"

Steele crosses his arms against his chest as his eyes narrow. "You might have Bridger fooled, but not me." The warmth filling his tone when he'd been talking to Willow is long gone. "I know you're involved with those messages."

I reel back, as if slapped. "You're wrong. I don't have anything to do with them."

"Bullshit," he snaps. "You're hiding something." I open my mouth to deny the accusation, but Steele cuts me off. "I think you and Garret orchestrated all of it. I saw you two together yesterday."

"It's not what you think," I say quietly as guilt constricts my chest.

"I care about Bridger, and I'd never want to hurt him. That might not have always been true, but it is now."

"Is that so?" His eyes narrow as he steps closer. "Just so you know, I'm aware of how he forced you into fake dating him in order to keep a closer eye on you. Maybe you've managed to snow him, but I'm not so easily fooled."

"You're right, he did blackmail me." The words burst out louder than I intend. I release a deep breath, trying to steady the storm churning inside me. "Look, I get why you'd think that. But things are different now. Bridger matters to me. I promise, I'm not the one trying to hurt him."

Steele's gaze narrows as he presses his lips into a tight line. His silence stretches, heavy with unspoken doubt, before he finally speaks. "I don't know what to believe," he says, his tone cautious. "But I'll tell you this—I'm not letting him get burned again."

"Neither am I." My voice is steady as I square my shoulders. "And I'm going to deal with it."

His brow furrows, suspicion flickering across his face. "What's that supposed to mean?"

"It means there's something I need to take care of," I say sharply, cutting off any further questions. Without waiting for Steele to respond, I turn on my heel and walk off, the urgency in my steps leaving no room for argument.

Instead of heading to class as planned, I veer toward the administration building on the other side of campus. My stomach churns with unease, a cocktail of adrenaline and dread swirling inside me. I don't have a plan or even the perfect words, but that doesn't matter.

I can't allow this to continue.

The closer I get, the heavier the air feels, like a weight pressing down on me. By the time I step through the double doors of the administration building, my palms are damp, and my breathing feels uneven. I straighten my spine as I approach the elevator.

The ride to the fifth floor is slow and agonizing. My reflection in the shiny metal doors stares back at me, pale and uncertain.

When the elevator dings, I step into the hall, the squeak of my

Chucks echoing in the quiet space. Each step toward his office at the end of the corridor makes my pulse thunder louder in my ears. Just before I reach the door, I pause, my fingers curling into fists at my sides. A small voice in my head whispers to turn back and avoid the confrontation altogether.

But I refuse to do that.

Summoning every ounce of courage I can muster, I push forward. The secretary at the desk looks up from her computer with a polite smile. Her perfectly pressed blazer and impeccable bun only make me feel more out of place.

"Hi," I say, my voice shakier than I'd like. I clear my throat and try again. "Is Mr. Sanderson available?"

Her smile tightens, and she tilts her head. "Do you have an appointment?"

"No, but it's important. I just need a few moments of his time." The words tumble out too quickly, betraying my nerves.

She studies me for a few seconds before picking up the phone on her desk. "One moment, please."

As she dials, I clutch the strap of my bag, my fingers digging into the worn leather. The muffled sound of her conversation reaches me, but I'm unable to focus on the words. My thoughts are a jumble of anxiety and resolve.

After a short exchange, she hangs up the phone and gestures toward the door. "You can go in. He has a few minutes."

My heart lurches as I nod, swallowing hard. "Thank you."

With a deep breath, I step toward the door, my hand hovering over the brass handle. I force myself to turn it and push the door open, ready to face whatever comes next.

Richard Sanderson sits behind a massive, polished desk. His sharp, calculating eyes snap up the moment I enter, narrowing with suspicion as they rake over me.

"Can I help you?" he asks, his tone clipped and unwelcoming.

I square my shoulders, willing the tremor in my hands to disappear. "Mr. Sanderson, my name is Holland Tate. I'm a friend of Bridger's."

His gaze hardens, and he leans back in his high-backed leather chair, folding his hands over his stomach. The faintest flicker of disdain plays at the corner of his mouth. "What about him?"

My heart hammers against my ribs as I take a hesitant step forward, gripping the strap of my bag like it's the only thing tethering me to the ground.

My throat feels like sandpaper as I force myself to speak. "I know about Garret."

The air in the room shifts. His expression freezes for a split second before his eyes narrow. "Excuse me?"

I lick my dry lips, summoning every ounce of courage I have left. "I know that Garret Akeman is your son," I say, the words slicing through the tense silence.

Richard's jaw tightens, and his fingers drum against the armrest of his chair. "You're overstepping, Miss Tate," he says in warning. "This is none of your concern."

"None of my concern?" I echo. "You're pitting two brothers against each other without one of them even knowing it. You've been lying to Bridger his entire life. He has a right to know the truth!"

His eyes flash with something that might be anger or something darker. My hands tremble, but I keep them at my sides, unwilling to show weakness.

"If you cared about him at all," I continue, my voice steady despite the storm brewing inside me, "you'd stop hiding the truth from him and do what's right."

"You have no idea what you're talking about," he snaps. "Bridger doesn't need your meddling. I suggest you stay out of matters that don't concern you."

I lift my chin. "I'm not meddling. I'm standing up for someone I care about. Someone who deserves better than the lies you've been feeding him."

The tension in the room turns suffocating.

"You're playing a dangerous game, Miss Tate. Be careful it doesn't backfire."

The threat in his words settles over me, heavy and oppressive.

"The only person playing games here is you," I say. "And I'm done letting you get away with it. If you won't tell him what's going on, I will."

"Tell me what?"

I whirl around so fast I nearly lose my balance, and my heart plummets to the floor when I see Bridger filling the doorway. His expression is a storm of confusion, shock, and anger. His eyes dart between me and his father, searching for answers.

"Bridger..." My voice is barely audible.

This isn't the way I wanted him to find out.

Without acknowledging me, he steps into the office, his movements deliberate. "Is it true?" His words hang heavy in the air as his gaze locks on his father. "Is Garret your son?"

Richard's cold glare shifts to me.

For a moment, the room is silent except for the heavy thudding of my pulse.

The older man rises from his chair, his expression unreadable, as he tugs at his tie to straighten it. "This is neither the time nor the place for this discussion."

Bridger's jaw clenches, and a muscle tics in his cheek. Anger radiates off him as he takes a step forward. "Don't give me that bullshit. Just answer the damn question."

Richard doesn't respond.

His silence is louder than any denial or confirmation could have been.

Bridger's bitter laugh echoes through the office. "Un-fucking-believable." He turns abruptly, brushing past me without so much as a glance, and heads for the door.

"Bridger, wait!" I call out, my voice cracking, as I chase after him.

He stops just outside the office, his shoulders rigid and his fists clenched at his sides. Slowly, he turns to face me. There's no way to escape the way his eyes blaze with hurt and betrayal.

"You knew?"

I falter under his piercing gaze. "Garret told me yesterday," I admit, my voice trembling. "I wanted to—"

"The messages," he interrupts, his voice raw and accusing. "They were from him, weren't they?"

I nod, the lump in my throat making it hard to speak. "Yes."

His face contorts with a mix of anger and disbelief. When I step closer, desperate to explain, he retreats, his body language screaming at me to stay away. The distance between us feels insurmountable.

"Don't," he snaps. "You should have told me."

"I'm so sorry," I whisper, my chest aching. "I was trying to do the right thing."

He shakes his head, his laugh devoid of humor. "Yeah, well, you didn't."

And just like that, he turns and walks away, his footsteps echoing down the hallway. I stand frozen, tears stinging my eyes as my heart shatters for the boy I've grown to care about.

And for the man who deserved so much better.

# WESTERN UNIVERSITY CHAT APP

FragileLikeABomb

Why do I get the feeling you're the type who secretly likes Taylor Swift?

ColdAsIce17

I'm offended by the "secretly."

FragileLikeABomb

So you do like her?

ColdAsIce17

I didn't say that.

FragileLikeABomb

You didn't deny it either. It's okay, Cold. You're safe here.

ColdAsIce17

Safe? Fragile, you're the last person I'd feel safe around.

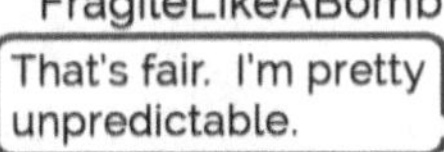

FragileLikeABomb

That's fair.  I'm pretty unpredictable.

# BRIDGER

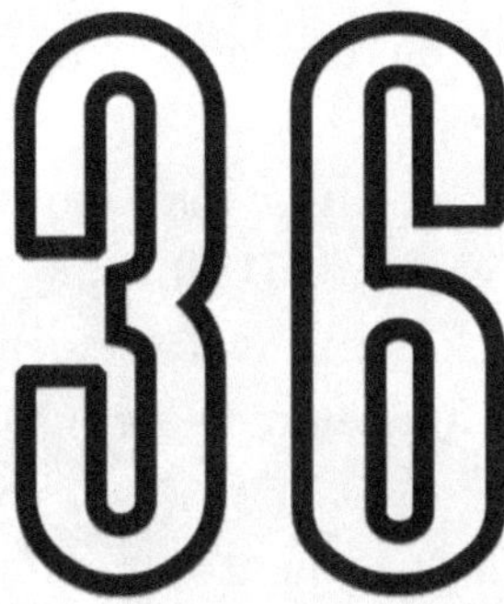

I stand outside Garret's apartment, staring at his door with its cheap paint and crooked numbers, trying to get my shit together. The night air seeps through my jacket, but the chill has nothing to do with why my hands are shaking.

I could bail. Turn around, go home, pretend I never found out the truth that's eating me alive.

But I didn't come this far to chicken out now.

Before I can overthink it, I knock. The sound echoes through the empty hallway, loud enough to make me wince. My knuckles sting, but I barely notice over the way my heart's trying to punch through my ribs. The seconds drag as I wait, counting breaths until I hear footsteps approaching from within the apartment.

My pulse jumps when Garret opens the door, his expression shifting from mild curiosity to a wall of ice.

"What do you want, Sanderson?" He blocks the doorway, arms crossed.

I clench my fists at my sides. There's no point in dancing around this. "I know."

For a split second, confusion clouds his face before his defenses snap back into place. "You... She told you?"

"No." A bitter laugh escapes. "Dick did."

Garret's jaw tightens, his posture going rigid. The air between us feels thick enough to choke on.

"Let me guess." He leans against the doorframe, his casualness belying the thick tension that radiates off him. "You're here to remind me that you'll be the one who gets the keys to the kingdom?"

"I don't want a damn thing from him. You want it? Take it."

Something flashes in his eyes. Doubt maybe, or disbelief.

"I came to talk," I say, keeping my voice steady. "Can I come in?"

There's a brief hesitation before he steps back and gestures for me to come inside. "Fine."

I step into the small apartment. The faint scent of stale coffee hangs in the air. The furniture is mismatched. There's an old plaid couch, a wobbly side table, and a chair that's seen better days. It feels oddly comforting in its imperfections. It's the kind of place that has been lived in, a stark contrast to the cold, museum-like perfection of Dick's mansion. Somehow, this feels more real.

Garret takes the chair by the window, leaving me the couch. I hesitate before sitting down, the cushion sagging slightly beneath my weight. The physical distance is nothing compared to the years of lies that stretch between us. His expression falters for a fraction of a second, and something vulnerable flashes in his eyes before the disdain returns.

I can't stop staring at him, searching for proof. Something in the jaw, maybe. The eyes. The kind of thing that should've told me we shared blood all along.

"What?" he snaps when he catches me looking.

I drag a hand through my hair, exhaling slowly. "Sorry. I just... I don't know where to start. This is a lot."

He leans back in the chair and crosses his arms over his chest. "Yeah, no kidding."

The tension in the room presses down on me until it becomes unbearable. "How long have you known?"

His lips curve into something that's not quite a smile. "I met Richard when I was ten. He'd show up every few months, have dinner, write a check, then disappear again. Real father-of-the-year material."

My stomach churns. "That was it?"

"He had his 'real' family." Garret's jaw clenches. "We were just an afterthought."

I think about Dick's cold presence in my life and how much I've hated it. And yet, sitting here, I realize that Garret might have traded places with me in a heartbeat, just for the chance to matter to him.

"I didn't know," I say quietly. "I never suspected—"

"Of course you didn't," Garret interrupts, his eyes hard. "Richard made damn sure of that. He keeps everything in nice, neat boxes so nothing spills over."

The bitterness in his tone lingers in the air, and I don't know what to say to make it better.

I lean forward, my elbows pressing into my knees as I search his face for answers. "Did you know about me? That you had a brother?"

"No." He shakes his head. "Richard never talked about his personal life. I just thought he was a businessman who traveled a lot. That's what I told people when they asked about my dad."

"What about freshman year?" The question burns on my tongue. "When we met?"

"Funny thing," he says, though there isn't a trace of humor in his voice. "He told me he didn't want me playing hockey, said it was a distraction or some bullshit like that. But I refused to budge. Hockey's the only thing I've ever had." His gaze hardens, his voice dropping. "Now I realize it was never about hockey. He didn't want us on the same ice, in the same room, figuring out the truth."

Another piece of the puzzle clicks into place, and I exhale slowly. "He didn't want me to play either. For years, he's been pushing me to quit."

Something sparks in Garret's eyes. Understanding maybe, or solidarity. "It didn't take long to put it together after we met."

I sit back as his words sink in. "Why didn't you tell me?"

Garret glances away as his jaw tightens. "Richard said he'd handle it when the time was right, and I believed him. Took a while to figure out the joke was on me." His voice cracks slightly as he pushes through it. "There was never going to be a right time. He was never going to acknowledge me. My mom had to threaten him just to get him to take responsibility at all. And even then, it was all behind closed doors. Like I didn't exist."

"I'm sorry," I say. The words feel inadequate. "You didn't deserve that shit."

Garret blinks, his expression unreadable. Then he leans back in his chair, the tension in his shoulders loosening. "All my life, I've been a dirty little secret," he says quietly. "And I got tired of it."

I nod, the air between us heavy with unspoken understanding. "No one should have to feel that way."

For a moment, neither of us speaks. The silence that stretches between us feels like a fragile thread.

I lean forward, locking eyes with Garret, my voice low but steady. "Is that why you started fucking with me?" For the first time, the anger that's been burning in my gut feels hollow.

He exhales slowly as his expression remains guarded. "I wanted him to see that you weren't the perfect son. That you weren't untouchable."

A humorless chuckle escapes from my throat. "Perfect? He never thought I was perfect. Hell, it was always the opposite. Most of the time, I was just a nuisance he had to deal with. Something to be fixed or ignored."

Garret's gaze sharpens, and his voice softens just enough to catch me off guard. "The bruises were from him, weren't they?"

It's not really a question. Even though part of me wants to deny it, to shove the truth back down where it can't be exposed, I refuse to cover anything our asshole father has done.

"Yeah," I admit quietly.

His face falls, guilt clouding his features like a shadow. "I'm sorry for dragging you through all of this."

I let out a slow breath, the animosity between us easing as I sit back. "I'm not."

"You aren't?"

I shake my head. "No. I'm glad the truth is out there. For what it's worth, I wish you'd just told me everything from the beginning. We could've had each other's backs instead of whatever the hell this has been."

He stares at me, his jaw working like he's struggling to find the right words. Finally, he nods, his voice rough. "That probably would have been better."

The silence between us feels heavy, but it's not suffocating. It's like the air has shifted. The tension replaced with something raw. Something real.

"We're brothers," I say softly. "We don't have to keep tearing each other down. We've got enough shit to deal with without that."

Garret drops his gaze to the floor. For a second, I think he might argue, but then he looks up. "Maybe it's time we stop."

It's not a resolution, but it feels like a start.

I push to my feet, sliding my hands into my pockets. "I should go."

He follows me to the door, leaning against the frame. The hostility from earlier is gone, replaced by something almost tentative. "I'm glad you stopped by."

"Me too." I hold his gaze. "We'll figure this out."

His nod feels real this time. No sarcasm, no bitterness. Just a quiet agreement to work through our relationship.

The cool air hits me as I step outside, clearing away the fog of tension that's been clouding my head. I walk to my BMW, each step measured, like I'm testing new ground. When I slide behind the wheel, my chest feels tight, but not in the usual way. There isn't the anger or frustration that's become my constant companion.

It's more like relief.

As if a missing piece has finally clicked into place.

My phone buzzes, and my stomach tightens when I see the name.

FRAGILELIKEABOMB

Just checking in to see how you are.

For the first time in years, I feel lighter.

ME

Truth?

FRAGILELIKEABOMB

Always.

ME

Feels like my life's been blown apart.

Three dots appear, and I find myself leaning forward, my heart inexplicably racing as I wait for her reply.

FRAGILELIKEABOMB

Must be something in the air. Same here.
Everything's falling apart.

Her words hit like a jolt of electricity. I hesitate, debating whether to take this conversation where my mind is already going. But I can't stop myself.

ME

The girl I've been seeing is amazing, but...

FRAGILELIKEABOMB

But what?

Something about her response makes my heart thump hard.

ME

I'm not sure I can trust her. She was keeping
shit from me.

The pause feels endless. I grip the phone tighter as my pulse pounds in my ears. When her message comes through, it hits like a punch.

FRAGILELIKEABOMB

Trust is hard. Especially when you're afraid of
getting hurt. But if she's worth it, you'll find a
way to work it out.

I stare at the screen, her words circling in my head. There's something about the way she writes, the understanding in her tone. It feels... familiar.

Too familiar.

For a second, I wonder...

Could *FragileLikeABomb* and the girl I can't stop thinking about be the same person?

I shake my head, trying to dislodge the thought.

No fucking way.

That's impossible.

It has to be, right?

As I start the car, the pieces keep trying to align themselves. The timing of her messages. The way she gets me. How she always seems to know exactly what to say.

Maybe impossible isn't the right word anymore.

After all, I just found out I have a brother.

What's one more life-changing revelation?

HOLLAND

The room feels emptier than it should, like a hollowed-out shell of what it was just days ago. Maybe it's because most of my belongings are already stuffed into the duffel bag on the bed. It's the same one I dragged here weeks ago when staying with Bridger felt like punishment.

At the time, I'd counted down the days until I could leave. I didn't want to be anywhere near him.

Now, the thought of walking out that door feels like a kick to the gut.

I smooth out a shirt before folding it neatly and placing it on top of the pile in my bag. My fingers linger on the fabric, and my throat tightens as I stare at the open zipper. Each piece of clothing I add feels like another goodbye I'm not ready for.

I don't want to go.

Not anymore.

At some point, without realizing it, being here with Bridger started to feel like home. Not the kind I grew up in, but the kind I'd always hoped for. Safe, warm, full of something I can't quite put into words.

With him.

But safe is a lie, isn't it?

A fleeting illusion.

Especially when the fragile trust we've been building is fractured.

A few days ago, everything felt precariously close to perfect. Now, it feels like I'm standing on shattered glass, every step slicing deeper.

The sharp buzz of my phone on the nightstand cuts through my thoughts, pulling me back to the present. I hesitate, my hand hovering in the air, my heart pounding.

I reach for it and swipe at the screen. *ColdAsIce17's* name lights it up like a beacon. The familiar sight makes my chest ache. It's a mix of comfort and something far more complicated.

I tap the message open and hold my breath as his words appear.

COLDASICE17

You've been seeing someone, right?

I frown.

ME

Yes. How did you know?

COLDASICE17

Not important. Do you care about him?

The message stares back at me, sharp and loaded. I sit down on the edge of the bed, my heart sinking like a stone, as my thoughts churn. Finally, I type out the truth, my chest tightening as I hit send.

ME

I do. But I'm pretty sure it's over.

The reply comes back immediately.

COLDASICE17

Is that what you want?

The weight of his question presses down on me, making it harder to breathe. I stare at the screen, my eyes burning with the threat of tears as I wrestle with the answer.

*Do I want this to be over?*

No. It's not what I want.

Not at all.

But what does it matter when everything feels broken beyond repair?

My thumbs move before I can stop them.

ME

No.

The silence that follows feels endless, each second stretching painfully thin. I wait, half hoping for another message, half terrified of what it might say. When my phone finally buzzes, the words on the screen make my heart stutter.

COLDASICE17

Do you think he cares for you?

My throat constricts as I reread the question.

Do I think Bridger cares for me?

After everything that's happened, I don't know anymore.

I force myself to type the truth.

ME

I'm not sure.

This time, the pause is longer.

Long enough for doubt to creep in and make me second-guess everything. My gaze drifts to the half-packed duffel bag on the bed. Maybe I should just grab it and go before Bridger returns.

It would be easier that way, wouldn't it?

Less messy. We can go back to avoiding each other.

That thought has a stab of pain pricking at me.

My phone buzzes, cutting through the storm in my head.

COLDASICE17

Maybe you should open the door and find out.

My brow furrows, confusion rippling through me. My fingers tremble as I type back.

ME
What?

The response is instant, almost demanding.

COLDASICE17
Open the door, Holland, and find out.

The air in the room seems to thin as realization slams into me. My pulse hammers in my ears, drowning out everything else as my gaze shoots to Bridger's bedroom door.

Another buzz.

COLDASICE17
Well? What are you waiting for?

The moment feels surreal, like it's happening to someone else as I push to my feet. My mind races with a thousand possibilities, but none of them make the least bit of sense. The knob feels cold under my hand, my palm clammy with sweat as I twist it slowly. Each second has my heart pounding harder.

The door swings open.

And there he is.

Bridger stands in the hallway with his phone in hand. His gray eyes are locked on mine, steady and unwavering, but there's something different in them. A softness I've never seen before.

Vulnerability.

I don't know who moves first, but suddenly, we're standing inches apart, unspoken words hanging between us.

"Hi," he says, his voice quiet.

A sob bursts free from my chest before I can stop it. Without thinking, I throw myself into his arms, my hands clutching at his neck as if he's a lifeline. He pulls me against him with a fierceness that undoes me.

"I'm sorry," I choke out against his shoulder, the words tumbling from my lips in a rush. "I should have told you the truth when I found out. I thought I was doing the right thing."

He pulls back just enough to look at me, his hands steadying me as his gaze meets mine. His expression is raw, stripped bare in a way that makes my heart ache. "I know," he says, his voice low and rough. "I talked to Garret. And now that I've had time to process it, I understand. I get why you didn't tell me."

As his hand holding the phone drops back to his side, my gaze follows. My heart thunders as the realization slams into me.

"It's you," I whisper, barely able to form the words. "It's been you all along."

His fingers tighten on my waist, his chest rising with a slow inhale. "I should have realized it earlier," he murmurs, his gaze searching mine. "Every message, every conversation... it was always you."

Tears blur my vision as a shaky laugh bubbles up from my throat. "Yeah," I say, voice thick with emotion. "It was me."

"Just so you know," he says, his tone dipping, "I care about you, Holland. I've always cared about you."

The air between us shifts, thickening with emotion and the pull that's been there from the start. A shiver races down my spine as his face moves closer, his eyes searching mine for the slightest hesitation. When he finds none, his lips brush against mine. The kiss is soft at first. Almost as if he's testing the waters. But then it deepens until it feels very much like coming home.

When we finally pull apart, I rest my forehead against his, our breaths mingling. For the first time in what feels like forever, the chaos quiets, and everything slides into place.

His gaze slices to my packed bag resting on the bed, and for a moment, fear ghosts across his face. He swallows hard before his eyes lock on mine again.

"Stay," he says in a low rumble that sends a shiver through me. "Don't leave."

A smile tugs at my lips, tentative at first but growing as warmth floods my body. "I wasn't planning on it," I admit, my voice steady.

A small smile breaks across his face, and just like that, the cracks between us begin to heal.

BRIDGER
SANDERSON
17
17
WILDCATS

The locker room buzzes with a frenzied energy that's impossible to ignore. Laughter bounces off the walls, mingling with the steady rhythm of chatter, the sharp rip of tape being peeled, and the metallic clink of skates being adjusted. The air is charged with the kind of electricity that comes with knowing the season hangs in the balance.

One game.

One shot at making the Frozen Four.

And yet, despite the stakes, my focus is split.

My gaze drifts to the far corner of the room where Garret sits alone, head bent as he tightens his laces. His movements are methodical, but there's a stiffness to his posture that gives him away. The guys have been giving him the cold shoulder for days. A silent punishment for the way he's acted. Most of them have had issues with him at one point or another, but none know the full story.

I think it's time to change that.

My stomach churns as I glance around the room. The thought of putting this out there feels heavy, almost suffocating, but it's a weight I can't keep carrying.

Not alone.

Taking a steadying breath, I push to my feet and step toward the center of the room. The hum of conversation doesn't immediately stop, so I clear my throat, loud enough to cut through the noise.

The guys pause as their attention shifts to me. Ryder leans against his locker, one brow arched in curiosity. "What's up, Sanderson? You got some pre-game pep talk locked and loaded?"

A few chuckles ripple through the room. My palms feel clammy, and I wipe them against my pants. "Not exactly." I glance at Garret, whose head jerks up at my words, his eyes narrowing in confusion.

The heaviness of the moment presses down harder.

Maybe I should've talked to him first.

Maybe I'm about to step over a line I have no business crossing.

But the truth matters, and it's time to let it out.

"Before we hit the ice, there's something I need to say. Something you all need to know."

The room falls completely silent, the buzz of energy replaced by a tense anticipation. All eyes are on me now. My heart pounds as I force myself to meet Garret's gaze, silently apologizing for not warning him beforehand.

Steele's expression never changes. He knows what I'm about to do. He's the only other person I told. After all, that makes Steele and Garret family.

It took a moment for my cousin to wrap his brain around that one.

I take another deep breath. "This isn't easy for me to talk about, but it's important."

Garret stiffens, his hands clenching into fists at his sides. "What are you doing, Sanderson?" His voice is quiet, but there's an edge to it.

I hold his gaze, willing him to trust me for just a second. "It's time they knew the truth."

A ripple of confusion spreads through the room, the guys exchanging glances, their expressions a mix of curiosity and concern.

"About what?" Ryder asks, his brow furrowing.

I square my shoulders, the words pressing against the back of my teeth, ready to spill out. "About Garret." My voice remains steady even though my pulse hammers in my ears. "He's not just a teammate." I pause, meeting Garret's surprised gaze. "He's my brother."

The room erupts in a chorus of shock.

Voices overlap as questions fly from every direction.

"You're hilarious, Sanderson!" Colby calls out with a roll of his eyes. "Now, stop screwing around. In case you weren't aware of it, we've got a game to win."

"It's official, he's lost it." Madden picks up his helmet before placing it on his head and fastening the chinstrap. "Is it too late to hold another intervention?"

"I'm not fucking around with you guys." My lips twitch despite the tension that rushes through my veins. "I just found out that Garret's my half-brother."

Hayes shakes his head. "You know what? I think he's being serious."

"Talk about a real plot twist," Ford adds.

Garret's jaw tightens, his expression unreadable as he looks away, his hands flexing against his thighs. Tension vibrates from every line of his body.

"Yes, I'm serious," I continue, cutting through the noise. "And no, I didn't know until recently. But this isn't about me or him. It's about us as a team. We've all been through enough this season. We need to stick together now more than ever."

The guys quiet down again, my confession settling over them.

Ryder is the first to speak, his voice carefully measured. "Is this true?" he asks, looking at Garret.

Garret lifts his head, his jaw tightening. For a long moment, he doesn't answer, and I think he might shut down completely. But then he nods, his voice clipped when he finally speaks. "Yeah, it is."

Another ripple of murmurs spreads through the room, but this time, it's softer.

Less judgmental.

More understanding.

"I know this is a lot," I say, my gaze sweeping over my teammates. "But Garret's one of us. He's family, in more ways than one. And if there's one thing I've learned this season, it's that family fights for each other. No matter what."

Silence stretches out, thick with unspoken words and emotions. Then Steele stands, stepping closer to me and clapping a hand on my shoulder. "Let's win this thing," he says simply.

The atmosphere in the room eases, the focus shifting back to the game. The guys nod in agreement, the chatter resuming as they finish gearing up.

Garret doesn't say anything as I move back to my locker, but as I sit down, I catch his gaze.

Coach Philips pokes his head into the locker room. "It's time, gentlemen. Are we ready to play some hockey tonight?"

The place ignites with energy as Ryder steps forward, his voice booming. "Wildcats on three!"

The team surges into action, gathering in a tight circle. Fists slam together with a resounding force, our voices blending into a unified roar that echoes off the walls. "One, two, three—Wildcats!"

The guys file out of the locker room as they head toward the ice. The air buzzes with anticipation and determination.

I linger behind, my attention locked on Garret as he stays rooted in place, his helmet cradled under his arm. His expression is difficult to read. It's a blend of tension, relief, and something that looks like gratitude.

When he finally looks at me, his voice comes out rough and low. "Thank you for saying all that and standing up for me."

I step closer, shaking my head. "You don't have to thank me," I say firmly, my tone leaving no room for argument. "You're my brother. That's all there is to it."

His throat bobs as he swallows, and he nods, his grip tightening on his helmet. "Still, it meant a lot. More than you know."

I reach out, clapping him on the shoulder with enough force to jolt him out of whatever spiral of emotions he's in. "Now, let's get out there and kick some Northwood ass."

His lips twitch into a small, hesitant smile before spreading into something genuine. He lets out a quiet laugh, and for the first time, it feels like we've finally broken through the wall that's stood between us.

"Yeah," he says, his voice steadier. "Let's do that."

Without another word, I pull him in for a quick hug before we head toward the door together, ready to take on the game as brothers.

As Garret and I step into the hallway, the sight of Dick leaning against the wall stops us both in our tracks.

"Bridger," he snaps. "I don't appreciate being ignored."

I exhale slowly as my jaw tightens. Without looking at Garret, I reach out and place a hand on his arm, silently signaling him to stay put. His muscles tense under my palm, but he doesn't move.

"There's nothing for us to talk about right now," I say evenly, meeting Dick's icy glare head-on. My tone is calm, but there's no mistaking the steel behind it. "When I'm ready, I'll reach out. Until then, I'd appreciate some space."

His face reddens as his composure cracks. "You listen to me—"

"Not today," I cut him off.

The hallway feels stifling, the air heavy with the tension that crackles between us. Dick opens his mouth, but I don't stick around to hear whatever venom he's about to spew. I give Garret's arm a nudge, and we move past him, our skates thudding softly against the rubber mat.

"Is he always like that?" Garret mutters under his breath, his voice low enough that only I can hear.

"Pretty much." I don't bother looking back as Dick's angry sputtering fades into the background.

For the first time in forever, I don't feel like I'm walking alone. Garret matches my stride, and the realization that I've got my brother beside me, hits me square in the chest. It's a strange, unfamiliar comfort, but one I'm willing to lean into.

When we reach the ice, Coach Philips is waiting, clipboard in hand and his expression all business. He glances between me and Garret before nodding to where the rest of the team is warming up.

"You ready, Sanderson?" he asks, his tone steady but expectant.

I pull my helmet over my head and glance at Garret. When he gives me a small nod, I turn back to Coach.

"More than ready," I say, my voice carrying a quiet determination.

With that, I step onto the ice, the sound of skates slicing into the frozen surface mingling with the deafening cheers of the crowd.

It's time to play.

HOLLAND

The arena vibrates with energy, the kind of electric buzz that thrums under your skin and sets your heart racing. There's a steady hum of excitement that ripples through the stands as fans decked out in Wildcats jerseys and face paint cheer. It's impossible not to get caught up in it.

I'm wedged between Willow and Juliette, the three of us packed tightly into a row surrounded by a sea of Wildcats fans. Around us, the rest of the girls—Carina, Viola, Stella, Fallyn, Britt, and Ava—are scattered in small groups, their laughter and shouts rising above the growing roar of the crowd.

For the first time in forever, I feel like I actually fit in somewhere.

I belong.

It's not that I've intentionally been a loner. Willow has always been my ride-or-die, the one constant in my life.

But outside of her?

Friends have never come easily. I've spent years building walls, bracing myself against the sting of disappointment and rejection. Sitting here with this group of girls who've embraced me without question feels different.

Nice in a way I wouldn't have expected.

"Wait a minute," Willow says, her tone one of playful disbelief as she leans toward me. Her elbow digs gently into my side. "Is that a smile on your face? It's almost like you're having a good time."

I snort, the sound turning into a laugh as I nudge her back. "Don't push it."

Juliette, seated on my other side, turns toward me. "Oh, she's definitely smiling. We need photographic evidence." She whips out her phone and holds it up, angling it for a selfie. "Come on, Holland, give me your best game-day grin."

"Absolutely not," I protest, ducking my head as Juliette snaps a photo anyway. The screen lights up with her triumphant laugh.

"Got it," she announces, showing Willow the blurry but unmistakable proof of my smile.

Carina spins around from the row in front of us, her glossy blonde ponytail swishing as she rests her arms on the back of her seat. Her eyes are bright with excitement as she grins at me. "Okay, can I just say how much I love that you and Bridger are a thing now? Like, we all saw the tension building, but still. I can't help feeling there's more to the story than you're letting on."

The group falls silent, and suddenly all eyes are on me. Heat creeps up my neck and into my cheeks as I shift in my seat.

I manage a wink, trying to play it cool. "Let's just say there's always more to the story."

Juliette's brows shoot up, and she leans in, practically vibrating with curiosity. "Well, now you have to spill. What happened between you two? We need details."

Before I can come up with a way to deflect, Fallyn saves me. "Forget Bridger for a second," she says, her voice laced with admiration. "Can we just talk about how badass you are for working at the Envy Room while taking a full course load? Like, seriously. I'd be flat on my face trying to do all that."

Laughter ripples through the group, and I roll my eyes, though I can't stop the grin that tugs at my lips. It's strange, this feeling of being accepted without hesitation or judgment. I spent so long assuming I had to keep parts of myself hidden, that friendships like this weren't meant for someone like me. But here they are, lifting me up instead of tearing me down.

"You want a lesson? Pole 101?"

Viola perks up, raising her hand like she's in class. "Sign me up. I've always wanted to learn how to spin without falling on my ass."

"You'd kill it," I say with a laugh. "Just don't come crying to me when you pull a hammy. Happens to me more than I'd like to admit."

"Deal," she says, her laughter joining the chorus around us. The group dissolves into playful chatter, and for a moment, the conversation shifts away from Bridger.

The lights in the arena dim slightly, and the hum of the crowd rises. The announcer's voice booms through the speakers, calling out the players' names as they skate onto the ice. My heart kicks into overdrive when Bridger's name is announced. He glides out with an easy confidence, his movements fluid and precise.

And then, as if he knows I'm here, he glances up into the stands. He can't possibly see me amidst the crowd, but for a fleeting second, it feels like his gaze locks on mine. A warmth envelops me, and a smile tugs at my lips.

The puck drops, and the game begins.

The arena comes alive, the roar of the crowd like a living, breathing thing that surges and swells with every play. I cheer louder than I ever have before, my voice mingling with the cheers and shouts around me. My eyes stay glued to Bridger as he commands the ice, blocking shots, making passes, and keeping the team in control. Every time the announcer calls his name, an undeniable sense of pride fills me.

He's incredible.

Strong, determined, relentless.

And mine.

As the game unfolds, it's no longer just about the Wildcats.

I'm not just cheering for the team.

I'm cheering for him.

The guy who's always held a piece of my heart.

BRIDGER
SANDERSON
17
17
WILDCATS

Slap Shotz is packed to the brim when we walk through the door. The air is thick with the buzz of celebration and the tang of beer. We're heading to the Frozen Four, and judging by the charged atmosphere in the bar, the whole town is riding high from the excitement.

I've got Holland tucked under my arm, and despite the chaos surrounding us, my attention keeps drifting to her. She laughs with Willow and the rest of the girls. Her eyes are bright and there's a smirk curving her lips.

It's a sight I'll never get tired of.

"Bridger," a voice interrupts, pulling me out of my thoughts.

I glance up to see Garret approaching. His hands are jammed into his pockets and his shoulders are hunched. Uncertainty is etched across his face as his gaze darts between us.

"Holland," he says, his voice quieter than usual, almost hesitant. "Do you have a moment to talk?"

She stiffens slightly as she nods.

"I just..." He exhales heavily, glancing at the floor before meeting her gaze. "I want to apologize for putting you in the position I did. Lying to Bridger, making you cover for me, dragging you into the messages. All of it. You didn't deserve that, and I'm sorry."

Holland studies him for a long moment as his apology lingers in the air. Just when I think she'll tell him to go fuck himself, she surprises me by reaching out and touching his arm.

"Thank you," she says softly, her tone steady. "I appreciate it. And I get it—you were hurting. But next time, maybe don't burn everything down around you to deal with it, okay?"

A quiet, self-deprecating laugh escapes him as he rubs the back of his neck. "Yeah. Lesson learned."

"Good." Her tone is resolute but not unkind. When her gaze meets mine, there's something in it that makes my breath catch.

Trust.

"All right," Garret says, shifting awkwardly. "I'm gonna grab a drink."

"Hey," I call after him. It's only when he stops, glancing back over his shoulder to meet my gaze that I say, "You're good, man. *We're* good."

His expression softens as he nods, and without another word, he disappears into the crowd.

Holland leans into me, her head resting against my shoulder. "I like this version of you."

"Yeah?" I tighten my arm around her, savoring the warmth of her against my side. "What version is that?"

"The one who forgives," she says, her lips curving into a small smile as she tips her face up to meet mine. "It's kind of hot."

I smirk, lowering my head so our foreheads nearly touch. "Only kind of?"

Her chuckle is soft, her breath warm against my skin. "Don't push your luck, Sanderson."

Around us, laughter and conversation fill the space, but there's something different in the air tonight. Something that feels more final. Not in a bad way, just in the way things shift when one chapter comes to an end and another one begins.

Ryder stands beside Juliette, his arm slung around her shoulders, his fingers absently playing with the ends of her hair. Ford and Carina are close by, hands clasped together, their eyes locked like they're in their own private world. Stella leans into Riggs, their grins matching as she whispers something in his ear. Viola nudges Madden playfully, her teasing met with a low chuckle as he pulls her against him.

Fallyn and Wolf are wrapped up in each other, her fingers resting lightly on his chest as he watches her as if she's the only person in the room. The only one he sees. Colby and Britt share a quiet moment, their hands linked, their smiles easy. Maverick tugs Willow closer, his lips pressing to her temple like he still can't believe she's his.

And Ava and Hayes?

They stand side by side, no grand gestures, just a quiet, undeniable certainty between them.

Out of everyone, their relationship is probably the biggest surprise of all.

The nine of us met as incoming freshmen, grew into men over the years, and found love stories none of us expected. Now, we're moving forward, each on our own path, ready to tackle whatever comes next.

One thing is for certain—no matter where life takes us, we've found something rare, something unshakable.

We started as teammates.

Now, we're family.

Not by blood but by choice. The kind of family you build and hold on to because they're the ones who truly matter.

My gaze shifts to Sully, the owner of Slap Shotz, when he hauls himself onto the small stage in the corner, his burly frame and booming voice instantly commanding everyone's attention. He raises his arms, palms out, and his deep voice cuts through the chatter like a knife.

"Hey!" Sully shouts, his grin as wide as the room itself. "Quiet down, you rowdy bunch, and listen up!"

The bar falls into a semi-silence, with only a few murmurs trailing off as all eyes turn to the stage. Sully points a finger toward our team, his expression full of pride.

"I couldn't be prouder of these guys and the season they've had. But let's get one thing straight—it ain't over yet, is it?"

The room erupts into cheers and whistles, the energy palpable. A grin tugs at my lips as Sully raises his hands again, motioning for everyone to settle.

"That's right! We've got a Frozen Four trophy to bring back to this town!" His voice grows louder, more animated. "But tonight? Tonight, we celebrate! So, who's gonna kick things off with some karaoke?"

The crowd roars in response, and my grin widens as Sully leans into the mic. "Come on! Don't be shy now!"

There's only one thing left to do to make this night complete.

Adrenaline hums through my veins, drowning out any nerves as I weave through the packed bar toward the stage.

"Bridger, what the hell are you doing?" Holland hisses, grabbing for my hand.

I glance over my shoulder with a smirk. Her wide eyes lock on mine, a mixture of amusement and panic in her expression. "Showing you—and everyone else—exactly how I feel."

Her mouth opens, but no words come out, as I pull away and hop up onto the stage. Sully claps me on the back with a hearty laugh.

"That's what I'm talking about!" he says, handing me the mic. "What'll it be, Sanderson?"

I lean in and whisper the song choice. His brows shoot up and then his grin returns, wider than ever. "You got it."

The moment the first notes of "Everything" by Michael Bublé fill the bar, a concoction of nerves and adrenaline surges through me. It's not like I'm afraid of a crowd. I've played in front of packed arenas, for fuck's sake. But this is different.

This isn't a game.

This is me, standing under dim stage lights, gripping a mic, and putting my feelings out there in the open.

I scan the crowd until I find Holland. She's frozen in place, her gaze pinned to me, lips parted in surprise. I smirk, letting the confidence settle over me as I ease into the song.

My voice is steady, but inside, my heart pounds against my ribs. I watch as Holland's hand flies to her mouth, her cheeks flushing. The noise of the bar dulls around me and everything fades until there's just her.

The girl who drives me crazy.

The very same one I can't stay away from.

The girl I'm probably half in love with already.

This one's for her.

And only her.

When the final notes drift off and the bar explodes into applause, I set the mic down and hop off the stage without hesitation. My sole focus is closing the distance between us. My feet barely touch the floor as I stride toward her.

She's still standing, cheeks flushed, her lips parted in surprise. The second I reach her, she buries her face in my chest and her arms wind around my waist.

"Thank you," she whispers, her voice muffled against my shirt.

I rest my chin on the top of her head and press a kiss against her hair. "No, baby. Thank *you*. For being mine."

Her arms tighten, and in that moment, surrounded by the riot of celebration, there's nothing but us.

Across the room, I spot Steele at the bar, his broad shoulders tense as he leans in toward the girl who has always been his best friend. Lilah's eyes are narrowed as she glares at him. If I had to guess, I'd say he just scared off the guy who was flirting with her earlier.

I chuckle under my breath and lean into Holland, brushing my lips against her ear. "Think she'll ever figure out his feelings go way beyond friendship?"

Holland's gaze follows mine, her brow arching as she watches Lilah jab a finger at Steele's chest, her frustration clear.

"I don't know," she murmurs, her tone thoughtful. "Think he'll ever grow a pair and tell her? Aren't they both graduating this spring?"

"Yup." I grin, shaking my head. "I told him the other day when he was whining about the date she went on that he better shit or get off the pot."

Holland lets out a laugh, her eyes twinkling as she looks up at me. "Charmingly put, as always. Kind of like you, huh? Finally deciding to take matters into your own hands?"

I slide an arm around her waist and pull her closer. "Hey, I'd say my master plan worked out pretty well in the end, wouldn't you?" My lips graze hers. "After all, I finally got the girl I've always wanted."

Her cheeks flush, and that teasing smile I love so much curves her lips. "Master plan, huh? And here I thought it was all spontaneous charm."

"Let me have my moment," I reply with a mock-serious expression, earning another laugh from her. My voice drops as I press my forehead to hers. "Now, what do you say we get out of here? After that hard win tonight, I was hoping you'd consider giving me a private dance."

Holland's eyes glint with mischief, her fingers trailing over my pecs. "I think that can be arranged," she whispers, her breath ghosting over my lips.

With a grin, I take her hand and lead her toward the exit until the noise of the bar fades behind us. Tonight, there's only one thing on my mind, and she's right here, her hand warm in mine.

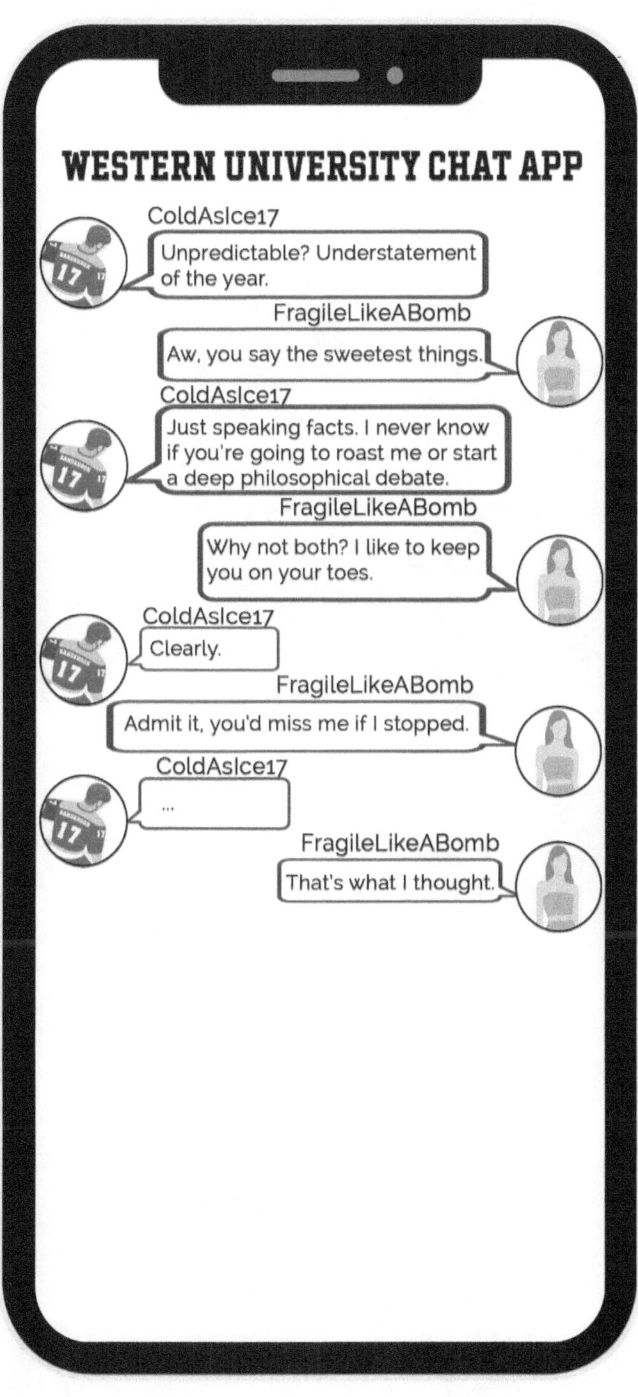
WESTERN UNIVERSITY CHAT APP
ColdAsIce17
Unpredictable? Understatement of the year.
FragileLikeABomb
Aw, you say the sweetest things.
ColdAsIce17
Just speaking facts. I never know if you're going to roast me or start a deep philosophical debate.
FragileLikeABomb
Why not both? I like to keep you on your toes.
ColdAsIce17
Clearly.
FragileLikeABomb
Admit it, you'd miss me if I stopped.
ColdAsIce17
...
FragileLikeABomb
That's what I thought.

BRIDGER
SANDERSON
17
17
WILDCATS

# EPILOGUE



*A year later...*

"**I**'m telling you, the idea is solid," I say, leaning back in my chair and tossing my pen onto the table with a flourish. "You're just salty because you didn't think of it first."

Holland's eyes narrow, and the corner of her mouth twitches in a way that tells me she's seconds away from letting loose a sarcastic retort. "Oh, please. Your groundbreaking plan involves, what, appealing to nostalgia with cheesy '90s references? Bold move, Sanderson. Really cutting-edge."

"Hey," I shoot back, folding my arms across my chest and leveling her with a look. "The '90s were iconic. If you knew anything about marketing—which, clearly, you don't—you'd know nostalgia sells. Admit it, you're scared I might be onto something."

With a snort, she rolls her eyes. "Scared? Of your Nickelodeon-themed campaign? That's rich. What's next, Sanderson? Are we going to pitch a *Rugrats* revival while we're at it?"

Before I can fire back, the door to the conference room swings open, and Uncle Joe strides in. His tie is slightly loosened, and he's cradling his usual oversized coffee mug with *World's Okayest Boss* emblazoned across it.

His gaze bounces between the two of us as a bemused expression tugs at his face. "Let me guess," he says, leaning casually against the edge of the table, "the great Sanderson-Tate marketing rivalry rages on?"

Holland leans back in her chair, crossing her legs and flashing a smug grin. "Don't worry. I'm winning, as usual."

"That's debatable," I mutter under my breath, earning a sharp elbow to the ribs for my trouble.

Joe chuckles, shaking his head as he takes a sip of coffee. "You two are something else, you know that? I'll say this, though, you've both been incredible assets to the company. But let me give you a word of advice."

Holland and I both sit up straighter, waiting for one of his infamous pearls of wisdom.

"Don't let whatever this is," he says, gesturing between us with his mug, "bleed into your personal lives. Trust me, my first two wives would tell you I did that a little too much."

Holland raises an eyebrow, and I can see the teasing retort forming on her lips, but before she can say anything, I jump in. "Don't worry, Uncle Joe," I say smoothly, draping an arm across the back of Holland's chair, "we never bring business home with us."

My fiancée nods in agreement, her tone as sweet as honey. "Absolutely. We know better than that."

Joe smirks, clearly unconvinced. "Then you're both smarter than I was at your age," he says, pushing off the table with a final nod. "Carry on. And try not to kill each other in here. You're scaring the interns."

The door clicks shut behind my uncle, leaving us alone again. A teasing smile quirks Holland's lips as she rises to her feet and gathers up her scattered notes.

I stand and loosen my tie from around my neck before tossing it onto the table. "You know," I start, stepping toward her, "he might actually be onto something. This rivalry of ours could get dangerous."

"Oh, please," she says, rolling her eyes, but the corner of her mouth twitches, betraying her amusement. "You and I both know it works for us. Besides, I'd never let it interfere with our personal lives."

"Good," I murmur, my voice dropping low as I close the space between us. My hands stray to her hips before I tug her closer. "Because I love you way too much to let some stupid work disagreement mess up what we've got."

Her breath catches as her hands rise to my chest, her fingers grazing the fabric of my shirt. "Way too much, huh?"

"That's right. Way too much," I confirm, brushing a kiss against her forehead. "More than I ever thought I could love someone."

Her teasing smile softens, and her gaze locks on mine, the usual sharp edge replaced with something deeper. "More than your '90s campaign?" she teases.

A chuckle slips free as I shake my head. "Even more than that."

My lips capture hers in a slow kiss. The world outside fades away as I lose myself in the feel of her. Her body molds perfectly to mine as her hands tangle in my shirt, anchoring me to her.

When we finally pull apart, her eyes stay closed for a beat longer, her forehead resting against mine. "I hate to ruin the moment, but," she says, her tone laced with humor, "don't forget we have my mom's wedding this weekend."

I groan, throwing my head back. "How could I forget? I've been counting down the days for months now."

With a laugh, she bites her lower lip as her eyes sparkle. "Don't worry," she says, her voice turning playful, "if you behave, I'll make it worth your while."

My head snaps down, and I raise an eyebrow, my interest piqued. "Oh, really? And what exactly did you have in mind?"

She smirks, her hands sliding up my chest. "Oh, you know... it might involve a private dance."

I tilt my head, pretending to consider her offer. "And?"

She swats my pec with a mock scowl. "What do you mean 'and'? Isn't that enough?"

I shake my head, grinning as I lower my voice to a husky whisper.

"I want a dance and a BJ. You know I like that swirly thing you do with your tongue."

With narrowed eyes, she swats at me again. "Now you're just being greedy."

"For you?" I say, leaning down until our noses are nearly touching. "Always. That's never going to change."

Her expression softens, her gaze searching mine. "I really hope it doesn't."

"It won't, baby," I promise, pulling her fully into my arms. "Not ever. This is just the beginning for us."

She buries her face in my chest. Her voice is muffled but full of emotion when she whispers, "I love you."

I hold her closer, savoring the moment and the feel of her against me. With her wrapped in my arms, and life waiting just outside the door, one thing's clear—whatever comes next in our lives, it'll be a wild ride.

And I wouldn't trade it for anything.

# WESTERN UNIVERSITY CHAT APP

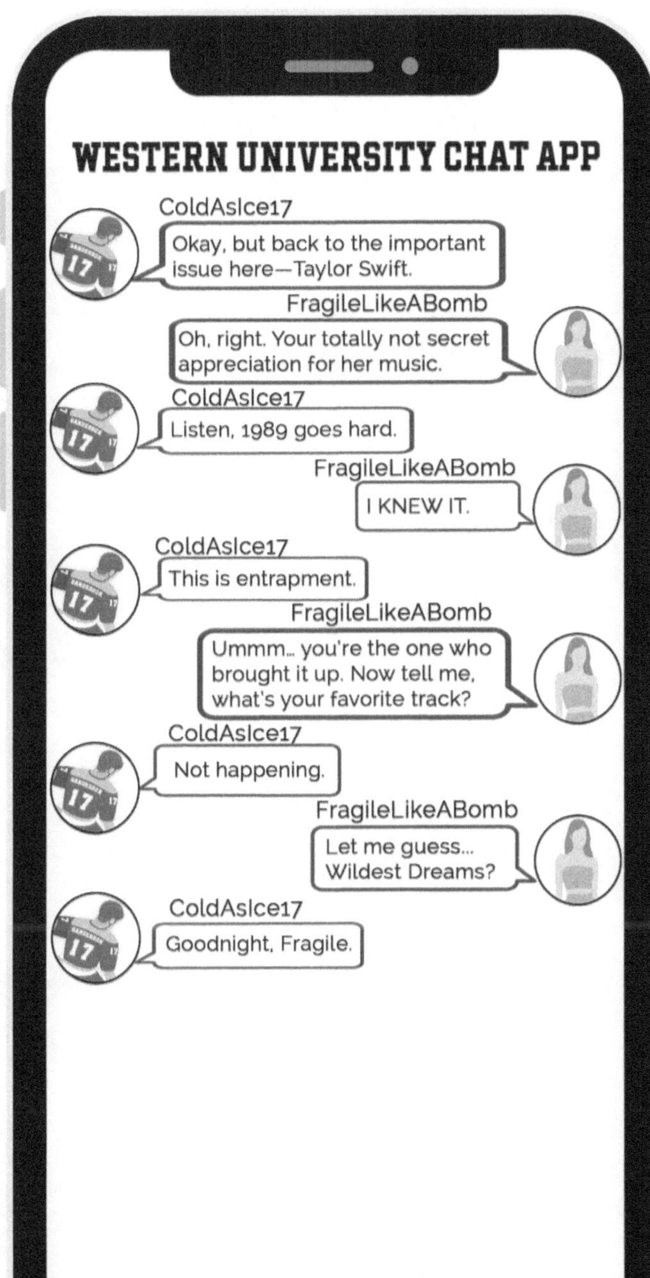

HOLLAND

*Three years later...*

The moment we step through the double doors of the Envy Room, Bridger halts and his hand tightens around mine. His gaze sweeps across the empty stage and his lips curve into a teasing grin. "Well, baby. You did it," he says, his voice warm. "There's no turning back now."

I glance up at him, a matching smile tugging at my lips as I squeeze his hand. "Nope, there isn't. Our names are officially on the dotted line. We're now the proud owners of a strip club."

With a snort, he tilts his head toward the stage with exaggerated flair. "Not just any strip club. *The* strip club."

I laugh softly, my smile fading into something more tender as I take in the room. The lights are dimmed, the tables and chairs neatly arranged, but the energy of the place still hums in the air the way it used to when it was jammed packed with customers and performers.

"It still feels surreal," I murmur, my voice quieter now. My gaze roams over the stage where countless memories were made.

"That you bought a strip club?" Bridger teases, his grin widening.

I roll my eyes and bump his hip with mine. "This place is so much more than that," I say as emotion creeps into my tone. My eyes glisten with tears as memories flood my mind. All the nights I spent hustling to pay tuition, all the laughter with my coworkers who became family, and the sense of belonging I'd always longed for. "It's the reason I could pay my way through college. It gave me a sense of family when I didn't have one. This place saved me."

Bridger's teasing expression softens as he steps closer, his arms circling me. His hands are warm, steady, and grounding. "I know, baby," he murmurs, his gray eyes locking on mine. He presses a gentle kiss to my forehead, the gesture full of affection. "I know exactly what this place means to you. For what it's worth, I couldn't be prouder of everything you've achieved."

The warmth of his words settles over me.

"You're a force to be reckoned with, Holland," he continues. "When you want something, you go after it and make it happen. That's just one of the reasons I love you."

A smile breaks free, and I let out a soft laugh, the heaviness in my chest easing. "Admit it, you just love being married to a boss bitch."

"Hundred percent," he says with a chuckle, brushing a strand of hair behind my ear. "And I can't see that ever changing."

The sharp click of heels echoes across the empty space, interrupting the moment. Bridger and I turn to see Randi, the club's former owner, striding toward us with her usual confident flair. She pauses a few feet away, her gaze sweeping over the room. A wistful smile tugs at her lips as she plants her hands on her hips.

"Well, kids, this is it," she says, her voice warm but tinged with nostalgia. "I'm really going to miss this place, but I can't say I'm not excited about spending my days sipping margaritas in Barbados."

I take a step forward, a mix of gratitude and sadness weighing on me. "You deserve it." I wrap my arms around her in a quick but heartfelt hug. "Thank you for everything. I promise we'll take good care of the Envy Room. And just so you know, you're welcome back anytime."

She squeezes me before pulling back, her eyes shimmering with unshed tears. "I never would've sold it to you if I didn't believe that." Her voice softens as she presses the keys into my hand. "You've got this, Holland. I'm proud of you."

Even though her words hit me square in the chest, I manage to nod. "Thank you."

With one last lingering glance around, Randi straightens her shoulders, gives us a small wave, and strides toward the door. As it clicks shut behind her, the quiet of the empty club settles over us.

I exhale, the gravity of the moment sinking in. "I'm really going to miss her," I admit, my voice barely above a whisper. My fingers trail along the smooth surface of the keys. "She's always been my sounding board. Anytime I doubted myself or needed guidance, she was there to steer me in the right direction."

Bridger steps closer, his gray eyes meeting mine, steady and reassuring. "Even in Barbados, she's only a phone call away," he murmurs, his tone soothing.

I nod, a small smile breaking through my lingering sadness. "You're right."

His lips curl into a grin as he tugs me closer, wrapping an arm around my waist. "And besides, you're not alone in this anymore. We've got each other, remember?"

My chest tightens, but this time, it's not from uncertainty. It's from the overwhelming comfort of knowing I don't have to carry this dream on my own anymore. "Yeah," I whisper, leaning into him. "We do."

My attention drifts to the stage, and before I realize what I'm doing, I take off in that direction. With a little hop, I'm up on the polished surface, the familiar feel of it grounding me in memories that rush back in a flood.

Gripping the pole, I swing around once. A laugh tumbles out before I can stop it. The motion feels as natural as breathing. It's been years, but in this moment, it's like I never left. I glance down at Bridger, who's leaning casually against one of the nearby tables, his arms crossed, a smirk tugging at his lips as he watches me.

"I remember seeing you in the crowd," I call out, my voice teasing but laced with fondness. "Dancing just for you."

His smirk deepens, his gray eyes gleaming with mischief. "Hard to forget, babe. You were unforgettable then, and you're just as unforgettable now."

I arch a brow, spinning around the pole again for good measure. "Think I still have what it takes to command your attention?"

His head tilts slightly, his gaze heating as it rakes over me. "There's only one way to find out," he murmurs, his voice dropping low.

With a chuckle, I tug off my sweater, letting it drop to the floor, leaving me in a snug tank top and jeans. "All right, let's see if I've still got it."

Bridger pulls his phone from his pocket, tapping the screen a few times before a familiar beat fills the room. The sound pulses through me, awakening muscle memory I didn't know I still had. Closing my eyes, I start to sway, allowing the rhythm to take over. My body moves instinctively, old routines merging with the present, each motion feeling freer than the last.

I peek through half-lidded eyes to find Bridger rooted in place, his jaw slack and his attention fixed on me. The awe and raw desire of his expression sends a thrill racing through me, igniting a spark I can't ignore. The performance builds to a crescendo as I finish with a playful flourish, leaning back against the pole, a triumphant grin lighting up my face.

Before I can say anything, Bridger is already moving, closing the distance between us in a few long strides. His hands grip my waist, lifting me off the stage like I weigh nothing.

His voice is low and rough as he leans in, his lips brushing against my ear. "Damn, Holland, that was the hottest thing I've ever seen. No question about it. You've still got it."

A laugh escapes me, breathless and exhilarated, as I wrap my arms around his neck. "Glad to know my husband approves."

"Approves?" He pulls back, his smirk softening into something more earnest. His hands tighten on my waist, grounding me in the moment. "I don't just approve. I adore and love you more than anything."

The sincerity in his voice steals the air from my lungs, and my heart swells, pushing past every wall I've built to protect myself. My hands slide to his face before pulling him down into a kiss that's as soft as it is consuming. I want to pour every ounce of what I feel for him into it.

When we break apart, my forehead rests against his, my breathing uneven. "I love you too," I whisper. "More than words could ever convey."

His arms tighten around me as his lips press against my temple.

In this moment, with Bridger holding me close, I know without a doubt that this is where I'm meant to be.

With the man who was always meant to be mine.

Thank you so much for reading Never Your Girl! I hope you enjoyed Holland and Bridger's story as much as I loved writing it! It's so hard to say goodbye to this world and the characters that fill it! I've loved getting to know the Western Wildcats and the women they've fallen head over heels for!

Curious about what comes next?

I'm starting a brand new series that follows characters you've already met at Western University and follow them up to the pros!

Ever hear of the Chicago Railers?

No?

You will soon!

*Make Me Yours* is a swoony, boy-obsessed, friends-to-lovers romance packed with forced proximity, undeniable tension, and a hero who has always been all in.

Any guesses as to who the couple is?

If you're looking for something to read in the meantime, check out

the parent books for some of the Western Wildcats characters! Hate to Love You, Just Friends, and the Breakup Plan are the parent books for Juliette, Maverick, Colby, and Ava!
There were also cameo appearances throughout the series by some of the Campus Series characters! The Campus Series starts with Campus Player!

*He has a reputation. She's about to discover the truth.*

Trust me when I say that Rowan Michaels fever is alive and well at Western University. His fanbase is legendary. The guy is a major player. Both on and off the field. Girls fall all over themselves to be with him. They fill the stands at football practice, show up at parties he's rumored to be at, and basically stalk him around campus.

It's a little nauseating.

Don't these girls have any self-respect when it comes to a hot guy?

Fine...I'll admit it, he's good looking. If you're into that kind of thing. Which I'm not. I've got school and soccer to keep me busy which is exactly why I avoid him like an unfortunate clap diagnosis.

Too bad for me that Rowan is my father's star quarterback. He's practically part of the family, attending Wednesday night dinners with us. To make matters worse, we're in the same major and get stuck together in classes every semester. It's like the universe is trying to play a cosmic joke on me. The one guy I'd like to steer clear of is the very same one I can't seem to get away from. But what if Rowan isn't the player I pegged him to be?

*What if one little secret has the capability to change everything between us?*

One-click Campus Player now!

# HATE TO LOVE YOU

## BRODY

"Dude, I thought you'd be back earlier." Cooper, one of my roommates, grins as I walk through the front door. There's a half-naked chick straddling his lap. "We had to get this party started without you." He shrugs as if he's just taken one for the team. "It couldn't be helped."

I snort as my gaze travels around the living room of the house we rent a few blocks off campus. Even though there are only four of us on the lease, our place seems to be a crash pad for half the team. By the looks of the beer bottles strewn around, they've been at it for a while. I'm seriously thinking about charging some of these assholes rent.

Although, I guess if I were stuck in a shoebox of a dorm, I'd be desperate for a way out, too. I played juniors straight out of high school for two years before coming in as a freshman at twenty. I skipped dorm living and went straight to renting a place nearby. There was no way I was bunking down with a bunch of random eighteen-year-olds who'd never lived away from home. Not to mention, having an RA up my ass telling me what I could and couldn't do.

That sounds about as much fun as ripping duct tape off my balls.

Which is, I might add, the complete opposite of fun. Hazing

sucks. And for future reference, you don't rip duct tape off your balls, you carefully cut it away with a steady hand while mother-fucking the entire team.

My other two roommates, Luke Anderson and Sawyer Stevens, are hunched at the edge of the couch, battling it out in an intense game of NHL. Their thumbs are jerking the controllers in lightning-quick movements, and their eyeballs are fastened to the seventy-inch HD screen hanging across the room.

I can only shake my head. Every time they play, it's like a freaking National Championship is at stake.

I arch a brow as the girl on Cooper's lap reaches around and unhooks her bra, dropping it to the floor. Apparently, she doesn't mind if there's an audience. Cooper's lazy grin stretches as his fingers zero in on her nips.

I'd love to say this scene isn't typical for a Sunday night, but I'd be lying through my teeth. Usually, it's much worse.

Deking out Luke with some impressive video game puck handling skills, Sawyer says, "Grab a beer, bro. You can take over for Luke after I make him cry again like a little bitch."

"Fuck you," Luke grumbles.

I glance at the score. Luke is getting his ass handed to him on a silver platter, and he knows it.

"Sure." Sawyer smirks. "Maybe later. But I should warn you, you're not really my type. I like a dude who's packing a little more meat than you."

My lips twitch as I drop my duffle to the floor.

"Hey, you see that bullshit text from Coach?" Cooper asks from between the girl's tits.

I groan, hoping I didn't miss anything important while I was out of town for the weekend. I'm already under contract with the Milwaukee Mavericks. My dad and I flew there to meet with the coaching staff. I also got to hang with a few of the defensive players. Saturday night was freaking crazy. Next season is going to rock.

"Nah, didn't see it," I say. "What's going on?"

"Practice times have changed," Cooper continues, all the while playing with the girl's body. "We're now at six o'clock in the morning and seven in the evening."

Fuck me. He's starting two-a-days already?

"You think he's just screwing around with us?" I wouldn't put it past Coach Lang. I don't think he has anything better to do than lie awake at night, dreaming up new ways to torture us. The guy is a real hard-ass.

Then again, that's why we're here.

But six in the morning...that sucks. Between school and hockey practice, I already feel like I don't get enough sleep. And it's only September. That means I'll need to be up and out the door by five to make it to the rink, get dressed, and be on the ice by six. By the time eleven o'clock at night rolls around, I'll fall into bed an exhausted heap.

Sawyer shrugs, not looking particularly put out by the time change.

Cooper pops the nipple out of his mouth and fixes his glassy-eyed gaze on me. "Can't you have your dad talk some freaking sense into the guy?"

Luke grumbles under his breath, "I can barely make it to the seven o'clock practice on time."

"Nope." I shake my head. I'd do just about anything for these guys, except run to my father with anything related to hockey. Coach and my dad go way back. They both played for the Detroit Redwings. I've known the man my entire life. He helped me lace up my first pair of Bauers. So, you'd think he'd have a soft spot for me. Maybe take it easy on me.

Yeah....fat chance of that happening.

If anything, he comes down on me like a ton of bricks *because* of our personal relationship. I think Lang doesn't want any of the guys to feel like he's playing favorites.

Mission accomplished, dude.

No one would ever accuse him of that.

"Then prepare to haul ass at the butt crack of dawn, my friend."

With that, Cooper turns his attention elsewhere, attacking the girl's mouth.

Luke eyes them for a moment before yelling, "Hey, you gonna take that shit to the bedroom or are we all being treated to a free show?"

Not bothering to come up for air, Cooper ignores the question.

Luke shakes his head and focuses his attention on making a comeback. Or at least knocking Sawyer's avatar on its ass. "Guess that means we should make some popcorn."

I pick up my duffel and hoist it over my shoulder, deciding to head upstairs for a while. I love hanging with these guys, but I'm not feeling it at the moment.

"Hi, Brody." A lush blonde slips her arms around me and presses her ample cleavage against my chest. "I was hoping you'd show up."

Given the fact that this is my house, the chances of that happening were extremely high.

I stare down into her big green eyes.

"Hey." She looks familiar. I do a quick mental search, trying to produce a name, but only come up with blanks.

Which probably means I haven't slept with her recently.

When it comes to the ladies, I've come up with an algorithm that I've perfected over the last three years. It's simple, yet foolproof. I never screw the same girl more than three times in a six-month period. If you do, you run the risk of entering into the murky territory of a quasi-relationship or a friends-with-benefits situation. I'm not looking for any attachments at this point.

Even casual ones.

I'm at Whitmore to earn a degree and prepare for the pros. I'm focused on getting bigger, faster, and stronger. The NHL is no place for pussies. If you can't hack it, the league will chew you up and spit you out before you can blink your eyes. I have no intention of allowing that to happen. I've worked too hard to crash and burn at this point.

Or get distracted.

In a surprisingly bold move, Blondie slides her hand from my chest to my package and gives it a firm squeeze to let me know she means business.

I have no doubts that if I asked her to drop to her knees and suck me off in front of all these people, she would do it in a heartbeat. Other than a thong, the girl grinding away on Cooper's lap is naked.

My first year playing juniors, when a girl offered to have no-strings-attached-sex, I'd thought I'd hit the flipping jackpot. Less than five minutes later, I'd blown my load and was ready for round two. Fast forward five years, and I don't even blink at a chick who's willing to drop her panties within minutes of me walking through the door. It happens far too often for it to be considered a novelty.

Which is just plain sad.

When I was in high school, I jumped at the chance to dip my wick.

Now?

Not so much.

It's like being fed a steady diet of steak and lobster. Sure, it's delicious the first couple of days. Maybe even a full week. You can't help but greedily devour every single bite and then lick your fingertips afterward. But, believe it or not, even steak and lobster become mundane.

Most guys, no matter what their age, would give their left nut to be in my skates.

To have their pick of any girl. Or, more often than not, *girls*.

And here I am...limp dick in hand.

Actually, limp dick in *her* hand.

Sex has become something I do to take the edge off when I'm feeling stressed. It's my version of a relaxation technique. For fuck's sake, I'm twenty-three years old. I'm in the sexual prime of my life. I should be ecstatic when any girl wants to spread her legs for me. What I shouldn't be is bored. And I sure as hell shouldn't be mentally running through the drills we'll be doing when I lead a captain's practice.

I pry her fingers from my junk and shake my head. "Sorry, I've got some shit to take care of."

And that shit would be school.  I have forty pages of reading that needs to be finished up by tomorrow morning.

Blondie pouts and bats her mascara-laden lashes.

"Maybe later?" she coos in a baby voice.

Fuck. That is such a turnoff.

Why do chicks do that?

No, seriously. It's a legitimate question. Why do they do that? It's like nails on a chalkboard. I'm tempted to answer back in a ridiculous, lispy-sounding voice.

But I don't.

I'm not that big of an asshole.

Plus, she might be into it.

Then I'd be screwed. I envision us cooing at each other in baby voices for the rest of the night and almost shudder.

"Maybe," I say noncommittally. Although I'm not going to lie, that toddler voice has killed any chance for a later hookup. But I'm smart enough not to tell her that. Chances are high that she'll end up finding another hockey player to latch on to and forget all about me. Because let's face it, that's what she's here for.

A little dick from a guy who skates with a stick.

Just to be sure, I run my eyes over the length of her again.

Toddler voice aside, she's got it going on.

And yet, that banging body is doing absolutely nothing for me.

Which is troublesome. I almost want to take her upstairs just to prove to myself that everything is in proper working order. But I won't.

As I hit the first step, Cooper breaks away from his girl. "WTF, McKinnon? Where you going?" He waves a hand around the room. "Can't you see we're in the middle of entertaining?"

"I'll leave you to take care of our guests," I say, trudging up the staircase.

"Well, if you insist," he slurs happily.

My bedroom is at the end of the hall, away from the noise of the first floor. As a general rule, no one is allowed on the second floor except for the guys who live here. I pull out my key and unlock the door before stepping inside.

My duffel gets tossed in the corner before I open my Managerial Finance book. I thought I'd have a chance to plow through some of the reading over the weekend, but my dad and I were on the go the entire time. Meeting people from the Milwaukee organization, hitting a team party, checking out a few condos near the lakefront. Just getting the general lay of the land. On the plane ride home, I had every intention of being productive, but ended up sacking out once we hit cruising altitude.

Three hours later, there's a knock on the door. Normally an interruption would piss me off, but after slogging through thirty pages, my eyes have glazed over, and I'm fighting to stay awake. This material is mind-numbingly boring, and that's not helping matters.

"It's open," I call out, expecting Cooper to try cajoling me back downstairs.

When that guy's shitfaced, he wants everyone else to be just as hammered as he is. I've never seen anyone put away alcohol the way he does. It's almost as impressive as it is scary. And yet, he's somehow able to wake up for morning practice bright-eyed and bushy-tailed like he wasn't just wasted six hours ago. Someone from the biology department really needs to do a case study on him, 'cause that shit just ain't normal.

When I suck down alcohol like that, the next morning I'm like a newborn colt on the ice who can't keep his legs under him.

It's not a pretty sight. Which is why I don't do it. Been there, done that. Moving on.

The door swings open to reveal Blondie-With-The-Toddler-Voice. And she's not alone. She's brought a friend.

I raise my brows in interest as they step inside the room.

In the three hours since I've seen her, Blondie has managed to lose most of her clothing. The brunette she's with appears to be in the same predicament. They stand in lacy bras and barely-there thongs with their hands entwined.

My gaze roves over them appreciatively.

How could it not?

Their tummies are flat and toned. Hips are nicely rounded. Tits jiggle enticingly as they saunter toward the bed where I'm currently sprawled.

I should be a man of steel over here. I haven't gotten laid in three weeks. Which is almost unheard of. I haven't gone that long without sex since I first started having it.

But there's nothing.

Not even a twitch.

Which begs the question—What the hell is wrong with me?

It must be the stress of school and the skating regimen I'm on. Even though I'm already under contract with Milwaukee and don't have to worry about the NHL draft later this year, I'm still under a lot of pressure to perform this season.

National Championships don't bring themselves home.

I'd be concerned that I have some serious erectile dysfunction issues happening except there's one chick who gets me hard every time I lay eyes on her. Rather ironically, she wants nothing to do with me. I think she'd claw my eyes out if I laid one solitary finger on her.

Actually, all I have to do is stare in her direction, and she bares her teeth at me.

Maybe these girls are exactly what I need to relieve some of my pent-up stress. It certainly can't hurt.

Decision made, I slam my finance book closed and toss it to the floor where it lands with a loud thud. I fold my arms behind my head and smile at the girls in silent invitation.

And the rest, shall we say, is history.

One-click Hate to Love You now!

# CAMPUS PLAYER

## DEMI

"**M**orning, Demi!" Gary, one of the stadium custodians, calls out with an easy smile and wave as he saunters toward me. "Up and at 'em bright and early this morning, I see."

My heart jackhammers beneath my ribcage from the twenty-minute run as I flash him a grin. "Always!"

"You have a good one! I'll see you tomorrow!"

Since I've already moved past him, I holler over my shoulder, "Same place, same time!"

Even with *The Killers* pumping through my earbuds, I almost hear the deep chuckle that slides from his lips. Our morning greetings are a ritual three years in the making. I've been running through the wide corridor that leads to the stadium football field since I stepped foot on campus freshman year. This will be something I miss when I graduate in the spring. Five days a week, I'm up at six, logging in a four-mile run before returning home, jumping in the shower, and heading off to class.

At this time of the day, the stadium is still relatively quiet, with only a few people wandering the hallways. There's something both serene and eerie about it. I've been here on game days when there are thirty thousand fans packed shoulder to shoulder, rooting on the Western Wildcats football team. Three-fourths of the stadium filled with black and orange is an amazing sight to behold. Football is a religion at Western. Unfortunately, the same can't be said for the women's soccer team. We're lucky if there are a couple of hundred spectators in the stands.

I've come to terms with it.

Sort of.

I keep my gaze trained on the light at the end of the tunnel and push myself faster. As soon as I burst out of the darkness, bright sunlight pours down on me, stroking over the bare skin of my arms and shoulders. It's late August, and summer is still in full swing. A whistle cuts through the silence of the stadium, and my gaze slices to the field. Nick Richards has been head coach of the Wildcats for the last decade. He also happens to be my father.

Two days a week, the guys are up at six in the morning for yoga. Dad is a big believer in flexibility. Even though I'm winded, a smirk lifts the corners of my lips. Watching two-hundred-and-eighty-pound linebackers contort their bodies into Downward-Facing Dog, the Warrior II Pose, and the Cobra is enough to bring a chuckle to my lips. Some of the guys actually like it, but most grumble when they think Dad isn't paying attention. Little do they know that he sees and hears everything.

My father catches sight of me and flashes a quick smile along with a wave in my direction. He has a black ball cap pulled low and aviators covering his eyes. There's a clipboard in one hand as he paces behind the instructor.

When I point to the field, he shakes his head. He might make the guys do yoga, but he refuses to participate. Something about old dogs and new tricks. Every once in a while, I'll tell him that he needs to get out there and set a good example for the team. He usually shoots me a glare in return.

Every Wednesday night, Dad and I get together. Our weekly dinners became a thing when I moved out of the house and into the dorms freshman year. He's busy coaching football, and my schedule is packed tight with school and soccer. Getting together once a week is the best way for us to stay connected. It doesn't matter if we're in the middle of our seasons; we always make time for each other. Especially since Mom lives in sunny California. After eighteen years of marriage, she got fed up with being a distant second to the Western University football program. She packed up her bags and walked out. I hate to say it, but Dad didn't notice her absence for a couple of days. Which only proved her point. Now she's remarried, learning to surf, and is a vegan. I visit for a couple of weeks during the summer before soccer training camp starts up at the end of June.

Even though it's only the two of us, our weekly dinners are set for three people.

I tell myself to stare straight ahead and not glance in his direction.

*Don't do it!*

*Don't you dare do it!*

Damn.

My gaze reluctantly zeros in on him like a heat-seeking missile. Long blond hair, bright blue eyes, sun-kissed skin, and muscles for miles. And he's tall, somewhere around six foot three.

I'm describing none other than Rowan Michaels.

Otherwise known as the bane of my existence.

My dad discovered the talented quarterback the summer before we entered high school and took him under his wing. Which has been...aggravating. In the seven years since, Rowan has become an irritatingly permanent fixture in my life. He's the brother I never wanted or asked for. He's the gift I wish I could give back. He's the son my father never had but secretly longed for.

On a campus with over thirty thousand students, one would think that avoidance would be easy to accomplish. That hasn't turned out to be the case. Somehow, we ended up in the same major—Exercise Science. I get stuck in at least one class with the guy each semester. This time it's statistics, which is a requirement. Three times a week, I'm forced to see him. And then there are the weekly dinners at Dad's house.

Every Wednesday, Rowan shows up without fail.

It's so annoying.

No, *he's* annoying!

Our gazes collide, and electricity sizzles through my veins before I immediately snuff it out and pretend it never happened.

*I am not attracted to Rowan Michaels.*

*I am not attracted to Rowan Michaels.*

*I am not attracted to Rowan Michaels.*

Maybe if I repeat the mantra enough times, it'll be true. That's the hope I cling to. I've made it through the last seven years trying to convince myself of this. I only have to get through our final year together, and then we'll go our separate ways—me to graduate school or maybe to the Women's National Soccer League, and Rowan to the NFL. He's one of the most talented quarterbacks in the conference. Hell, probably the country. There is little doubt in my mind that he'll be a first-round draft pick come next spring.

Trust me when I say that Rowan Michaels fever is alive and well at Western University. His fanbase is legendary. The guy is a major player.

Both on and off the field.

Girls fall all over themselves to be with him. They fill the stands at football practice, show up at parties he's rumored to be at, and basically stalk him around campus.

It's a little nauseating. Don't these girls have any self-respect when it comes to a hot guy?

I wince at that unchecked thought.

Fine...I'll begrudgingly admit it; he's good-looking.

I shake my head as if that will banish the insidious thoughts currently invading my brain. Enough about Rowan. It's time to focus on the reason I'm at the stadium at this ungodly hour. I rip my gaze from him as I hit the cement staircase. After half a flight, all thoughts of the blond quarterback vanish from my mind. How could they not when my quads, glutes, and calves are on fire, screaming for mercy as I force myself to the nosebleed section. By the time I finish, my legs are Jell-O, and I still have a two-mile run back to the apartment I share with my best friend off-campus.

I give Dad a half-hearted wave before leaving. It's the most I can muster. His lips quirk at the corners as he shakes his head. He thinks I'm crazy. At the moment, I can't argue with his assessment of the situation. Although, it's the extra training I put in that helps me run circles around the other team in the second half of the game.

The jog home feels like it will last forever. By the time I unlock the apartment door, I'm ready to collapse. I beeline for the shower and jump in before it's fully warm. My skin prickles with goose flesh, but it feels so damn good. Twenty minutes later, I'm dressed and ready to take on the day. My hair has been thrown up in a messy bun, and I'm making a protein smoothie that will fuel me for my morning classes.

Just before taking off, I poke my head into Sydney's room. I know exactly how I'll find her, and that's buried beneath a small mountain of blankets. She doesn't disappoint. We met the summer before freshman year in training camp and have been besties ever since. She's the yin to my yang. The peanut butter to my jelly. The Thelma to my Louise. Where I'm more introverted and cautious, she's loud and boisterous. She's been known to leap without necessarily looking at what she's jumping into. Every so often, it gets us into trouble. Sydney and I have lived together since sophomore year. I gave up trying to cajole her ass out of bed for a six o'clock run after the first week of us cohabitating when she nearly took my head off with an alarm clock.

"It's that time again," I sing-song obnoxiously, "rise and shine."

There's a grunt and then some shifting from under the blankets that tells me she's alive.

When I chant her name repeatedly, each time escalating in volume, she growls, "Get the fuck out!"

"Awww," I mock, "that's so sweet. I love you, too."

Sydney snorts before a hand snakes out from beneath the blankets to give me a one-fingered salute. Then she grabs a pillow and tosses it in my general vicinity. It falls about five feet short of its mark.

I stare at the dismal attempt. "If you're trying to cause bodily harm, you'll have to do better than that."

"Piss off."

"All right then." I shrug. "See you after class." With that, I close the door behind me.

My farewell is met with another indecipherable mouthful. If this weren't something we went through on the daily, I'd worry she was in the midst of a stroke. Sydney is definitely not a morning person. She's more of an early afternoon person. Another thing I've learned over the years? The action of waking up to a brand-new day is a gradual process. She's like a bear rousing prematurely from hibernation. It's not a pretty sight. She's lucky I don't take her insults personally.

I grab my backpack from the small table crammed into the breakfast nook area along with a coffee before heading out the door. The apartment I share with Sydney is located three blocks from campus, which is highly sought out real estate. We're fortunate Dad is friends with the guy who manages the building. It's probably one of the only perks of having a father who is a head coach of a college football team.

You'd think there would be more, but you'd be wrong. Honestly, being Nick Richard's daughter is more of a hindrance than anything else. People assume you receive special treatment on campus, from professors, or that you have an in with all the football players.

Or worse...

*Much worse.*

After a bunch of ugly—not to mention untrue—rumors circulated freshman year, I've done my best to distance myself from the Wildcats football team. They're a great bunch of guys, but I don't need all the ugly gossip and speculation that comes along with being friends with them.

As I reach Corbin Hall, the mathematics building for my stats class, my gaze is drawn to a clump of students standing around outside the three-story, red-brick building. In the center of that crowd is Rowan. I don't have to see him physically to know that he's close. The muscles in my belly contract with awareness. It's like a sixth sense. One I wish would go away. He's the last person I want to be cognizant of.

As I jog up the wide stone stairs to the entrance, my gaze fastens on him. A smirk twists the edges of his lips, and my eyes narrow before I drag them away and yank open the door to the building. Relief rushes through me as I step inside the air conditioning and disappear from sight.

"Hey, Demi, wait up!"

I turn at the sound of my name before slowing my step. The dark-haired guy jogging to catch up smiles before falling in line with me.

Justin Fischer.

He's a baseball player and teammates with Sydney's boyfriend, Ethan. We've been seeing each other for about a month. It's still casual at this point. With school and soccer, I don't have a ton of time to invest in a relationship. He seems to understand that and isn't pushing to be more serious.

When he leans in for a kiss, I angle my head. At the last moment, he tilts in the opposite direction, and we end up bumping teeth instead of locking lips. With a grunt, I pull away and chuckle. My fingers fly to my mouth to make sure I haven't chipped a tooth.

Maybe I've been reluctant to admit it to myself, but that kiss sums up our relationship perfectly.

Awkward and a step out of sync with each other.

"Sorry," he murmurs with a slight smile. I search his face and wait for any telltale sign of sexual chemistry to ping inside me. Unfortunately, my insides remain completely unfazed, which is disappointing but not altogether unexpected. I had a sneaking suspicion when we first got together that it might turn out this way.

"No problem," I say, hoisting my smile and brushing aside those thoughts.

"I haven't seen you for a couple of days," he remarks as we turn a corner and continue walking.

"It's been busy." Which isn't a lie. School might have recently started, but the academics at Western are rigorous. And being a Division I athlete is more like a job. If you're not ready to put in the work, don't bother showing up. There's no half-assing it around this place.

"When's your next game?" he asks.

"Tomorrow at six." My gaze flickers in his direction. Not that I expect him to come, but...

Fine, so maybe I do. If he wants to be my boyfriend, then he needs to show a little support.

His dark brows draw together. "That sucks. I've got a mandatory study hour I have to attend."

I shrug off the disappointment. It's another nail in the coffin of this relationship as far as I'm concerned. "That's cool. It's not a big deal."

"But I'll see you tonight?"

Oh. Right.

*Tonight.*

Well, damn. In a moment of weakness, I threw out an invitation to join our Wednesday evening dinner. It's one I now regret. If only there were a gracious way to rescind the offer.

"If you're busy, I totally understand—"

"Are you kidding? No way." With a grin, he shakes his head. "I wouldn't miss it for the world. I'm looking forward to meeting Coach Richards."

Great. So this is more about my father than me? Exactly what every girl wants to hear.

I force a brittle smile. "Awesome. He's excited, too."

That might be something of an overstatement.

Justin nods toward the end of the corridor. "I better get moving. Professor Andrews is a real stickler for punctuality."

"Yup. See you later."

This time, when he leans in, our lips align perfectly. The kiss is nothing more than a fleeting caress. There and gone before I can sink into it.

And I'm left feeling...absolutely nothing.

I bury the disappointment where I can't inspect it too closely before giving him a wave as he takes off. For a moment, I stand rooted in the hallway and watch as he disappears through the crowd. There's nothing to distinguish Justin from the thousands of guys who look exactly like him on campus. He's of average height and build with dark hair and espresso-colored eyes. He's nice enough. Although, if I'm completely honest, he's a little self-absorbed. He talks about baseball all the time. If Ethan hadn't introduced us, he's not someone I would have looked twice at. We don't have a ton in common.

As much as I hate to admit it, this relationship has probably reached its expiration date.

Now it's a matter of pulling the plug.

Ugh. I hate breakups. Although, it's doubtful this will end up destroying him. I'll have to make it through tonight and figure out the rest.

With a sigh of resignation, I head to the classroom and find a seat tucked away in the far corner of the small lecture hall. A lanky guy I recognize from a few of my other classes settles beside me. He flashes a dimpled smile as we empty our backpacks.

The tiny hair at the nape of my neck rises seconds before Rowan enters the room. It's like my body knows when he's within a thirty-foot radius. I glance at him from beneath the thick fringe of my lashes before shifting away. Air becomes wedged in my lungs as I wait for him to take a seat. And it won't be next to me because I'm—

"Hey man, would you mind moving?"

*Surrounded on both sides.*

Damnit. I'm hoping the cutie next to me will tell Rowan to go take a flying leap.

What? It could happen. Not everyone at this university is enamored of the football-playing god. Although I realize the odds aren't stacked in my favor. Rowan is the most recognized athlete on campus. People fall all over themselves to accommodate him.

It's a little sickening.

Okay, maybe more than a little.

"Sure, no problem, Michaels." The guy next to me hastily packs up his books before vacating the desk. Unable to ignore him any longer, I glare as Rowan slides onto the seat next to me.

"Did you really think you could evade me that easily?" Laughter brims in his deep voice. A voice, I might add, that does funny things to my insides.

"One can always hope, right?"

"Oh, answering a question with a question." He leans closer, eating up some of the much-needed distance between us. "I like it."

I roll my eyes as his lips stretch into a satisfied grin. Irritation bubbles up inside me when sexual tension blooms at the bottom of my belly. Or maybe that tension has settled a little lower.

*It's definitely lower.*

I'm tempted to swear like a sailor. How is it possible that I feel nothing for the guy I'm actually dating, and yet my pulse skitters out of control for someone I don't even like? It's so freaking ironic. It's been this way since we met, and nothing I do stomps it out. I can try to fool myself into believing it's not there, but that doesn't make it any less true.

It's a relief when Professor Peters takes his place at the podium and clears his throat. Once he's captured everyone's attention, he delves headfirst into the probability of dependent and independent events.

Grateful for the excuse to ignore Rowan for the next fifty minutes, I open my textbook and concentrate on the lesson. Just as the blond boy fades into the background, his bare knee bumps into mine. Electricity ricochets through my entire being. I glance at him to see if he's noticed the strange energy we always seem to generate and find his ocean-colored gaze fastened to mine.

My guess is that he does.

*Damnation.*

One-click Campus Player now!

# MORE BOOKS BY JENNIFER SUCEVIC

**<u>The Campus Series</u> (football)**

Campus Player (Demi & Rowan)

Campus Heartthrob (Sydney & Brayden)

Campus Flirt (Sasha & Easton)

Campus Hottie (Elle & Carson)

Campus God (Brooke & Crosby)

Campus Legend (Lola & Asher)

**<u>Western Wildcats Hockey</u>**

Hate You Always (Juliette & Ryder)

Love You Never (Carina & Ford)

Always My Girl (Viola & Madden)

Dare You to Love Me (Stella & Riggs)

Never Mine to Hold (Fallyn & Wolf)

Never Say Never (Britt & Colby)

Mine to Take (Willow & Maverick)

Break my Heart (Ava & Hayes)

Never Your Girl (Holland & Bridger)

**<u>Parent Books for the Western Wildcats</u>**

Hate to Love You (Hockey) (Natalie & Brody)

Just Friends (Hockey) (Emerson & Reed)

The Breakup Plan (Hockey) (Whitney & Gray)

**<u>The Barnett Bulldogs</u> (football)**

King of Campus (Ivy & Roan)

Friend Zoned (Violet & Sam)

One Night Stand (Gia & Liam)

If You Were Mine (Claire & JT)

**<u>The Claremont Cougars</u> (football)**

Heartless Summer (Skye & Hunter)

Heartless (Skye & Hunter)

Shameless (Poppy & Mason)

**<u>Hawthorne Prep Series</u> (bully/football)**

King of Hawthorne Prep (Summer & Kingsley)

Queen of Hawthorne Prep (Summer & Kingsley)

Prince of Hawthorne Prep (Delilah & Austin)

Princess of Hawthorne Prep (Delilah & Austin)

**<u>The Next Door Duet</u> (football)**

The Girl Next Door (Mia & Beck)

The Boy Next Door (Alyssa & Colton)

**<u>What's Mine Duet</u> (Suspense)**

Protecting What's Mine (Grace & Matteo)

Claiming What's Mine (Sofia & Roman)

**<u>Stay Duet</u> (hockey)**

Stay (Cassidy & Cole)

Don't Leave (Cassidy & Cole)

**<u>Standalone Football</u>**

Love to Hate You (Daisy & Carter)

**<u>Collections</u>**

Claremont Cougars

The Barnett Bulldogs

The Football Hotties Collection

The Hockey Hotties Collection

The Next Door Duet

# ABOUT THE AUTHOR

Jennifer Sucevic is a USA Today bestselling author who has captivated readers worldwide with her sizzling new adult romances. With over thirty novels to her name, her stories of love, heartbreak, and swoon-worthy heroes have been translated into six languages, including German, Italian, and Portuguese, making her a truly global voice in the genre. Armed with a bachelor's degree in history and a master's in educational psychology from the University of Wisconsin-Milwaukee, Jen initially worked as a high school counselor before embracing her passion for writing full-time. Her background in psychology lends a depth to her characters that resonates with fans everywhere.
When she's not crafting irresistible love stories, Jen enjoys biking along scenic trails and soaking up the sun at the beach. She currently resides in Michigan with her family, where she continues to dream up heroes and heroines you'll want to fall in love with again and again.

If you would like to receive regular updates regarding new releases, please subscribe to her newsletter here-
Jennifer Sucevic Newsletter

Or contact Jen through email, at her website, or on Facebook.
sucevicjennifer@gmail.com

Want to join her reader group? Do it here -)
J Sucevic's Book Boyfriends | Facebook

Social media links-
https://www.tiktok.com/@jennifersucevicauthor
www.jennifersucevic.com
https://www.instagram.com/jennifersucevicauthor
https://www.facebook.com/jennifer.sucevic
Amazon.com: Jennifer Sucevic: Books, Biography, Blog, Audiobooks, Kindle
Jennifer Sucevic Books - BookBub

www.ingramcontent.com/pod-product-compliance
Lightning Source LLC
Chambersburg PA
CBHW030747310726
48969CB00005B/1335